THE CARTON CHRONICLES

escapades and adventures

of Charles Dickens'

most romantic hero,

after his execution

Keith Laidler 2010

First published 2010   Aziloth Books
Copyright © 2010   Keith Laidler

Every effort has been made to contact all copyright holders. The
publisher will be glad to make good in future editions any errors
or omissions brought to their attention.

This publication is designed to provide authoritative and
accurate information in regard to the subject matter covered. It
is sold on the understanding that the Publisher is not engaged in
rendering professional services.

British Library Cataloguing in Publication Data

A catalogue record for this book is available from the British
Library

ISBN-13: 978-1-907523-01-4

Printed and bound in Great Britain by Lightning Souce UK Ltd.,
6 Precedent Drive, Rooksley, Milton Keynes MK13 8PR.

Contents

'Treasure' in the Wall

Builders renovating an 18th Century cottage at Lintzgarth, Teesdale were surprised yesterday to find a carved square stone beneath thick plaster in the north wall of the dwelling. The owner of the house, Arnold Patterson, 66, told our reporter how he had cleaned the marks on the mysterious slab: "At first we thought it were three numbers, 0-1-6" said Mr Patterson, a retired farmer who has lived all his life in the dale. "but that didn't really make any sense. Then our lass said they might be letters. Seeing as how we were stumped, we tried looking at them like that, and realised the zero were a funny sort of 'D' and the six were really a 'G'. That made the one an 'I'. And there it was, plain as day: 'DIG'. So we did".

After an hour's excavation, the stone was pulled clear to reveal a well-built cavity, containing several dozen sheaves of dusty papers, yellow with age, to each of which was appended the signature 'Sidney Carton'. Parish records show that Mr Carton retired to the dale in 1855, dying in the cottage at the venerable age of 102. Old people in Lintzgarth still remember tales of a much-travelled man with rakish ways and dubious morals, including an apparently well-founded rumour that he had been a spy in the pay of both the British and French during Napoleonic times.

Editing of Mr Carton's literary treasure trove is to be undertaken by local antiquarian Francis de Turville. Hopefully, more about this mysterious personage, and the secret of his Hidden papers, will become apparent when the contents of the manuscripts have been collated and published.

Teesdale Gazette 21st August 2009

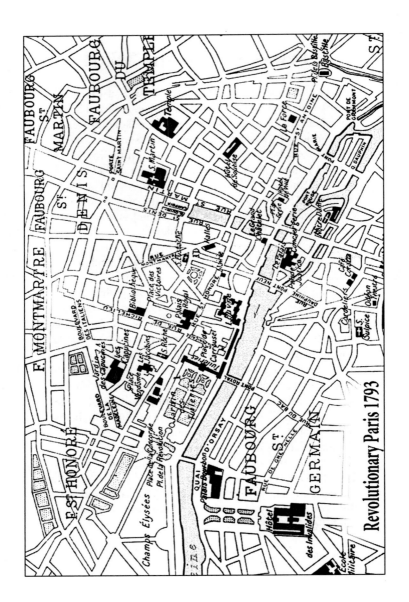

Revolutionary Paris 1793

Chapter One

"The supposed Evremonde descends, and the seamstress is lifted out next after him. He has not relinquished her patient hand in getting out, but still holds it as he promised. He gently places her with her back to the crashing engine that constantly whirrs up and falls, and she looks into his face and thanks him.

She kisses his lips; he kisses hers; they solemnly bless each other. The spare hand does not tremble as he releases it; nothing worse than a sweet, bright constancy is in the patient face. She goes next before him -

They said of him, about the city that night, that it was the peacefullest man's face ever beheld there. Many added that he looked sublime and prophetic...

"It is a far, far better thing that I do, than I have ever done; it is a far, far better rest that I go to than I have ever known."

Well that, at least, is how young Dickens sees it in his latest tome; but then he always is happiest scrawling sentimental guff, piping his eye over a starving orphan but not quite managing to find enough pelf to succour the poor creature

3

himself. All pious hand-wringing and sermonising while the cash rolls into his account. Not averse to lying by omission neither, especially in aid of a good line or a grand finale. Mind you, he is writing sixty years and more after the event, (and mis-spelling my name - Sidney with an 'i' if you please, Charles dear boy) so perhaps he don't know the full story. Unlike myself. I'm well over ninety now, but the mind's still sharp and I remember it all, clear as day: the sun, the noise, the crowds, the tumbrils. The hideous confusion of the Terror.

Chapter Two

The blade descended with horrible swiftness. I had never seen the guillotine at work close to. Christ, what horror! The poor girl's head literally flew into the basket, which being full gave me a better view of her features than I might have wished. The same face that, moments before, had been so full of expression and emotion, had spoken to me so tenderly, now jiggled like a puppet, the eyelids flickering, the teeth chattering, the dead lips moving convulsively, as if to speak. And above, the bound, headless trunk of the seamstress sprayed blood against the wide flat blade, feet and legs juddering despite the restraining bands.

It was as if a veil had been lifted from my eyes. I had brought myself to this? Voluntarily? So that Evremonde might be free? Free to escape judgement, to walk and love and laugh with Lucie? Beautiful, delightful Lucie, who I would see no more! I was to die, so that pathetic imbecile, that polite, boring excuse for a man, that aristocrat! could flee with my love to England and enjoy her for the rest of his days. While I took his place, wallowing in martyrdom, dreaming that they would remember me, would call their son after me in gratitude. Fool that I was! Evremonde had duped me into this, substituting my life for his, stealing my darling from me. The cunning conniving bastard! She would be with him now. And in moments, even as they spoke and smiled together en route for Calais, my head would be held up to the mob and reviled and spat on - as his! It was past bearing.

They had me now; the two jailers had taken my arms, leading me up the rough stairs of the scaffold. "No, No!" I yelled desperately "It's a mistake, I'm not Evremonde!" Jeers and laughter greeted my wild clamouring. "Please, no please, listen. You fools, I'm not even French! I'm Sidney Carton, I'm English". More laughter. Someone threw a stone. They were binding my arms and feet. Too tightly; it was painful. I tried to break free, writhing, blaspheming, screaming oaths. One of the men leaned forward and put his mouth to my ear.. "Come now, Evremonde", he whispered. His breath stank of garlic. "There is no escaping this. You must look through the little window. Do not put yourself to shame. Play the man. Die well".

Strong arms lifted me onto the wooden slide and fastened me down. I was on my stomach, immobilised, it was all I could do to turn my head. Oh Christ, my head! "One, two, heave!" Dear God, they were pushing me forward, my head was through the hideous, blood-dried gap, I screwed my lids shut as the wooden top-piece dropped into place with a noise like the crack o' doom. And suddenly, all at once, I was very calm. The man had been right. There was no escape, it was over, Evremonde had won. I opened my eyes and stared placidly at the crowd, not six feet distant, the cricateurs busy at their work, the rest eyeing me eagerly, their faces aglow with murderous anticipation. The noise, their catcalls and jeering seemed strangely dulled, their movements slow and dream-like. This would be the last sight I would see, these street scum, painted whores, bearded soldiers in the dirty blue and white uniform of the republic, food vendors, coffee sellers, Defarge locked in discussion with another man, vacant-faced farmers visiting the city for the first time ...

Defarge! From the tail of my eye I saw the executioner's hand grip the blade-release bar. "Defarge!" He ignored me, engrossed in his conversation. Desperately, I screamed again, my voice breaking, "Defarge! It's me. Sidney Carton. For God's sake stop this, tell them who I am"

In the brief silence that followed he looked up, staring at me, puzzled. Then a voice in the crowd called out "You're a dead man talking, that's who you are" and the moment was gone. The mob erupted. "Death to the aristos" "A bas le tyran". "Get on with it". But Defarge was frowning, and the man beside him, a slight, pinch-faced fellow with wired spectacles and a neat powdered wig perched atop his narrow head, had raised a restraining arm. He seemed to have some authority, for the executioner stayed his hand despite the mob's protests. Sweat was pouring from me, running into my eyes; my left shoulder had spasmed with the effort of holding up my head. I had to convince them, now! they could not restrain the mob for long. Think! Desperately I cudgelled my brains for proof. "I was in your wine shop last night! Don't you recall? Your wife thought I was Evremonde! But I'm not! For the love of Christ, I'm not!"

"By God! Carton? Stop, I know this man!" Defarge was trying to push his way forward through the crowd "In the name of the Revolution, Stop!" But it was too late, I could hear the scrape of the handle being pulled, I let my head fall forward against the rough planking, and darkness descended on my eyes.

Chapter Three

And that, gentle reader, is as close as I ever wish to come to being executed. I've had some nasty scrapes since then, more than I care to remember, but none where I was certain surer of my own extinction. So you can imagine my surprise when I opened my eyes and, instead of a greeting from Lucifer and his myrmidons, found myself within a foot of the most winsome female face I'd seen for some time, and being primed with a dram of the best Cognac to boot! I decided dreamily that I must have escaped t'other place and somehow slipped past St Peter, but the sight of Defarge behind this angelic vision, standing tense and anxious, brought me quickly to my senses. The other chap was with him too, looking down his nose at me through his wired spectacles as if I was one of the multitudinous pieces of filth the Parisians are so fond of leaving in their disgusting streets, and he'd just stepped on me.

Their presence boded ill so I decided to ignore them for as long as I could. "Thank you mam'selle" I gasped, choking slightly as the raw burn of the brandy seared my throat, but managing all the same to cast an admiring glance towards the delightful cleavage, just inches from my face. Her eyes followed my gaze; she smiled, and obligingly leaned even farther forward, wayward wisps of her chestnut hair caressing my forehead for the briefest moment before she pulled away. Corking the brandy bottle, she swayed off to stand by the glowing hearth, eyes demurely downcast, just to the right of Defarge and Spectacles, both of whom continued to regard me with undisguised disgust. They were an odd brace of birds, those two: Defarge huge, formidable and feculent in his obligatory sans-culotte uniform of rough peasant's blouse, blue bandanna, striped workman's trousers and the red Phrygian cap of the revolutionary, while his companion was tiny by comparison, a wee bantam just an inch or two over five feet and flawlessly attired in an elegant jacket of olive green, resplendent with lace cuffs and a robin's-egg blue waistcoat beneath. Impeccable black trousers covered his thin shanks, from which peeped spotless white stockings that slid into silver-buckled shoes so highly polished I could just make out a double image of my own slumped figure, reflected in each of his shining leathers. Quite a dapper little man, his brown hair carefully powdered after the fashion of the time, and you would have passed him for just another petit-bourgeois, a dandified provincial lawyer of no real account, until he lifted his pince-nez (which he did quite often) and impaled you with his eyes. Grey-green they were, quite large for such a small narrow face, and so full of malignant malice and disdain my innards dissolved beneath his silent icy gaze. Suddenly terrified, I realised I was in the presence of one of the Giants of the Revolution, bellwether of the Jacobin Club and lodestone of the Committee of Public Safety. A name that now, sixty years on, is steeped in infamy, but who was then spoken of with a mixture of awe and admiration. A man who had already sent hundreds to look through the little window of *La Guillotine*. This was the Incorruptible himself. Robespierre.

"So Defarge" the voice was weak, high-pitched, ill matched with those tigerish eyes, which continued their transfixing stare, coldly interested, as if I was some novel prey beneath

9

his paws. His skin was pale, with a greenish cast. "You are certain?"

"*Bien sur*, Citizen Deputy". Defarge was a changed character; gone was the surly arrogance I'd seen the night before in his wine shop, he was all obsequious deference. "He is not Evremonde but a known friend of the accursed aristo. One Sidney Carton. English. This much is certain. Why he remained in Paris, why he impersonated Evremonde, why he seemed willing - until the last moment - to have died in his place, all these things we do not know. Defarge's broad face took on a knowing, vulpine look. "Perhaps" he said hopefully, his rough voice hoarse with excitement "he is an English spy, an agent of Pitt!"

For an instant the terror of the last few hours rose up again to overwhelm me - spies were Guillotined as a matter of course. I gasped my innocence, then realised Robespierre was staring contemptuously at Defarge "A spy you say? And what spy voluntarily places himself under the blade? Pray enlighten us Defarge. What possible advantage would England derive from the self-immolation of this ... wretch?"

Well, 'wretch' was a bit much, but I was all in favour of the main thrust of his argument, and subsided into wounded silence. While Defarge spluttered into his beard, Robespierre ignored him and turned those horrid eyes back in my direction. "No, that will not march. This is... Do you speak French monsieur?"

It was a technique I was later to see him use often: the sudden *non sequitur*, the surprise question. I was so taken aback the thought of dissembling never crossed my mind. "Yes, your eminence" I stuttered "I..."

"A simple 'Citizen' will do monsieur" There was something horribly unsettling about the shrill insistence of the man's voice, like a rabbit with a weasel at its throat. "Good. Then we can continue our discussion in my native tongue. As I was saying to friend Defarge, this whole *affaire* hardly appears of national importance, nor does it seem at all political, no..... it smacks to me of a personal nature". He was walking up and down in front of me now, his carefully manicured hands held behind his back. A lawyer before the jury as ever was. "Yes... I will be frank with you monsieur. I have had you watched since the moment you arrived in Paris. Your activities aroused my suspicion. At first. But the reports that reached my desk soon allayed my fears: you were spoken of as a melancholy, as morose, listless; and all your endeavours orbited around a certain female... Lucie Manette, married to the *emigré* Evremonde, known also as Charles Darnay. Several of my informants reported on your "doleful expression" or commented on the 'longing' in your eyes, when this female was present in your company. Hmm? No, no, no, this is emphatically not about politics, is it monsieur? It is an affair of the heart. *N'est-ce pas?*"

The look on my face must have sufficed him for an answer. "Ah, it is true. Then, monsieur, I salute you. You were willing to lay down your life for the happiness of the woman you love, is this not so?"

"Yes, it is so" I returned slowly, and heard a gasp of admiration from the Angel of the Brandy. I essayed a look in her direction and she was standing there open-mouthed (and a lovely mouth it was too) staring at me. *"Quelle courage. Quelle amour!"* she whispered admiringly, her bounteous bosom quivering deliciously with suppressed emotion.

Robespierre too seemed visibly overcome by my admission. He had turned away from me, towards the hearth, leaning heavily against the mantle-piece with his right hand. Sharp now, thinks I, he's plainly moved by your plight; play the loverlorn hero and it could be your passport out of this God-forsaken city with its lawless soldiers, sanguinary mobs, its *carmagnole*, executions and the constant daily fear and suspicion. Let him think that I still....., and then I became aware of a horrible continuous snorting noise and realised with horror that the slight lawyer at the hearth, Robespierre, the Incorruptible, was blowing his nose into the fire! Directly into the fire, mark you, flicking it off the end of his pointed beak with his fingers - you could hear the snot sizzle on the coals. Wouldn't credit my eyes, at first, but it was gospel. I discovered later he'd actually written a poem, a diatribe in verse against - of all things - the use of handkerchiefs. It's God's truth. He'd entitled the ode *"The Art of Spitting and Blowing One's Nose"* and he recited the whole ridiculous piece to me a few weeks after. Of course I was fulsome in my praise (the Incorruptible was a jealous bastard at the best of times and very conscious of his *amour-propre* besides). I can still recall one passage:

> *No, no, never would a Roman of courage inflexible*
> *Submit his bold, free and majestic nose*
> *To the caresses of soft cotton as he blows* [1]

As I say, moronic nonsense. But no doubt it loses something in translation.

He'd finished his Classical ablutions by now, and glanced briefly at the girl, wiping his fingers discreetly on the inside of his jacket. "Quite so, my dear child. It is a courage rare, and most admirable. But now, Citizeness Defarge - Suzanne - Monsieur Carton and I must talk of weighty matters. You may leave us". Dutifully, she left the room, swaying delightfully, casting sorrowful eyes in my direction, in which she somehow contrived to incorporate as much promise as melancholy, and which turned up my temperature nicely, despite the predicament I was in. And she was a Defarge? Surely not kin to the towering boor of a sans-culotte who still stood, subdued and obedient, next to the fireplace? God, she was lovely. How old? Not more than sixteeen, seventeen at the most. Tiny waist. And such bouncers...

"Monsieur, I too, know what it is to love!" Robespierre's piping voice broke into my erotic reverie and brought me up short. He was staring earnestly at me, hands clasped, his thin hams all a-quiver. I knew then that, if I wished to see tomorrow's dawn, I had in some wise to gain this man's favour, his forbearance at least. Well, he admired my courage, as he saw it, and it seemed that, like me, he had been unlucky in love. A good start. I composed my features to rapt interest and leaned forward, my mind whirring. "You, too, Monsi... Citizen Robespierre?"

"Yes, yes! I am consumed with love", he gasped earnestly, his mean eyes afire in his narrow lawyer face, and I gave what I hoped was a sympathetic and understanding half-smile to this most unexpected baring of his soul. And with a total stranger to boot; but then again, sometimes it is easier..... .

"But my love is not for a single woman..." (I shook my head, puzzled).

"It is love for every woman, every woman in France..." (vigorous head bobbing on my part at this juncture: shoulder to shoulder with you there my lad, thinks I)

"...and for every man!" (steady now Robespierre! Mind you, he could be the type...),

"My passion, my love, is for the whole of Humanity. My desire is to raise them all to Virtue, to Felicity"

I sighed inwardly with relief at this revelation and increased the nodding rate markedly. I could see his line of march now, the man was a zealot, a fanatic. Like all cold intellects he felt far more at home with abstract concepts. I knew the type; until my meeting with Madame Guillotine I had been in much the same case, preferring the ideal of being in love with Lucie to the terrifyingly complicated and slightly sordid business of actually making love to Miss Manette. Robespierre too, felt easier above such squalid matters as human love or individuals - his concern was not with people, but with The People. For the Incorruptible, Ideas were far safer to handle than the powder keg of real human emotions. A sou to a sovereign he was chaste as a monk. Permanently. They always are. *Virgo intacto*, no error.

"Virtues are simple" he proclaimed to the ceiling, which was, I noticed, rather charmingly ornate. "They are modest and poor... they are the patrimony of the People. Vices, on the other hand are rich. They are adorned by the love of pleasure and the snares of perfidy; they are escorted by all the dangerous talents; they are escorted by Crime."

You know, if I had heard this gammon just two days ago it might have had power to sway me. But since then, *non sum qualis eram**[1] - I had undergone a powerful initiation at the hands of Samson and his awful machine, and now I was a convert to a much more practical philosophy, one that Robespierre obviously found abhorrent - epicurean pleasures, wine, song, idle chatter, carnal love. *Carpe Diem* as his nose-blowing Romans would have said, though what I wished to seize might not have met with their commendation. For from this time on I was resolved to grab every moment of each day by the scruff of the neck and shake and worry the last morsel of pleasure and excitement and joy that I could from it. I'd wasted too much of my life in melancholy introspection - just as Robespierre was playing out his own days with dreams of dry, barren Idealism as the route to human happiness. You sapless sterile fool, I wanted to shout, logic and reason and intellect aren't even half the story - mental shields, nothing more, to guard us from the strength of our true feelings, our emotions, our passions. Lord, he was so wide of the mark he wasn't even facing the target.

Not that I was going to tell him. Too dangerous by half. Besides, he'd never have heard me for he was still in full cry: "Whoever does not hate Crime is incapable of loving Virtue" he intoned. "There are some who call for leniency for the royalists, and pity for the scoundrels. No!" his face was an implacable mask, the eyes like flint behind his glass lenses. "Pity instead the innocent, pity for the weak, pity for the unfortunate. Pity for Humanity." He completed his preoration in fine style, head half-bowed, his hands clenched with compassionate frustrated rage. It would have been quite moving if it wasn't for the fact that this angry little man was a blood-soaked monster, and the route

---

[1]   *I am not what I once was*

14

to death for countless hundreds of ordinary people, for all of whom he affected to profess so much love.

The head came up and he was off again like a coursed hare. "The Revolution elevates Virtue, it cannot be allowed to fail. Yet it is beset with enemies, both without and within. The slaves that Europe's monarchs sent against us have been successfully held at bay, we have beaten their armies at Handschoote, at Menin and on many another field of arms. But within, Sir, within! There are enemies everywhere, in the provinces, in Paris, within the Sections, even inside our beloved Assembly. Is this not so Defarge?

"*Certainement*, Citizen Deputy" returned Defarge dutifully, scowling his suspicion in my direction.

"And they must be rooted out, ground down, destroyed." He had worked himself up into a fine paddy by now; there was a slight froth of spittle at both corners of his mouth, and his breathing was laboured "Those that poison Virtue must pay the ultimate price. But for that we need information, details of their dalliance with Crime! Only then-"

An insistent rapping at the door finally put paid to this elevating homily, and not before time. Any more about Virtue and I might have given that morally-constipated moron the same riposte that Danton delivered some months later.[2] If I'd dared. As it was I said nothing as Defarge rushed to the door, turned the lock and stepped swiftly back as yet another overdressed dandy barged in, tall this time, and much younger than the Incorruptible, but with the same cold disdainful look about him. The light glanced from heavy gold ear-rings as he stalked purposefully across the room, his handsome head, the features almost feminine in their perfection, held high above a huge cravat, staring around him with the look of one for whom the rest of the human race are just so much cattle. Three stalwart Republican guard stood on the threshold, eyeing me leerily, bristling with pike, musket and sabre. The tall man took Robespierre by the arm and drew him into a corner, where they conferred mightily together, heads knocking. After a while Robespierre came up for air and beckoned Defarge into their little conclave. All I could hear were worried mutterings, so I gave up trying to listen in on their conversation, and contented myself with appraising the delectable Purveyor of Brandy, who had re-entered in the wake of the tall chap; she returned my gaze boldly enough, which gave me hope that I might number at least one admirer among the ranks of the *famille Defarge*.

After a space Robespierre broke away from the group and came towards me, brow furrowed, his thin lips pursed. "You must excuse me. Monsieur" he murmured distractedly. "St Just" he gestured towards the tall young popinjay who was already making for the door - so this was the infamous St Just, disciple of Robespierre's frigid philosophy, whose implacable pursuit of suspects and traitors had earned him the chilling soubriquet 'Angel of Death' - "St Just has brought distressing news... Important business of State calls me away.... We will speak again tomorrow, but for tonight you will be a guest of the Republic". St Just was already at the top of the stairs, standing there taut and chafing, the very picture of respectful impatience. "I will send someone to direct you to your lodgings in an hour or so. Citizeness Defarge can see to your needs until then. Please do not try to escape, it would be foolish in the extreme. There is a guard at the door, one in the street below and a third in the alley. Until tomorrow... ." and he was gone, out through the door like a whippet from the slips, calling on Defarge to follow. The sans-culotte made an ill-graced exit, his eyes bouncing suspiciously between the Citizeness and my sprawled figure. But go he must - in those days it was death to ignore a summons from Robespierre.

As the sound of their footsteps receded on the narrow staircase I lost no time in engaging the Citizeness in polite conversation. "Mademoiselle", (I guessed that, like all but the most republican of females, she would find the older, more gracious form of address more flattering) "you are kin to Citizen Defarge?

She blushed charmingly. "Yes... Monsieur. I have the honour to be his daughter". That stomached me, I swear. I could hardly believe my ears. That old goat had sired such beauty? "But, Sir, I do not think father likes you".

"It is of no matter", I answered, looking her frankly up and down. "What gives me greater concern is how I may stand with another, far more beguiling, Defarge."

"I am sure" says she archly "that you are capable of standing very well, should the occasion demand". She had somehow contrived to move closer to me, and suddenly I no longer felt exhausted. Quite the contrary.

"That I can" I said, affecting to ignore the delicious implication of her last remark, and raised myself swiftly from the chair, only to sway unsteadily on my feet. I allowed myself a small groan, and made great show of staying my tottering figure against the nearby card-table with one hand, frowning in pain, my eyes screwed closed, and drawing my other hand across my brow, in a passable imitation of a man on the point of collapse. It had the desired effect. She ran to my side and I allowed her to support my arm, resting my head against the wonderful scented softness of her hair. "Oh my brave Monsieur, but you are greatly fatigued by your *essai d'amour*." Not yet, thinks I, gazing down into those wide, adoring blue eyes, and swelling décolletage, but if my plans speed we both shall be, and very soon.

"Yes, yes" I gasped in what I hoped was a reasonable counterfeit of a spirit in agony, letting my hand drop exhaustedly onto her curved rump. "I desire only peace for my tormented soul, and solace from my woes"

"It would be my honour to help you" she whispered earnestly, her breathing laboured as I absently fondled her bounteous bosom. "The example of courage and true adoration you displayed today is worthy of any sacrifice, any reward....ooohhh Monsieur! .... Please, Monsieur...be patient....please, the door!" but I was ahead of her there and had already shot the bolt with my free hand, while my other pulled eagerly at her blouse. Praise be for the virtuous simplicity of Republican garb: she was in a state of lustful *deshabille* in no time, and moments later we were buckled to on the floor, with me pumping away merrily as we exchanged garbled endearments in French and English. She was most easy to please and we completed the engagement simultaneously in grand style. It must have been a bravura performance on my part, for no sooner had our duet finished than she slipped her tongue in my ear and whispered "Bravo Monsieur. Encore, encore..." and to the sound of tumultuous gasps and groans we mounted joyously into the second movement of our symphony. I'd heard it said that a close brush with death has the invariable effect of stimulating the generative capacities, and I can attest, on my oath, to the truth of the old saw. No sooner had we finished mixing French rump with English giblets than I found myself capable of a third bout with my delighted, appreciative partner.

God knows how long we would have gone on (though I'd have cried craven first, no question; Citizeness Defarge - or Suzanne as I now felt able to call her - was as avid a minx as ever played the two-backed beast), but as we lay there, in a state of amorous lassitude following our third encounter, I was startled from pleasant musings on the correctness of my new path in life by something heavy, probably a musket butt, crashing against the lock. The door shook twice more on its hinges. "Open, Open!" a rough voice called insistently through the panelling. "Open in the name of the Republic!" We disengaged in some panic, and while the Citizeness repaired to the kitchen to renew her revolutionary credentials, I dragged up my breeks and drew back the bolt to find myself facing a diminutive sergeant-at-arms, and clustered around him on the threshold a ragged company of revolutionary guard. "You are Carton?" he enquired brusquely.

"*Mr* Carton" I returned, in as dignified a manner as I could muster considering I was half-naked with my britches threatening imminent collapse.

"You will come with us"

"So, my man, my rooms are prepared?" I asked, as loftily as the situation would allow. No harm in keeping the little bugger firmly in his place.

He seemed to find the question amusing. "oh yes, *Mees-ter* Carton" he shot a glance at the squad behind him, raising his eyebrows at their suppressed Gallic giggles. But the voice was laced with menace as he turned back to look at me, his eyes contemptuous. "Yes, we have your room quite ready".

Something was dreadfully amiss. "Where am I to be lodged?" I blustered.

"You do not know?" He was smiling openly now, black teeth and bad breath. "You have a reservation - at the Conciergerie"

"What!" I took a step back from the door, my heart hammering, the bile rising in my throat. This could not be happening. "Th... The Conciergerie?" I stammered, "bu...bu.... but there is some mistake.. for God's sake - it's a prison for traitors!".

"Bien sur Mees-ter Anglais. But do not worry. Perhaps..." he drew his finger meaningfully across his throat "perhaps you will not lodge there long".

Chapter Four

One of the big mistakes these young writers - like our friend Dickens - make when they describe France during the '90s, is to view the whole show in black and white, as a simple conflict between revolutionary and royalist, a Manichean drama of Good against Evil, of the generous king and his noble friends and ministers overwhelmed and trampled down by the wicked revolutionaries, who live only to chop off aristocratic heads and sing the Marseillais in chorus. It is the most utter tosh, all of it. For a beginning the nobles, *Les Grands,* as they delighted in being called, merited everything that happened to them - most of 'em did, anyway. I mean, every country has its elite, who tend to accumulate privilege and keep the hoi-polloi at bay, but what civilised land would allow their blue-bloods exemption from taxes that even the poorest must pay, or the right to impose forced labour on their tenants. *Droit de seigneur* hadn't entirely disappeared from the list of traditional privileges either. Mind you, the clergy were no better, with their total tax exemption (except for the piddling *don gratuit*). The Church was the biggest landowner in France before the Bastille was stormed. Every bishop was a noble, most of 'em with two or three mistresses and a dozen or so bastards to their credit. Celibacy indeed.

But worse, much worse, than this wilful portrayal of high-born numbskulls and impious priests as innocent martyrs in the cause of freedom, is the image of the cohesion of their opponents, of the awful, evil unity of the Revolutionaries. Puffed up with ridiculous notions of Liberty, Equality and Fraternity, they are shown dedicated to the overthrow of everything civilised men (for which read Britons) hold dear, viz.: the holy trinity of royalty, property and wealth. Total galimatias. The leading lights of the Glorious Republic were as flawed a set of heroes as ever walked God's earth, and I should know for I met nearly all of 'em. Most, (Robespierre was an exception), were steeped to their hocks in intrigue, corruption and graft. And as for Unity - these giants of the revolution were forever at each other's throats, and hated and intrigued and conspired against their revolutionary brothers with far greater relish than they ever did the *ancien regime*. Power changed partners in Paris faster than a tu'penny whore, and it was hard to know from one day to the next who was master.

On the 17th December 1793, the night I found myself an unwilling guest of the Conciergerie, matters stood in this wise. The revolution had been running full tilt since 1789 and for many it had become a way of life. The bastille had been stormed on July 14th of that year and the prisoners released from their foul, mephitic cells (including old Manette, Lucie's sad, mad father); the privileges of the Church were swiftly swept away; the nobles had been dispossessed of their lands and fine chateaux, and had either fled or been executed; the Baker was dead, his head taken off by my old playmate Madame Guillotine, and the Baker's Wife had been given an identical revolutionary haircut a few months later, following a trial in which she was accused *inter alia* of Aggripina's crime with her son. She rode the tumbril in October; a Wednesday it was, if memory serves[3]. The regicide had stirred up a fine old storm beyond the Republic's borders - until then most European nations had been content to leave France to her revolution, but killing Kings just wasn't done in polite society, you see, and the Crowned Heads of Europe suddenly began to feel a lot less secure about their own necks. Austria and Prussia were soon at war with the fledgling republic. But far from cowing the revolutionaries, they replied with The Edict of Fraternity, claiming for France the 'natural frontiers' of the Rhine, Alps and Pyrenees. This had had been the last straw for Britain, who felt both its Channel security and its trade links to India threatened: together with Holland, Britain joined the alliance in the spring of '93, with Spain following suit in March. The outcome of all this was that revolutionary France now found herself at war with all of the great powers of Europe.

Within France things were in an even greater stew. There were almost constant insurrections in the provinces, either supporting royalist factions, or against the increasingly draconian edicts that issued from the Convention, the self-styled 'Guardians of the Revolution' who ruled from Paris. The rebels were strong in many of the provincial towns: Marseilles, Toulon and Lyon had all risen and repudiated the Convention. The Vendee was in flames. Desperate times, you'll allow, but 'comes the time, comes the man' as they say these days, and the crisis of Revolution had thrown up a whole series of remarkable men: scheming, careful Mirabeau; Marat, the scrofulous firebrand editor; Carnot the engineer, whom Napoleon was to call his 'organiser of victories'; George Jacques Danton, weak and courageous in equal measure; icy, impenetrable St Just and, of course, Citizen Robespierre.

Some, like the Incorruptible himself, (and the Angel of Death too, I fancy), were sincere in their own way - cold idealogues, yet holding firmly to their own perverse vision of a Better Future; but far, far more were lifelong devotees, high initiates, of the philosophy to which I had only recently become a convert. For such men, all the weighty problems of the day resolved themselves into a single simple question -

'How can I benefit?' Not that I blame them, you understand. Within the space of a few brief years their whole world had been turned upside down, the ancient social fabric of France was rent asunder, the established order abolished, and in its place, instead of the promised Equality, Freedom and Fraternity, there was only denunciation, arbitrary arrest and endless executions. The lack of what an Englishmen (or even a Prussian for that matter) would call a fair trial meant that life was precarious in the extreme, and *sauve qui peut* was undoubtedly the order of the day. Sensible too.

The upshot was internecine strife, chaos and faction, with endless sub-groups forming within and between the various cliques, and a constant shifting of alliances. I won't bore you with the details - can't remember them at this distance anyway - but the essentials were these: early on the new government had divided into three main parties or groupings, based loosely on their level of revolutionary fervour. Those tending towards some sort of reconciliation with the rump of the *ancien regime* were the Girondin, so named because many of their leaders came from the Gironde region of France. Opposing them were the extremists of the revolution, the Montagnards, the Mountain Men, who sat on the upper benches of the Assemby and believed they alone held the ethical heights of the revolt. The Montagnards were led by the true zealots of rebellion, the radical Jacobins, of which friend Robespierre was the leading light. In between these extreme positions lay a wide swathe of moderate deputies, known to the lofty Montagnards as The Plain, or more scathingly *Le Marais* (the Swamp). Nowithstanding their apparent differences, a high degree of moral panic pervaded the whole convention, with each group desperately trying to prove and maintain their own revolutionary credentials by ever more fearsome restrictions to liberty and justice (all in the name of freedom of course) while at the same time declaiming loudly against their opponents' monstrous failings and deceitful intentions to undermine the regime from within. There was, despite this, a kind of balance within the government, until, just two months before my own brush with French justice, Robespierre had organised the denunciation and execution of the Girondist leaders. It was the beginning of the Terror. Within days Brissot, Madame Roland and a score of others had been tried, condemned and given their quietus by Doctor Guillotine's fearsome engine.[4]

But a revolution is a hydra-headed beast and no sooner had Robespierre destroyed one 'moderate' party (I use the term loosely), than another rose up to take its place. This new group was led by Danton, a huge bull of a man with strong sensualist tendencies, a square pock-marked face and the voice of Stentor. Danton had been bosom friend to Robespierre in the beginning, as had Danton's second-in-command, Camille Desmoulins, a rather unstable young writer who I always found a particularly disagreeable companion, though Danton liked him well enough. But both men had grown weary of the incessant denunciations and beheadings and wanted an end to the Terror, a position which Robespierre seemed to take as a personal affront. Such pettiness was the norm for these 'united revolutionaries'; more often than not personal animosities took precedent over national interest, and throughout the years of '92 and '93 it was only the appalling incompetence of the Austrians and Prussians that prevented the speedy arrival of foreign troops in Paris and a swift end to the new nation. Xenophobia was rife; people of all political persuasions saw signs of British or Austrian or Prussian sabotage wherever they looked, and foreigners stood in no little peril of denunciation as a spy.

Which made my lodgings at the Conciergerie all the more repugnant and disquieting. The journey thither, along cobbled streets on an unsprung cart surrounded by pike-wielding citizen-soldiers, did nothing to assuage my fears. It was late dusk when we left and black night by the time we drew rein before a massive building, shadowed and shapeless in the gloom. Two men came forward with lanterns and, trembling and protesting, I was half-dragged along flickering torch-lit corridors and up bare stone stairways smelling of piss and vomit, always with a set of strong hands guiding my elbows and a couple of likely lads front and rear to forestall any chance of escape. We stopped suddenly, hard by a huge oaken door with a tiny, heavily barred window. Two sets of locks were turned and with a cheery *"bon nuit, Mees-ter Anglais"* from the despicable sergeant-dwarf, I was cast unceremoniously into the darkness, collapsing on my hands and knees against a stone floor covered with filthy straw and God knows what else. Shaking, cursing, I rushed to the tiny grille, screaming madly that they must let me out, it was all a mistake, I was a friend of the Revolution, an intimate of Robespierre, we had taken tea together only today. If they would just let me speak with him....

"They will not listen Monsieur". At first I thought I had imagined the words - the voice was calm, cultured, distinctly feminine, with a delicious lilt of creole *patois*, and the last thing I expected to find in this house of death. I had believed myself alone in the cell, but as I turned back from the door and accustomed my eyes to the heavy darkness, I discerned the form of a well-dressed female, sitting primly on the low trestle that offered the only piece of furniture in the room.

"Madame, your pardon" I murmured, bowing low in a forlorn attempt to restore my tattered dignity. "I did not realise I was in the presence of a lady. Pray excuse the vehemence of my protests". She was not young, I noted. But nor was she too old - I placed here somewhere around thirty, perhaps a little younger.

She inclined her head in acknowledgement. "It is only to be expected Monsieur. To be dragged from one's home, and thrown into this rat's nest of a place, without appeal, on the basis of the slightest suspicion..." her voice trailed off, seemingly in resignation, then suddenly she was on her feet, sounding forth, rigid with tension , shaking her fist at the door and those beyond it "It is intolerable! What else can one do but scream out one's anger at these revolutionary frauds who espouse Liberty and imprison the Innocent!"

True enough, but not perhaps the most politic of statements given our present peck o'troubles. Despite the danger I had to admit that I was drawn by her fiery anger, by what I can only describe as her presence. She was not a conventional beauty - a rather angular face, I remember, with a slightly aquiline nose - but she was one of your statuesque fillies, tall, high-breasted, with an abundant mane of chestnut hair, fairly radiating health and life and female fecundity. Ripe, you might say. In spite of my own depleted energies I was quite taken with her.

I inclined my head in solemn agreement as she ended her tirade "Indeed Madame. Your feelings echo my own. But how comes it that a lady of your undoubted breeding finds herself in such a plight? "

She smiled then, her teeth a flash of white in the darkness of the cell. "Ah good sir, it is truly a sorry tale, but not uncommon. My husband, Alexander, Comte de Beauhharnais - we are estranged - ", she added helpfully, casting me an odd sideways glance, as if secretly weighing me up, "the Count has been a faithful servant of the revolution since the beginning; did he not serve against the enemies of the Republic and rise on his own merit to command the Army of the Rhine? Yet he has been forced to resign his commission - his 'hereditary taint', as they call it here, has placed him under suspicion. It is despicable! Honesty and honour count for nothing, nothing! Slowly, so slowly, the net that will catch us all closes in!" She span to face me, her handsome features distorted with misery. "Not three weeks ago my cousin, Francoise, was arrested under the contemptible Law of Suspects and held at Sainte-Pelagie. And then... then the stroke I had feared all these past months fell....They came for me, this very night, and brought me here!" She flung herself into my arms, despair

personified. "I know not if the Count too is arrested, if he lives or dies! What will become of us?". God she was tall, our eyes were almost on a level. And such eyes - large and blue and beautiful, filled with tears and sadness and horror. "Oh Monsieur, I fear we are doomed. Marked for death. Both of us! I tremble to think of the fate that awaits us tomorrow. We shall not live to see another day".[5]
I surmised as much myself but to hear my worst forebodings confirmed in such stark terms set my innards seething. She was clinging to me like a drowning man to a spar, her head against my shoulder, sobbing, and it was only the delightful sensation of her bosom pressing against my chest that helped me turn my thoughts from my own imminent demise to matters of a more pleasant and uplifting nature. She really was quite lovely from the neck down. And suddenly, as if reading my own thoughts, she had dropped her hand and began the most intimate of caresses .
"Monsieur..." she breathed, not raising her head, nor ceasing her stroking, "kind Monsieur... I am estranged from my spouse... Alexander...we have not...the Count has not ... has not been a true husband to me for over a year" She was moving faster now, pressing herself against me. I've said earlier that escaping a hideous death makes you monstrous horny, and there was no question that, for the Countess, the reverse was also true - thoughts of her own impending dissolution seemed to have set the dear lady alight. "if I am to die tomorrow I should like, just once more, to enjoy the delights of the conjugal bed, even with a stranger. Dear Monsieur... kind Monsieur...you will oblige me...? "

Well, how could I refuse? Condemned man's last request and all that. Truth was, she had already worked me up into such a fine state of excitement that nothing short of the guillotine or firing squad could have prevented me having my way with her, whether she wished it or not. We disrobed swiftly, in a lather of excitement, and I'm proud to say that, despite my exertions earlier that evening, and regardless of the threat of a horrible death just hours away, I was still able to oblige the Countess Beauharnis to her evident satisfaction. In fact, I obliged her twice.

Which was just as well, for they came for her not long after, about an hour before dawn. She dressed calmly, taking as great a care with her *toilette* as if she had been off to a reception at Court, and it was a stab in the heart each time she turned to me and asked if her gown was too creased or if her ear-rings hung correctly. She kissed me on the forehead just before they took her away. "Do not worry Monsieur" she whispered, "I will remember you, and our night together, all my life". Which, as far as I recalled from my own tumbril ride, would be about another thirty minutes. I'm not ashamed to admit that I was crying as they led her away. Such a pointless waste of a fine spirited mount.

Not that I had much time to ponder the pathos and injustice of it all. They called me out a few hours later, and the sheer awfulness of what they planned, and what I was about to endure - again - simply overwhelmed me. Images of the seamstress's head chittering in the basket, of her decapitated, blood-soaked body with its shuddering twitching limbs, returned to me with hideous clarity. I could not, I would not, face that horror again! I was seized by a howling panic and rushed blindly from the voice that called me to death, leaping towards the high cell window, scrabbling up the rough stonework, laying hold of the bars and hanging on with the strength of a maniac. It took four of them to prise my fingers loose and carry me, screaming and flailing, from that fetid little room. I lashed out blindly as I was set down on my feet, howling curses, stumbling and blinking in the bright light. Then, gradually, it dawned on me that my hands were not being pinioned, that there were no other prisoners assembled, that the usual guards were absent, and that the Angel of Death - tall, suave St

Just - was watching me as I gasped and panted and swore, an amused smile on his handsome face. He held a fine linen handkerchief to his chiselled features - its perfume carried to me across the span or so which separated us - the monstrous revolutionary realities which his theories provoked were obviously distasteful to a man of his refined sensibilities. He preferred his verbal revolution at the Convention, abstract and sanitised. I hated him then - smiling and secure amid the hetacomb his beliefs sustained - with a fervour that seared my soul. I still do, though he's long dead. Hard to believe that his sand ran out a bare six months later, that I've outlasted the supercilious bastard some threescore years and more. Perhaps there is Divine Justice, after all.

But at the time St Just appeared to hold all the cards. "Come, come, Monsieur Carton" he said sardonically "it ill behoves love's hero of yesterday to unman himself in this way. *Du calme...du calme mon ami....* you will not die this day", and the lofty smile was like a knife in my stomach "Tomorrow?" his shoulders rose in an almost imperceptible shrug "Who can say? We live in perilous times, you and I. Come now, compose yourself. Citizen Robespierre wishes to renew your acquaintance."

Chapter Five

And that was as much as I could extract from him on the long carriage ride to Robespierre's private quarters at number 396 on the squalid Rue St Honoré. For all his power, the Incorruptible lived spartan fashion, in an obscure house smack in the middle of a timber yard, owned by a carpenter named Duplay, to whom he paid rent and board. As we rattled towards the entrance, I noticed a large imperial eagle carved over the archway, for all the world like that atop a Roman standard; a small thing, you'll say, but a singular coincidence in the dwelling of a man who, for all his democratic fustian, aimed at nothing less than the crown of Caesar. At the time all I could see was the aptness of the thing, for Robespierre looked set fair to seize absolute power. But it should have warned me, even then, of his eventual fate.

We were received most kindly by a serious young man with a wooden leg, the son of Carpenter Duplay, who ushered me quickly upstairs into Robespierre's *cabinet*, which, like the great Denounciateur himself, was small and impeccably clean, though not without charm. The place was full of flowers, set in vases in various parts of the room, and several cages containing song-birds adorned the walls near the window, which opened onto a small blossom-filled garden. There were at least two framed portraits on the walls, and two more in prominent positions about the room, all of Robespierre himself, eloquent testimony to the monumental egoism of this dangerous little dwarf of a man, who made bold to rule all France in the name of the People. The great man himself was in an armchair, reading. He rose at once, pushing his spectacles up onto his forehead, and received me graciously, as if I had not just endured a night of terror (Countess Beauharnais excepted) at his express command. I was handed to one of the hard straight-backed chairs by the window, and offered wine, which I accepted gratefully. I needed something to steady my nerves. Robespierre took the seat opposite, and again I was struck by the singular appearance of this intense, extraordinary man, with his low flattened forehead and awful fawn-coloured eyes. He smiled towards me with an affected look of kindness, but there remained something sardonic, even demonic, in his countenance, the deep marks of smallpox adding to the repulsive nature of his physiognomy. Knowing how totally I was in his power, he seemed to me like a bird of prey, a vulture eyeing its next meal.

"Mon cher ami" he began, and immediately the tocsin rang loudly in my brain. At what point had I become his dear friend? The Incorruptible wanted something of me, doubtless - I should already be a headless corpse otherwise - why else his smiling interest and this second meeting?

"You know of my admiration for you," the small neat figure in front of me continued smoothly "and of - your very good health, sir, the wine is to your taste? Excellent - of your courageous attempt at self-immolation. It was an act most noble, full of Virtue. But you must compose yourself, *mon brave*, for I have news that will test your courage once again....." He allowed the sentence to hang and the silence extend - ever the lawyer, playing for effect - then let the blow fall. "I must inform you that none of the suspects your sacrifice was designed to save have escaped Revolutionary Justice. They are taken - all of them".

I sat bolt upright in my chair, my glass falling unnoticed to the floor. "Lucie?" I croaked, gasping for air as if I'd been kicked in the midriff. Since my hedonistic conversion in the shadow of the axe the day before, and my vow to live for pleasure alone, I'd believed myself liberated from the sweet torment of the infatuation (as I'd persuaded myself it was) with Lucie Darnay, née Manette. Citizeness Defarge and the Countess had each in their way been tokens (and delectable tokens too) that I was free from all attachment. If I had given Lucie any thought at all, it had been to assume that she and Darnay and their companions had safely taken ship for London. But now! Knowing she might remain in peril shattered at a blow the carefully constructed wall of indifference I had been at such pains to erect. All the wretched longing, the vain, incurable love I felt for her sweet, innocent person flooded through me, filling me body and soul with a hopeless yearning. "Lucie? Monsieur Manette, Miss Pross, Jerry, Mr Lorry? All taken?"

"Indeed. They were apprehended in a forest outside of Amiens, on the Somme, just thirty leagues from Calais. Your brave scheme almost succeeded. You must be greatly disappointed".

I sank back into my seat, nodding disconsolately, yet inwardly ecstatic. For another thought had suddenly occurred to me, a thought that swept away much of my fear and despair. It was this: if all were taken, then Charles Darnay must also be back in French custody! This was cause for rejoicing, for whatever happened now, it was the end of the aristocratic buffoon - there was only the Guillotine, the lime pit, and an unmarked grave for him now. My mind raced ahead in joyous anticipation. He would never, never! have my darling again. His fate was sealed, and the spectre of widowhood now beckoned Lucie, a widowhood in which she would need comfort and support. And who better to comfort her - and to receive whatever gratitude she chose eventually to bestow - than the brave soul who had selflessly given his life - almost - for her happiness?

Of course, there were still enormous obstacles to this most devoutly to be wished outcome; not least that, as a suspect, captured while attempting escape, Lucie's life must be forfeit with the rest, (for there was not a shred of doubt in my mind that Lorry, Pross and Jerry would shortly receive their revolutionary haircut). But I had a shrewd suspicion that Robespierre, knowing he held Lucie's life in his gift, had carefully orchestrated my night in prison, and this meeting, in order to extract some service from me. But for the life of me I couldn't see how I might fit into his schemes. What, I puzzled, could he plan that needed my help? All he knew of me, surely, was my infatuation with Lucie, and my misconceived attempt to save Darnay - Darnay! I realised with a sudden spasm of dismay that there had been no word of Charles Darnay in Robespierre's report, that the Incorruptible had yet to confirm the Frenchman as a captive. Surely, of them all, he had not escaped? "Darnay?" I ventured , my heart beating just behind my teeth "Evremonde. What of him?"

Robespierre shook his head, looking at the carpet, and took his time to respond. "Alas..." he replied, the lilt in his strange, piping voice belying his words. "He is not with the rest.... Again, you will not find what I am about to say to your liking..." and the little weasel took a slow pull on his wine before continuing "...When the coach was stopped by our patriots, coward that he was, Darnay fled alone into the woods, abandoning his family and his friends to their fate. Three brave republicans pressed on his heels, under strict orders to capture him alive. The chase went on for over an hour, but the strength of desperation was with him and he began to draw away from his pursuers. To avoid his escape the fugitive was brought down with musket fire". He looked straight at me then, and the eyes were dagger points of barely concealed triumph as he watched me slump back, my head in my hands. "Charles Darnay is dead, we have his body. Unfortunately, the honest patriots were too... too enthusiastic. They used their sabres on him, Darnay's body received many cuts, his face was unrecognisable". He shook his head sadly, and for once the remorse was sincere. "A great pity. I should have liked to see his head on a pike, along with rest of the traitors and emigrés, as a warning to others. We must be implacable, adamantine, without pity, or Virtue will be submerged-"

I was watching his performance through my fingers, listening to him prate on and praying the sanctimonious little runt could not see the grin that threatened to split my face. It was true then, valid, sealed and confirmed. He was gone. That bastard Darnay was with the Choir Invisible, at last, and probably already demanding a position as chief baritone. All that remained was to save my beloved Lucie and to finesse her and myself far, far way from this homicidal pygmy and the fatal lunacies of Republican France.

No easy task, you'll allow. But, as I suspected, the weasel-faced homunculus in front of me was thinking along very similar lines - though for his own ends entirely. Once his latest Republican Rant had exhausted itself, he approached the real subject of our meeting slantwise, first informing me that I should not worry unduly, the prisoners were being held "for the moment" in rooms at a nearby inn, heavily guarded of course, but well cared for with the best their captors could provide in vittals and wine.

I caught at that. "For the moment you say. What then, will become of them?"

Robespierre spread his hands. "What else? They conspired to evade Revolutionary Justice, to aid the *emigré* Darnay to escape. As you did yourself. This Monsieur Lorry, his servant, and the woman, Madame Pross" his right hand flicked repeatedly, waving away their lives, "It is the Place de la Revolution for them, and Samson's ministrations. The Order of Execution lacks only my signature". The omission of Lucie and her father - and myself - from this heartless, casual proscription hadn't escaped my notice. I leaned forward, letting hope shine from my eyes. "But what of Monsieur Manette, and his daughter?" I thought it best not to mention yours truly - Robespierre laboured under the preconception that I still held my life at nought, and it was important he continue in his folly. "Can they be saved?" The Incorruptible's stern, pinched features softened slightly. "Their case is somewhat different" he sniffed "As a former prisoner of the Bastille, Manette is held in high esteem by the People. And his sufferings there, as you are aware, have affected him deeply, most deeply, disturbing the equilibrium of his mind, so that he is now quite unaware of his surroundings or even of the presence of his own daughter". Well that was true enough, I'd seen him - the poor cull was *non compos mentis* and then some.

He paused, and I let the silence lengthen, awaiting his offer (for an offer there would be, I was certain of it) and unwilling to say anything that might jeapordise the way his mind was running. After what seemed an age, he began again: "To place under trial and to execute" (the two actions seemed inseparable in Robespierre's mind) "such a hero of the Revolution, especially in his present condition, would be a scandal... we might be seen as over-zealous, even inhumane" (a little late for that, laddie, I thought, my tongue near bitten through). "It has therefore been decided" says this hypocritical Holy William, "that for the good of the Republic it is best to give out that Manette was unaware of the conspiracy that surrounded him and remains blameless." He paused again.

I knew he had baited his hook but I threw myself willingly upon it. "And Lucie?" I demanded "what of her?"

"Ah, the widow Darnay" says the devious, dandified dwarf, and I must say it sounded well, the widow part, at least. "She is as deep in this as the rest and, unlike her father, the People are indifferent to her fate. Her guilt is beyond cavil. It is the Guillotine for her." I groaned aloud at this, falling back into my chair, truly mortified, but with all my faculties alert, waiting, hoping, for Robespierre to spring his trap. He was watching me carefully, his eyes hard behind his spectacles as he held up a restraining, well manicured hand. "Or perhaps I should say... it *ought well to be the guillotine.* However... matters may perchance be modified..... ". I sat up at this, rigid with a tension that was only partly simulated, making my expression glow with a new-found optimism. He too sat forward, steepling his fingers, our heads just a span apart. God, but he was an ugly little man, with breath to match. "The truth is" the piping voice continued "that I am very much moved by your actions of yesterday. You have melted my heart."

In a pig's eye, but I nodded attentively, never taking my eyes from his own gimlets. "Your selfless sacrifice deserves reward. For myself, I would for your sake allow Manettte and his daughter, and yourself, safe conduct to England this instant", he shook his sallow-green head in counterfeit regret. "But the Committee of Public Safety... the members would never allow it. I should lose my own head, and that would mean disaster. Without my guiding hand, my careful counsel, who knows what disasters the Republic may endure".

It was my turn to shake my head, lowering my eyes as we both contemplated the horror, the barrenness, of a world without Robespierre. Simultaneously I puzzled to myself what the diminutive intriguer was leading up to, for this whole performance was certainly part of some guileful device to mould my will to his. What could he want of me? "No, it is not possible" he continued. Unless...."

"Yes?" I exploded, seizing his hands desperately. I knew my role, you see - the more so as, for the most part, my concern for Lucie's safety, and my own, was real enough. "Yes? Tell me, sir, I pray you! What can be done?"

"Unless..." says the Incorruptible, quickly detaching his hands from my own, distaste curling his narrow features (hated physical contact, you see - *virgo intacto*, as I said) "...Unless there were extenuating circumstances. If, shall we say, you were able to perform some valuable service

36

to the Republic, some task dangerous that would put the Committee forever in your debt, and make them as charitably inclined towards you as I am myself. This could, in fact I am sure it would, change everything vis-à-vis Miss Mannette".

And without so much as a by your leave he launched himself into a detailed description of his murderous plans for me. The Committee of Public Safety was filled with 'traitors' - by which he meant any whose revolutionary vision differed from his own - all of whom it was his duty to 'purge'. As he spoke it became clear that Robespierre saw himself as a centrist, holding the middle ground between the moderates (the chief of which, as I've said, were Danton and his scribbler friend, Desmoulins) and the *enragés*, also known as Hebertists, extremists led by the firebrand orator Jacques Rene Hébert. Strangely enough, seen in those terms, there was much truth in what Robespierre said. Since the sudden death of his wife and its hideous aftermath Danton[6] had become disillusioned by the endless bloodshed and had tried to force through a policy of reconciliation within the nation and peace overtures abroad (there were even rumours of a restoration of the monarchy). By contrast, Hebert and his minions believed that only a savage repression, a ten-fold increase in Terror could save the 'purity' of the Revolution and secure the safety of the Republic. Robespierre sat between these extremes: he had little truck with reconciliation with enemies of the state, but he wanted to use the Terror sparingly (in his terms) to execute only those who had led the masses astray and not, as one noted Hebertist had seriously suggested, to indulge in an orgy of beheadings designed to reduce the population of France from 27 to just 10 million souls. As his briefing progressed, it became obvious that Robespierre regarded the *enragés* as by far the most present danger. And that he intended to destroy them.

Hebert's men were especially active in Lyon, doing bloody murder in the aftermath of the city's failed insurrection. It had been decided to make an example of Lyon, but few in the Committee of Public Safety had realised their decision would unleash such an endless wave of atrocities. This was where the most damning proof of the Hebertist guilt would be found and thence, I discovered with my heart beating retreat and my innards dissolving, I was to go as a spy to amass the evidence that he, Robespierre, would put to the Committee of Public Safety and so bring about the Hebertists downfall. A good plan, yes? asked this miniature Machiavelli, then pressed on without awaiting a reply (which was just as well; I had known something was in the wind, but these sudden revelations had left me utterly unmanned, speechless with fright). I was, I discovered, perfect for this important role: I spoke good French and what little accent I possessed could be put down to regional dialect - people from all over France were on the move, my arrival would excite no suspicion. And my *cher ami* Robespierre could help me further. He had an associate - Proteus - whose skill in disguise was unparalleled. This master of dissimulation would train me in the rudiments of the art so that my true identity would remain forever inviolable. I should be in the Incorruptible's employ for no more than a month, two at the most. Then, with the Hebertists humbled and Robespierre a rung closer to absolute power, then at last, Lucie and I (with old Mad Manette safely in tow) would be given safe conduct to Calais, where it would be all aboard and up anchor for Merry England. I had his word on it. Could anything be easier?

"What then, Monsieur, is your answer? Are you willing to aid the Republic? It will not be for long"

So there it was; a 'task dangerous' (for which read suicidal, for I did not share the Incorruptible's impregnable confidence that I could pass unnoticed as a Frenchman) and in exchange I was offered my own, and Lucie's, release. I was in bad bread right enough, and I didn't like it above half, and nor did my deliquescing bowels. I closed my eyes, clasping my hands to disguise their shaking, and tried desperately to think my way out of this nightmare. For all his talk of aiding the Republic, Robespierre was finagling me into a personal vendetta, into a power struggle with his political enemies, dangerous men who knew of the Incorruptible's enmity and who would stop at nothing to turn the tables and see him mount the scaffold in their stead. They knew, you see, that if they did not guillotine him he would certainly send them to look through the small window. It was war to the death, albeit a battle fought slowly with unctuous phrases and midnight cabals and sudden denunciations

One thing was certain, once I took this step there could be no turning back. I should be Robespierre's man and were he to fall, I and all his followers and allies would follow him to execution. It was madness.

On the other hand, only yesterday I had believed my life to be over, had quite literally had my head upon the block. And I had come off - by blind chance or the mysterious workings of destiny I couldn't tell, but I had somehow won through and, britches soiled but otherwise whole, I had escaped. Besides, in the space of the last twelve hours I had blown the grounsels with two of the most beautiful women in revolutionary France, several times over. My spirits rose at the thought of their embraces - there was danger in Lyon, doubtless, but who knew what other sweet possibilities might await me if I risked it all on this one desperate throw. A man with quick wits and a ready tongue might yet escape the fickle sweep of the Reaper, even in such a place. And there was the equally delightful prospect, should I outlast these perils (and if Robespierre's word could be trusted, which I doubted) of a joyful reunion with Lucie, and of carrying her back, like some Classical hero in the books she delighted to read, from the mouth of death to England and safety. Could she then be anything other than grateful?

Then again, was that what I wanted - *domus et placens*

uxor?*² Lucie and quiet domesticity? Yesterday morning I would have gladly sold my soul for such a prize; but by evening of the same day, schooled by Madame Guillotine and sated with Miss Defarge, I despised it; and yet now, just minutes since, the simple mention of Lucie's name had recalled all the old yearning. Were my feelings for Miss Manette real? or merely an emotional spasm, a cloud passing before the sun of my true (and much baser) emotions? My mind was in turmoil, betwaddled, and who could blame me after all the horrors I had endured in the past day and a half?

Besides, it was all one. For, whatever else was true, and whatever imagined, one certainty stood foremost: although all-unspoken, the threat that lurked behind Robespierre's offer was real enough: Refusal would lead Lucie only one way - to trial, condemnation, and an early appointment with Samson, the pitiless state executioner. And while that was bad enough, an even worse fate would be in prospect. I, too, must be executed; in fact, there was little hope I would survive another night, should I spurn this last avenue to safety. Put that way, the riddle was easily told. There could be only one response. I opened my eyes, lifted my chin and stared boldly into Robespierre's unblinking, sphinx-like face.

"My answer, Citoyen? *Vive le Republique!*"

---

²   * *home and a pleasant wife*

Chapter Six

Dante. It was the first thought I had after breasting a rise
on the northern coach road and gazing across at the once
fair city of Lyon, set upon its many hills. The place was
an inferno: fires everywhere, casting tongues of flame high
above the rooftops, licking out from doors and windows,
while the winter clouds hung in a solid mass over the
city, casting back a dull red glow, as if heaven itself was
attempting to draw a veil over this hellish scene. The faces
of my escort were bathed in the sickening, flickering light as
we sat our horses, breath smoking in the frosty January air,
and stared all unbelieving at that dreadful conflagration.
"Sweet Jesu" the sergeant at my elbow muttered in horror,
then remembered himself, coughed, and turned in his
saddle to face me. "Sir, this is as far as we go. You must
make the rest of the journey alone, for your own safety."
And for yours, I thought sourly, dismounting with ill
grace, my movements still uncomfortable in the stiff, dirt-
begrimed weeds of my chosen disguise. The sound of a
collapsing building carried to us on the still night air and
with it the unmistakable mournful keening of humans in
torment. The horses shied nervously as the sergeant took
the reins of my mount from my unwilling hands; he saluted

briefly, then he and his four-trooper escort turned and were thundering away northwards, leaving me standing alone in the freezing, doom-laden darkness. I continued to stare down the road long after they had gone, hoping against hope that, even now, it was all some dreadful mistake and that they'd come riding back, laughing and joking, to whisk me away to Paris and.... to what? Robespierre's tender mercies? There was no help for it. Sighing, I hefted the clutch of packages onto my shoulders and rode Bayard of the ten toes towards the forbidding vision of hell to which my own idiocy, and Robespierre's mad scheming, had condemned me.

Though I dreaded my mission, I was quite confident of my disguise. My two weeks with Robespierre's associate Master Proteus had been a revelation, and had revealed in me a quite unlooked for ability in dissimulation. Why he insisted on his classical *nom de guerre* I've no idea - everyone knew the gentleman in question as Jean-Marie Forez, a famous thespian of the Proissard. He was lodged in a narrow alley, just off the Rue de Grenelle, hard by the Champs de Mars, and when, the day after my final interview with Robespierre, I arrived there and hammered on his portal, I was received by an old, bent grandfather with a voice as thin and whispery as his hair, and ushered upstairs into a spacious drawing room. As I seated myself on the handsome chaise longue and accepted a brimming glass of wine, the old boy bustled unsteadily about the room, muttering away to himself, clearing wine glasses and plates (there had obviously been some sort of soirée the previous evening) and stacking them on a nearby card table.

"Will the Monsi...the Citizen be long?" I enquired, by way of conversation.

" Eh? Whassat?" Methusaleh returned creakily. "Did'ee say something, eh?"

"The Citizen, your master?" I enunciated the words slowly and carefully, in deference to his antique lugs. "will... I... see...him ... soon?

"Eh? What? Oh! yes, yes..." gasps this wizened bag-o'-bones, and then suddenly, without warning, Methuselah absolutely metamorphosed before my astonished gaze. As God's my Maker, he seemed to grow twelve inches or more in height, his voice deepening, girth widening, and the years somehow dropping away "You may, Monsieur Anglais, see Proteus at once!" And now, there before me, was a figure of middle height, somewhat corpulent, fresh complexioned, his countenance bright and beaming with satisfaction at the success of his transformation and the look of stupefaction on my face.

"Good God!" I gasped with heartfelt amazement. "You're Monsieur Forez. Yes, you are, of course you are, I've seen you at the theatre. How in the name of Heaven did you do that?" My confusion was genuine. The man was a genius. "You're either in league with the Devil or...." I looked down at the glass in my hand, "...has my wine been doctored?"

Proteus drew himself up in one of his famous theatrical poses, legs wide, his right hand raised "Neither wizard nor poisoner, my dear sir" The hand flirted gracefully in an exaggerated bow in my direction. "Merely a skilled practitioner of my humble craft, to wit, the art of masquerade, of bending reality to my will, of persuading an observer to see that which I wish him, or her, to see.... The rudiments of which, I am commanded - by the illustrious Citizen Robespierre, (something in the way he delivered this phrase imbued it with a definite flavour of irony) - to teach to your good self over the next few days."

We began that same afternoon, following a sumptuous lunch at which Proteus bombarded me with endless tales of his theatrical triumphs. But for all his bombast this mincing Roscius knew his trade, and in those few days I learned a skill which has served me well all my life and has preserved this old carcase from destruction on diverse desperate occasions, as you'll hear, if God spares me long enough. But what was really amazing was the utter simplicity of Proteus' technique. He taught me early that my notion of

disguise as puttied cheeks, counterfeit moustachios and
false beards was naïve, and worse, downright dangerous.

"You see my dear, it is all a matter of perception". He was
sitting cross-legged on the mahogany table of his workshop,
its top strewn with wigs, toupées and a gallimaufry of
powders and face paints such as you might see in any
actor's dressing room. Huge mirrors on every wall threw a
multitude of infinite, reflected images of the Maestro between
the glass, slowly fading in the flickering candlelight. He
had taken pains with his toilet since our first meeting, all
silks and lace, and his florid face was carefully powdered,
the cheeks rouged, and his lips seemed more than naturally
coloured, especially for a man approaching fifty. A back
gammon player[7], right enough, his fancy ran more toward
Ganymede than Venus, that much was plain. And - from
the coy sideways glances he continually threw my way -
deeply unsettling. "I say again, dear boy, Perception is
all". He slipped from the table and ripperty-tippertied
to the seat next to my own, affecting what I'm sure the
old backslider believed was his most alluring smile. "You
must forget these fancies, this concern with changing your
physiognomy. Unless you have ears like windmill sails or
the nose of a gargoyle - and you are, I see, blessed with
pleasingly regular features..." he was patting my knee most
disconcertingly "...Quite handsome in fact, in the Classical
style... but I am digressing dear boy, business first - Now,
as I say, unless you are preternaturally ugly, the question of
your features is secondary. Watch now..." and he turned to
the nearest mirror and spent the next few minutes carefully
fitting a false nose to his face, before swinging back towards
me in triumph, beaming his pleasure. "Voila! I have
changed my appearance, have I not?" Well, his look had
altered somewhat and, eager to ingratiate myself, I nodded
assent. His smile vanished. "Non! Non, non, non - I have
not.!" and he leaned forward, wagging an admonishing
finger in my face "You think the different nose produces
the disguise? *Idiot!* No, not if I continue to walk in my

usual style, to retain my normal mannerisms, to hold my body in its accustomed posture, to laugh, to smile, even cough or spit in the same way, or keep the same tone to my voice. Then, I have changed *nothing*, because I am still recognisable as myself, because what constitutes 'myself' is the combination of all these things that others perceive and know about me. And my 'cunning disguise', with its puttied nose, or ridiculous false beard is, *sans aucun doute*, a farce." He paused, considering "Such a ploy is not entirely useless; it may help in certain extenuating circumstances - should you need to pass by someone who is excessively familiar with your features, shall we say. At a distance. But close to..." and here he thrust his face within a hand's breadth of my own, nor, I noticed, did he miss the opportunity this afforded him to place a hand higher up my thigh "See! It is too blatant, too obvious a fake, *n'est-ce pas?*"

It was true. Despite being so carefully applied, seen at close quarters the false nose would have fooled no one. I'd never considered the matter carefully before, but I could not fault his argument. Where we normally see such disguises, at the theatre or in street-plays, we voluntarily enter a very different world, a place in which each of us cheerfully suspends our critical faculties and accepts all manner of false simulation, eager to escape reality and submerge ourselves in the hamfatters' happy illusion. It's the same with so-called masters of modern literature - Dickens and his ilk - the hero is forever donning a moustache or hairpiece, walking incognito into the Jaws of Death, and snatching his ladylove from a fate worse than death at the hands of the dastardly (and presumably myopic) villain. The trouble is, we tend to carry over these dramatic tableau into the real world, and assume that the techniques of the theatre and novella will do duty in our own lives. But of course, it is all so much wishful thinking. As Proteus had so ably demonstrated, they don't pass muster. Something else is needed. But first, with the old quean's fingers half-way up my thigh, it was necessary to set out plainly the terms of our mutual cooperation.

"The thrust of your argument is strong, Citizen Proteus" I whispered, leaning back from that gross, over-painted visage, "you make your point well and I will not forget. But one thing.... if you do not remove your hand from my leg, at once, then, Robespierre or no, *this point* ..." and I slid the tip of my poignard swiftly against his wattled throat "...will be the last you ever remember"

He whipped his hand away as if it had been burned and sat back, pouting grotesquely. "Oh anger! Such strength, so vigorous.... but I do like that. I had cherished the hope" he continued a moment later, eyelids fluttering "that I might have made acquaintance with the strong thrust of quite another dagger in your possession." He gave an exaggerated sigh "Ah me! Alas. But not everyone.... and that other Anglais... he was so much more accommodating."

My ears pricked at this. "What? One of my countrymen? Here? In Paris? Say on..." And I laid the dagger's point close to his crotch "Speak now, or before I'm done you'll trill an octave higher, by God you will!. Say on damn you!"

"Oh rough and wicked" breathed this ageing pederast, hands fluttering on his chest. I believe he was enjoying himself immensely "It is of no great moment. Nothing to concern the Incorruptible, or the security of the Republic. Just a rich *Anglais* seeking amusement."

This was news indeed! A fellow countryman, who might well provide the chance of succour; for, despite the risks involved, what freeborn Englishman would allow another to languish under Robespierre's wicked heel? Well I, for one, but there were plenty more brave lads besides, all puffed up with patriotic zeal, who would count it their bounden duty to lend a hand. If this chap was a bold enough fellow, we might together formulate a plan of escape for myself, and for Lucie. Yes, the more I considered it, the more it seemed a God-sent opportunity to flee Robespierre's pernicious grasp. I was in a lather of frustration. "For the Love of God, man, speak plainly! Who was this Englishman?"

"A nobleman. He came sometimes with his friend, Sir Andrew Ffoulkes. Such fine, firm-limbed young men." Proteus had an expression on his face such as I'd seen earlier that morning in my shaving mirror, as I recalled Citizeness Defarge and the Comtesse. "Yes, Sir Percy was a very apt pupil. And so very keen. We spent several, productive - and creative - afternoons together. Oh indeed, he was very creative."

I had no doubt he was, for I was now pretty certain I knew the blueblood whom Proteus found so amenable. Not socially you understand; he existed in far too rarified a social strata for us ever to have met. But I'd seen him right enough, strutting in the streets or branking at the theatre, surrounded by his catamites, tricked out in silk and satin, the conceited overweening fop, gold cane, snobbish looks and mincing gait. Ignored his wife too, by all accounts, though she was as sweet a piece of crackling as you could wish to set your teeth to. Though just why Sir Percy Blakeney might wish to avail himself of this fellow's art was beyond me.

To fool his friends in some imbecile jape, doubtless, the preening coxcomb. But -

"You would like me to contact him, perhaps?" Proteus' voice broke in on my disappointed ruminations, and I noticed absently that he had taken the opportunity to place his hand tentatively on my shoulder. "We remain in contact, Sir Percy and I" he went on, "Discreetly of course, considering the tenor of the times. It would be a simple matter for me to send a short missive" the rheumy old eyes had taken on a dreamy expresssion, "it would be good to see him once more, to reactivate our friendship."

Watching him simper away, I came close to laying the ridiculous old fruit out cold. Sir Percy Blakeney? Aid in escape? The very idea was ridiculous. Involving that addled-pated peacock in any scheme would simply invite disaster. "Thank you, Proteus" I answered coldly, sheathing my stiletto and looking through the glacial panes at the icy hail falling on the cobbles outside, suddenly chilled, despite the warmth of the hearthfire . "I have no wish to meet the gentleman at present" Aid and succour from Blakeney? I'd sooner trust my life to a drunken donkey.

Now, I've always been a firm believer in the old adage: "what you can't get out of, get into", and so, with this brief candle of hope extinguished, I damned Sir Percy to hell, and fell to my studies with a will. And once we'd established the terms of our teaching contract, that I was in no wise a Gentleman of the Back Door, nor wished to be, Proteus and I got along well enough, and I quickly mastered the essentials of his craft. This was, as I've already indicated, that successful disguise has nothing to do with those things most people consider absolutely indispensable to impersonation, and that it was almost exclusively a question of thinking yourself into the character of the person, or rather the class of persons, you wish to mimic.

I found the whole thing rather easy - any lawyer would, I suppose, my profession being stuffed to the gills with fraudsters. In truth, the whole judicial process is based on deceit and dissimulation, with prosecuting and defending counsels spending their time pretending (subject to who is paying) a certainty of guilt, or an assurance of innocence, that they naturally do not feel and yet - to be successful - must of necessity convey to the jury as the genuine sentiments of their heart. Dissimulation is bred in the bone of all true lawyers, they suck it with their mother's milk, and I took to Proteus' training like David's Sow to drink. Half my hours were spent idling on the frigid cobbles of Paris, freezing my nether regions as I observed the fishwives, farriers, butchers and water carriers, the coal sellers, card sharps, cut-purses and footpads, all the myriad bustling, jostling, cursing street life of the capital, carefully making notes on mannerisms, argot, clothing and custom. The remainder of the day was passed indoors, under the Maestro's baleful eye, togging myself up in their various vestments and affecting to enter into the spirit of each trader or petty criminal.

And shirt-lifter though he undoubtedly was, wasn't he the martinet when it came to performing? Nothing was ever perfect. Everything, each piddling little detail, had to be rehearsed with infinite patience, a score of times or more. I hated the long hours, the boring repetition of movements, the interminable reiteration of regional accents (I even tolerated Proteus' occasional erotic sally in my direction - the old reprobate couldn't keep his hands to himself - and unwelcome as his attention was, at least it alleviated the tedium of my existence).

But most of all I detested the fact that everything I did was performed under duress, that I was not my own master, and little better than a slave; I was a vassal of Robespierre, in thrall to that weasel-faced pygmy, and subject to his slightest whim. I swore then that, should I get the chance to free Lucie from her imprisonment, she and I would flee France at all hazards.

But for my very life I could not set the Incorruptible at defiance, nor refrain from attending to the task the cold-eyed sphinx had contrived for me, and gradually my studies began to bear fruit. Building on my natural aptitude for dissimulation, I could soon camouflage my own character completely, and take on another with an ease that astonished my tutor and wrung from him the grudging soubriquet 'Chameleon'. I would, no doubt, have benefited from further schooling, but under the impatient promptings of Robespierre (who was himself hard pressed by his enemies, and required a return on his investment sooner rather than later), Proteus pronounced himself tolerably satisfied with my progress and, following one last forlorn attempt on my virtue, discharged me from his school for stage-craft and like deviancies.

Two days later, I was escorted to the outskirts of Lyon by the five horsemen aforesaid, and unceremoniously launched into my new career as republican spy. And so complete was my disguise that my own mother, God rest her, would not have seen the son she bore in the itinerant barber-surgeon who trudged stolidly towards what remained of that unfortunate city. Certainly, no one gave me more than a passing glance as I made my way among the cannon-shattered, smouldering ruins. Despite the carnage, many folk were making their way thither. An army of looting, raping, murdering revolutionaries still needs feeding, still demands clothes for their backs, and warmth, and entertainment, and - given humanity's limitless vanity, even amid the horror of hades - they still require their beards shorn and their hair cut. So there was no shortage of bold entrepreneurs upon the road, each willing to brave the barbarisms of revolutionary justice to turn a fine profit. I would hardly be noticed among the horde of vultures flocking to feed upon the corpse of Lyon.

No, entering Lyon was not the problem - surviving, and returning scatheless from the inferno - that was the real trick of it. For there was death everywhere. I carry with me a series of nightmare images that refuse to fade: a mother crooning a lullaby to a dead infant amid a heap of decapitated corpses; a young man crawling on the frozen ground, desperately trying to remake his stomach, pressing lengths of yellow-green bowel back into the yawning sabre gash across his belly, screaming the while; two emaciated waifs playing catch-as-catch-can around a hideously bloated cadaver, their bare feet black with blood; the city square, lit by the flickering glow of burning buildings, its cobbles strewn with over a hundred corpses, their features hideously mangled by grape-shot; Revolutionary Guard, grim and well-turned out, leather and brass-work polished, bayonets gleaming redly and throwing back the flames, marching yet another score of the condemned - men and women of all ages, some with infants clinging to their mother's skirts - to the killing ground in front of the cannon; young lads and maids bound together in an obscene parody of a lover's embrace and driven to the *Brotteaux* to be blown to fragments; the river running so red with blood that the jest went round its scarlet hue would prove a warning to counter-revolutionaries in Marseille, nearly two hundred miles to the south. *Lyon n'est plus* they said, and dear God, they were right.

But more unsettling than all these sights is the memory of the hideous reek of the place - the stench of smoke and gunpowder mixed with entrails and blood and shit, and the roast-pork odour of charred human flesh . Dead bodies - intact dead bodies - you can get used to; they're not too unsettling after a while; often, you can pretend they're asleep. But for true horror nothing compares with soiling your boot in the dark, and finding that the sticky mess you are cleaning off is a squashed human liver, or a gelatinous mass that was once someone's brain; or again, knocking your head against an obstruction that turns out to be a kidney - for all the world like that of an ox - but a kidney that belonged to some unfortunate enemy of the Republic, hanging from a rafter by the long white strand of whatever it is that comes from the centre of its ghastly bean-shaped mass. Body parts strewn everywhere - for me they came to symbolise the harrowing torment of Lyon in its death-throes. I remember sitting uncomfortably on a stool one evening, rummaging irritably about in the half-light, and finding a hand lodged beneath my buttocks - well, part of a hand, three fingers and half a palm it was. I threw the horrid thing off into the darkness somewhere and continued eating my supper with hardly a thought. The continual disgust numbs your senses, you see, and you shut down all finer feelings in an attempt to cope. It's only later, months later, that the nightmares begin.

But for all the atrocities and death, a life of sorts went busily on. The People, in the form of avenging sans-cullotte or stern republican soldier, continued to eat, drink, sing and fornicate amidst the hetacomb. More importantly, their hair and beards continued to grow, and as all Froggies - most of them anyway - are punctilious about their appearance, my newly assumed tonsorial skills were greatly in demand.

My first salon was a single chair, set on a shattered street corner, but so successful was this initial foray into the world of business that Gaston Dupré (my fledgling alter ego), very soon removed to a tiny closet above a boisterous tavern. What was more, my choice of occupation proved inspired, for who has heard of a taciturn barber? I engaged my patrons in constant conversation, swapping witticisms, gossiping, but always careful, amid the general badinage, to sound each client out, to discover in what gainful employment they were engaged, and to extract from each the maximum amount information for my weekly report to Robespierre. Within a fortnight - as word of my expertise spread - I was able to hire a tolerably clean ground floor room with upholstered chairs and a cracked mirror in which to host my increasingly grand clientele. Eventually I had Revolutionary Judges, Officers of the Guard, bureaucrats of note, and even bigwigs from the Paris Commissioners themselves as patrons, which suited my schemes wonderfully.

My establishment was next to a knocking shop - bad for business you might think, but nothing of the sort: there's nought as garrulous and slip-tongued as a self-righteous sans-culotte who has just enjoyed a skinful of *vin ordinaire* along with his oats. The contact to whom I delivered my reports whispered that the Incorruptible was tolerably pleased with my work, which I took to mean that his collating of damning evidence against the Hebertists was progressing well, and that old weasel-face would soon be mounting the rostrum at the Convention and denouncing his foes in terms that would lead them, ineluctably, to an appointment with the Blade of Equality. Bad luck, but I can't say I was too bothered. The bastards who destroyed Lyon deserved no-one's pity. The guillotine? Too good for them.

So the days went by, and there was I, shaving away diligently at the corpulent neck of some sweating minor bureaucrat and trying to pry from him what information I could, when the door behind me burst open - and suddenly all the noisy banter in my little establishment faded to silence. It was as if an icy hand had frozen the mouths of everyone in the place, and it had precious little to do with the cold blast of air that had entered along with a most singularly unpleasant ruffian. The pompous old greywhiskers I'd been shaving took a quick, wide-eyed look in the mirror, and burst from his seat like a rocket, hurriedly offering his place to the newcomer, a squat, gotch-gutted knave, bat-eared, unkempt and slovenly in mud-smeared morning coat and breeks, with a three day beard and a long black mane restrained in a greasy pigtail.

He flopped himself down and eyed me dispassionately through the mirror, as if I were a particularly large louse he'd spied crawling beneath his shirt. "Shave" says he peremptorily "trim the sidewhiskers". Nothing else, but it was enough to make me jump, for beneath his taciturn demeanour you could absolutely feel the malign hatred of the man, a white hot furnace of anger that threatened at any moment to burst its bounds and spread fatal destruction through the world. I could almost smell the rage and see the smoke rising, like looking at a volcano through a glacier, and a damned thin sheet of ice at that. A rare cull this, and one who'd bear careful handling.

That said, I couldn't just shave him in silence, now could I? So I attempted a little conversation, essaying him with two of my standard verbal gambits, on the coldness of the weather, and how well maintained our local Guillotine was, compared to that of Paris. One innocuous, you see, and t'other designed to display my impeccable revolutionary credentials. Both got nowhere. The first he simply ignored. At my second sally I was graced with a low grunt, which in a man of his humour probably passed for a sudden attack of eloquence.

Knowing my place, I thought it best to follow his example and the rest of the cut was completed in a stony silence that fairly rang the echoes of the room. For it was not just our little *tete-a-tete* that had run aground, everyone in the room had stopped their mouths and continued to sit silently, glumly avoiding each other's eyes, as I completed the brooding Volcano's coiffeur. He, however, had obviously been meditating on my final comment, for as he stood up and passed over the five sou payment (without, I might add, even so much as a *merci*), his tongue suddenly ran away with him "Better maintained, you say? And why? Because in one day at Lyon the blade of equality is oiled with more greasy aristo heads than those fools in Paris can manage in a week". He stared about him truculently " That's what's lacking in the capital - more lubrication!"

A chorus of approbation from the mass of hitherto mute clientele followed his progress to the exit, but this squat whirlwind of hate looked neither left nor right, and slammed the door with such force that he cracked one of the coloured glass panels that, (to give the place a more festive air), I'd gathered only that morning from the ruins of the City's Cathedral. That was too much. I made to follow, intending complaint, but one of my customers was fleeter, and before I'd gone six paces my path was blocked and my arms pinioned by a brawny bluff cove with an enormous beard. "*Doucement*, Gaston" he muttered through his face fungus, though not unkindly, I noticed. "That's it, *mon brave,* easy now, you don't want to be rubbing that particular gentleman up the wrong way, devil a doubt o' that."

"Whyever not?" I answered hotly, pulling at the restraining hands "Who in hell does he think he is, by God! that -"

"-That *gentleman*..." beardie interrupted quickly, flicking his eyes warningly towards the rest of the crew, who hadn't moved from their seats and were observing our conversation with every sign of interest. "...that gentleman who so graciously patronised your establishment was the Commissioner himself, Citoyen Collot d'Herbois".

For a moment I believe I blacked out, certainly the room dimmed before my vision and it was only the fact that Beardie had refused to relinquish his grip on me that

I managed to stay upright. Herbois the Butcher! The instigator of a thousand deaths - Here - and I was about to give him a verbal whipping! Oh Jesus! My head would have been on a pike before morning.

My bearded saviour turned out to be another of Robespierre's creatures - he had hundreds of 'em scattered all over the country - sent to bring orders from his lord and master, though he was keener by far to spread the most recent Paris gossip, of which he seemed to have a inexhaustible fund. One topic in particularly held me spellbound, and set my teeth on edge at the same time. It seemed that Defarge's daughter, the beautiful Suzanne, had 'sprained her ankle'*[3], and the proud *grandpère*-to-be was taking the news rather badly.

"He's in his cups most days" says beardie after my last customer had left, settling himself on a cracket and wrapping himself around another glass of my best vintage "sits there in his grog-shop, surrounded with empty flagons and broken bottles, lamenting the awful fate of his 'poor angel' and swearing bloody vengeance on the motherless son of a bitch that deflowered his daughter and ruined his honour. Pot valiant, eh?"

My blood froze at the news. Could it be...might I...? but surely not. "When is she due?" I asked with pretended indifference, nonchalantly trimming my nails with a poignard.

End of Vendemaire, or so they say" he replies, taking a refill. He was no sluggard himself with the claret, that was his fourth glass - but *in vino veritas,* and he was welcome to a score or more if it helped loosen his tongue.

Vendemaire? God how I hated this stupid revolutionary calendar - what was that as a good Christian date? It would be..... I calculated hard, and very nearly cut my finger to the bone in shock. Oh Christ! ... Late September.....The timing was most horribly exact! Nine months since my Christmas liaison with la belle Suzanne. Oh God, did

---

3   * *a euphemism for falling pregnant out of wedlock*

Defarge know? "The father...?" and I let the question hang, yawning with affected ennui.

He leaned forward, leering through his furze "Ah, but that's the best part of the tale. You'll never guess... it makes no sense..." he took a long pull at his glass, wiped a hand across his beard, belched loudly, and stared off vacantly into the distance.

I was near bursting, red faced with the effort of suppressing my fear and frustration. "The father...?" I prompted gently.

"What? Oh" he came back with an effort. "Yes, well, it's like this, as I said, you'll never believe it when I tell you-"

I was close to striking him. "Never believe what? Come on man, it grows late and I must to bed, finish your tale and sharp about it"

"But that's just it, you see... I can't finish the tale.. for she won't".

"What? What in God's name are you blathering about? She won't ?"

"Exactly.... That's right...She won't finish the tale ... won't say who gave her the babe". He spat on the floor, wiping his mouth on his sleeve. "Swears she'll die before his name will pass her lips. And she means it too, by all accounts"

Well thanks be to God for that, thinks I, the throbbing in my head receding and my stomach settling somewhat. It would not do to have a drunken Defarge on my heels, demanding that I call him Papa and do the right thing by his girl. Mind you, she was an Athanasian wench, M'am'selle Defarge, and given her voracius appetite, and her stamina, I'd wager there might be another three or four possible sires for her whelp. But if I was to blame, and I wasn't admitting I was, mind you, it was no wonder she was tight-lipped. To have enjoyed carnal relations with an Englishman would immediately make her suspect; and in France at that time, to be suspect was to be as good as dead. No, even were she sure it was I who had slipped a bun in her oven, she'd do well to keep her bone-box shut. I was safe for the moment, then, but this was ill news just the same, and yet another matter to concern myself with - for what if she was suddenly seized with an unfortunate fit of conscience and blurted out the truth? It was all very inconvenient and on top of all my other woes, did nothing to help me sleep well o'nights.

Besides which, it was the first time I'd fathered a bastard. I married early y'see, in the Colonies, and been the very image of a faithful husband, only to have my dreams of happiness crushed to dust and blown to the four quarters. Since that disastrous time I'd lived like a monk, celibate as the Pope – until, that is, my recent epiphany on the steps of the guillotine. That revelation set me on a path of lifelong travel and philandering, and who's to say how many white, brown, black and yellow little Sidneys now frolic in far flung corners of our Empire. Not a few, doubtless, but of them all, there's only one of whose paternity I'm certain.

His mother was married (for a wonder) and an aristocrat to boot, but no whit less willing for all her high birth. Her husband, she confessed to me, was monstrously disinclined to "any form of intimacy", preferring the pleasures of the chase to the marital bed. Well, *chacun à son goût*, as our French cousins say, and I was more than happy to stand *in loco mariti* for the foolish old dommerer, enjoying many a happy bout with the lady in the hayricks on their Leicestershire pile, while he spent his hours with horse and hound, 'view halooing' to his heart's content.

That was the autumn of 1821, I recall, and the time past pleasantly enough until she left for the London Season. Nine months later The Times announced that she had been safely delivered of a boychild, on May 5th it was, and because of the timing I always wondered, and kept an ear cocked for news from that quarter. She died early, poor spoilt lass, and the husband sent the boy to Rugby, but he was expelled for drunkenness some years later, which given my own alcoholic tendencies, set me thinking again. Tom Hughes' book gives a brief account of the lad – Flashman by name and nature – but considering what followed it can only have been a very biased account.[8] Because young

Flashman did well for himself in the military, fighting for the Empire in all corners of the globe and covering himself in glory. Still at it too, by all accounts. That set me back, you may imagine, for I'd no idea how the lily-livered Carton blood could have produced such a hero. So I went to view him, quiet-like; just for curiosity you understand. And to settle my mind.

I caught up with him at Horse Guards in '42, descending from a carriage, just after his audience with young Vicky. And there was no doubt in my mind. Leaving aside one or two traits that were obviously gifted from his mother, it was almost like looking in a mirror: the same height, same dark features, and the same sardonic smile. I incline to leanness, and he was a little more muscular than me – but then his mother was a buxom lass with plenty of meat on her bones. He even walked like me. No, he was mine, devil of a doubt. A son, and one to be proud of. Though I could never own him.

Chapter Seven

But all that was some twenty years hence, and I must return to my present tale of revolutionary tribulation. It seemed I was to be the father of a Frog, and as if the pregnancy of the beauteous Suzanne were not problem enough, the bearded Hermes also brought harsh words from my master Robespierre - and the sum and substance of his tale was that the odious Hop-o'er-my-Thumb found my latest report uninspiring. I was reminded that the primary targets of my mission were the Hebertist captains in Lyon, and through them their leaders in Paris. Robespierre was now tired of "street chatter and rumour masquerading as fact", and demanded - demanded no less! - that I find some new employment that would better satisfy his more exacting requirements. It seemed my barbering days were done.

So, were you abroad on the steep streets of Lyon that following evening, you would see barber Dupré taking the air, looking neither right nor left as he strides boldly down the avenue, a heavy bundle tucked beneath one arm. Gaston pauses awhile, looks round and, judging himself alone, ducks swiftly into a shadowed alley. Five minutes later, a tall young clerk, Francois Laborde, emerges from the self-same side street, and who would guess that this clean-limbed Adonis, resplendent in silks and satin shirt and with a cravat so high it was already strangling the bejesus out of him, had quietly compassed the death of our dear barber, and carried under his arm the very body (well, the outer garments) of Gaston Dupré, deceased.

The next day, with Gaston's worldly goods deposited safely in the flowing waters of the Rhone, Francois presents himself at the *Mairie**[*]. He is welcomed with open arms, for even a raving, genocidal revolution needs its bureaucrats, and clerks are in short supply in the city, most of the earlier incumbents having been butchered singly by Collot d'Herbois' death squads, or scragged in batches of twenty beneath the muzzles of Revolutionary cannon.

That old poof Proteus would have been proud of my successful transformation, and the ease with which I slid into a new character and a new life. Better yet, my latest career bid fair to provide Robespierre with the intelligence he craved, and to keep the Incorruptible's Damoclean sword from impaling either myself or my beloved Lucie.

Not that I was prepared to allow my affection for the widow Darnay to deter me completely from the delights of the flesh, and here I hit a vein of good luck that, once found, I worked with a will. It came about like this. For the first week of my bureaucratic duties I was occupied as junior investigator, issuing certificates of *civisme*, a document which guaranteed your sansculotte affiliations, and which was essential if you were to remain in good odour with the new revolutionary regime (and - to speak bluntly - to stand an even chance of remaining in sole possession of your head). A handy job it was too, for, as you may imagine, there was no shortage of supplicants for these revolutionary dispensations which, like the Catholic kind, were a guarantee of freedom from all manner of pain and suffering, in this world anyway. And, again in common with the Pope's Heavenly Passports, a hefty payment was required to ensure a safe passage to the land of peace and plenty - and you can be sure I took my share of the gelt. The men were eager to part with good red gold, not the useless *assignats*[9], to obtain this little slip of safety, and the females (the young and pretty ones at least)

---

could always count on me to endorse a similar testimonial - provided of course that, when it came to a choice between their moral and civic virtue, they could demonstrate just how ardently they preferred the latter. I was always willing to be persuaded - an hour or so of passionate discussion in my private office at lunchtime was usually sufficient to solve even the most intractable problem.

So engrossing were these intimate investigations of mine, and so enjoyable, that it was with mixed feelings that, less than a week into the job, I obtained the entré I sought to the inner circle of revolutionary justice. The powers that be were apparently so well pleased with my work that I was seconded to the topmost level of the judicial system, the Holy of Holies, to the *Tribunal Criminel Revolutionnaire*, on the third floor of the Mairie, where, for three days each week, I must busy myself in collating the names and addresses and occupations of all those 'counter-revolutionaries' and ne'er-do-wells who had already fallen beneath Madame Guillotine's broad blade, or the grapeshot of the militia.

This was brain-benumbing stuff, tedious in the extreme, and depressing too, for it entailed working my way through ream upon ream of death warrants, most of them signed by barber Dupré's erstwhile customer, Collot d'Herbois, or by his bosom companion and revolutionary peer, Joseph Fouché. I was a model employee, working at my battered wooden desk in the freezing office until late into the evening, ruining my eyes in the single candle allowed; and happy to do it, for this was Manna from Heaven as ever was; everything that Robespierre required was now passing through my hands, and I lost no time in making duplicate lists of all these unfortunates for the edification of the Incorruptible and the doom of his enemies. With the information I was amassing the destruction of the Hebertistes was assured, which must give the miserable dwarf more pleasure than the proscription of a million handkerchiefs. And a happy Robespierre was the nearest thing that Lucie and I possessed to a passport out of France.

For despite my weekly spate of philandering, (as you'll recall, I still had two full days devoted to *civisme* applications), I discovered that my thoughts returned continually to Lucie; more especially, it seemed, after an amorous bout with yet another willing postulant for revolutionary favour; in that dark period of post-coital despondency, I'd find myself picturing her lovely blonde, blue-eyed, angelic face, her superb lithe figure. And I'd ask myself for the hundredth time why I was wasting myself with these other, less virtuous females.

Mainly, of course, because they were less virtuous. And they were *here,* while Lucie was, for the moment, quite beyond my reach. But that did nothing to stop me chastising myself for a debauched rakehell and libertine, despising my venery, and swearing eternal fidelity to this paragon of womanhood. Until the next applicant showed up, sporting her dairies.

My new position brought me into constant, close proximity with the revolutionary élite charged with the continued annihilation of Lyon. The venomous Collot d'Herbois had by this time been recalled to Paris, where he soon inveigled himself a place on the Committee for Public Safety in an attempt to wrest control of this powerful organ of state from the Robespierrists. I saw him but rarely after his departure, and so was denied the equivocal delight of dealing with him without his ever realising that, as Gaston Dupré, I had held a razor to his throat and shaved him in silence. By God, had I known then the extent of his crimes, and how he would forever mar my own happiness, he'd never have left that chair, but would have sat there permanently silent, a second mouth across his neck; as I hope for salvation I'd have backed him there and then.

As a result of his departure I now made the acquaintance of his fellow inquisitor and partner in crime, Joseph Fouché. Chalk and cheese they were, these two, for despite working hand in glove to compass the obliteration of Lyon, the characters of the two men could not have been more different. Everything I observed of Collot d'Herbois conformed to my first impressions and bespoke his mental instability - the man was an Abram of the first water, a raving, homicidal bedlamite, and a sadist to boot, a blood-drinking ogre who would rather sign death warrants than take breakfast, a choice which, as God's my witness, he often made.

But Fouché struck me as an altogether different cove, tall, smooth-faced and quietly elegant. He was a man after my own heart, an opportunist whom fate, or his own careful machinations, had settled for the moment at the top of the pile, and who - again like me - would do whatever was necessary to maintain his position and to save his own skin. For make no mistake, in revolutionary France there was no retiring from public life (Danton tried it, and look what happened to him). No, for those who had achieved high position it was a case of *tout ou rien*, all or nothing. Look at the histories if you doubt me; how many of the revolutionary grandees laid down their high office and survived? Damn few; and they more by luck than judgement. The revolution was a tiger they all bestrode, clinging tightly and in most cases despairingly to that striped tricolored pelt, and any who lost their grip fell straightway into its ravening maw. It was triumph or die, simple as that. And with Fouché I had the impression that, while he found the total annihilation of an ancient city and its population distasteful, nevertheless, if it was a question of their obliteration or his, he would destroy away with the best of them. Which he did, reluctantly perhaps, but quite as efficiently as Monster Herbois. As I say, much like yours truly, and I could not help but warm to that.

Besides, he had taken a shine to me himself, probably because he, too, could recognise a kindred spirit. We conversed often - carefully avoiding all political topics - and I discovered that we had a mutual love for the intricacies of the law, and, of all things, for fishing. I had found the art of angling a wonderful solace for the melancholy state that had subdued me following my return from the Colonies, and the disasters that had overtaken me there.[10] Fouché too, had discovered the balm that rod, line and an hour or two by the water's edge could bring to a troubled soul. And while the new-found me had now no time for the fisher's art, I still retained sufficient knowledge to converse intelligently enough on a subject which he obviously considered fascinating.

It was strange to sit there of an evening, around the hearth with a pipe and a glass of good wine, discussing the intricacies of casting or ground-baiting, or hearing his latest tale of a particularly wily pike - "Hercule" he called the beast, (a very Leviathan according to Fouché, at least a span in length and possessed of preternatural cunning), that he had spent the best part of three months trying to land - and we'd be yarning and bantering away for all the world like two jovial yokels in a rustic inn, and then suddenly I'd realise that the smiling, jocular man in front of me had spent the day arraigning prisoners and sending scores of men and women to their deaths. Had he known my true identity, and my connection to Robespierre, I've no doubt I'd have been first up before the muskets next morning. But it did not seem to bother me too much at the time; I discovered I had the happy facility (indispensible in one of my new calling) of actually believing, for hours at a time, that I *was* Francois Laborde, clerk to the Tribunal Criminel Revolutionnaire, and a willing helper in the destruction of Lyon and its counter-revolutionary criminals. So, except for the occasional nightmare of disclosure and death, which I suppose is a natural adjunct to this profession, the time passed pleasantly enough.

I had lunch with him one afternoon in late February, (no ladies having arrived that day to present their civic credentials or engage me in lively debate) and the talk slid round, as it usually did, to his latest unsuccessful attempt to outwit Hercule. After this discourse he sighed and stared at the fire, and there came one of those easy silences that occasionally falls between good friends who are perfectly at ease in each other's company. I was taking a satisfied pull at my pipe when Fouché suddenly looked up from the blaze, fastened me with his eyes, and said quietly: "What are your thoughts on Citoyen Robespierre?"

My jaws spasmed around the pipe stem at so unexpected a mention of that hateful name, and my bowels span wildly with such shock and terror that I almost bewrayed myself in my panic. He knew! I could tell straightway. He absolutely knew I was Robespierre's spy. He was watching me with a half-smile on his smooth, shrewd face, and my fright must have been obvious for he leaned forward and patted my arm in an oddly compassionate gesture. I tried to smile but managed only a ghastly grimace, the pipe still clamped between my teeth. Oh God, It was all up; would it be the axe or the firing squad? Please, not the Guillotine again! He was still smiling, the bastard, enjoying my torment. When would he call for the Guard to drag me off? Why didn't he just get it over with?

His hand tightened on my forearm. "Don't concern yourself so, Francois", he said, almost kindly. "I'm just asking your opinion. Between friends...."

In my funk-befuddled state I hardly heard him as I cast around desperately for some means of escape, a window, an attic, a closet to hide in, anything to avoid the coming doom. So it took some time for the import of his words to penetrate my fear-cramped brain. But then, suddenly, with a great flowering of blissful relief, I realised he was totally sincere. There were no guards waiting in the corridor, no last requests, no bullet in the brain. He knew nothing of my double life, of my treachery, and I was safe. Fouché, as he had said, was simply seeking my opinion.

Even so, I had to be cautious. This was revolutionary France and loose-tongued talkers were likely gibbet-fodder. I mumbled something vaguely complimentary about the Incorruptible, balancing it immediately with equally ambiguous maunderings on the virtues of Hebert and his friends. Danton, too, I rambled, was a reasonably good egg... then again....

When I dared sneak a glance to judge how my words were speeding it was to see Fouché staring at his feet, shaking his head - and he was positively grinning. I stuttered to a stop, and he looked up, flagging a reproving finger before my face "You, monsieur, are temporising. You are sitting the fence, yes?" The smile subsided a little as he sat back, staring at me, still half-amused "this is a wise precaution, normally. But these are not normal times, Francois, they are extraordinary." There was a look of deadly earnest on his face now. "In a revolution, it is sometimes an error to sit the fence, a fatal error. For everyone is vying with everyone else and each looks around and thinks: 'if he is not for me, he is against me'. And the poor fence-sitter is seen as an enemy by everyone. Is this not so?"

By God, he was right. I had spent my time trying to blend in, to be innocuous, to have no real affiliations. But perhaps it had served only to point me out as a man without convictions, to-

"No, even those of us with no convictions" he broke in, mirroring my thoughts, "even we are forced in this situation to choose a side. The trick" Fouché continued, warming to his subject " is to choose the right horse, the mount that will carry us through to the winning post, covered in fortune and glory." He suddenly pushed himself forward so that his mouth was almost touching my ear, and whispered a single word: "Hebert". Then he had flopped back in his chair, watching me carefully. I can see him now, his silver-blonde hair falling across his eyes, his unnaturally smooth face creased for a moment in a sardonic smile. "This is the winning horse. His faction is ruthless, he controls the *enragés*; can you honestly believe that the others..." and here he mouthed the words 'Robespierre' and 'Danton", "....can you believe they will overcome such a hellish and bestial force of nature? No, these madmen will wade in blood until they are sated with it, or they destroy themselves with their hatred and malice. And until that happy hour arrives, those who wish to survive must make show of supporting their aims, even to the extent of destroying a city". His voice dropped to a whisper. "Why else do I kill these innocents and commit such hideous crimes..... for my own survival. But to sit the fence, it is worse than a crime. It is a mistake. This is my advice. You must choose, for your very life - choose wisely."

In the event, Fouché was wrong, and right, as you'll come to know. But it was decent of him, to take such a chance and reveal his own feelings so clearly. Why he did I'll never know, for he was ever famed as a close-lipped schemer. And he wasn't to know that, because of Lucie, I was wedded irrevocably to Robespierre's cause come plague, death or damnation. But I appreciated the gesture all the same, and while I eventually sent two despatches with details of Collot-d'Herbois' part in the massacres to Robespierre, I contrived to lose any mention of Fouché each time. His part in the atrocities was already well known, but it was a way of repaying him for his kindness - and besides, his comments had unsettled me. There was no downier bird in the revolution than Fouché, as events proved full well, and the thought that sure-footed Robespierre might slip, and that I might find myself on the losing side filled me with dreadful foreboding. If shielding Fouché was an act of gratitude, it also allowed me to hedge my bets. And paid off very nicely it did too, as I hope to tell.

And so my double life continued for upwards of three months, during which time little of import occurred at Lyon, but great matters were afoot in Paris. For, in just the same way that Robespierre was massing his artillery against Hebert, so too, from their headquarters at the Cordeliers Club, Hebert and his cronies were planning their own coup against the Incorruptible and his friends St Just, Hanriot and Couthon the Cripple. And as Fouché had intimated, Hebert was a formidable foe: he controlled the *Père Duchesne*, a newspaper boasting a 600,000 circulation; Bouchette, the Minister of War, was a staunch ally, and he had filled this important ministry with Hebert sympathisers. Collot d'Herbois, newly returned from Lyon, was now ensconced as Robespierre's rival on the Committee for Public Safety, and Hebert looked to the Butcher of Lyon, and to that gross-bodied fanatic Billaude-Varenne, for support when the time came. He forgot that Collot d'Herbois was quite literally a madman, swollen with pride and jealousy, and that he hated the great-voiced vagabond Danton more than he loved life. That error was to cost Hebert dear.

Hebert saw only his own dream of greatness. The leader of the extremists envisioned himself at the head of another 31st May insurrection, when the Jacobins had risen against the Convention and ousted the Girondin deputies. Now he foresaw a second insurrection of the masses, with himself at their head, a revolt that would sweep away the power of the Jacobins, sending Robespierre, St Just, Couthon and the rest to pay their devotions to Sainte Guillotine.

As was normal in these intrigue-laden times, battle was joined without any overt declaration of war, nor were the combatants named. At the Convention, Hebert began speaking of men who were "greedy for the power they were accumulating" while his lieutenant Vincent talked incessantly of unmasking plotters the names of whom "people would be amazed to know". Another Hebertist enthusiast stigmatised "the worn out men of the Republic, who look on us as extremists because we are patriots and they no longer wish to be patriotic." All this, you'll note, without referring to any Jacobin by name, much less a mention of the Incorruptible himself. At the beginning of March posters began appearing all over Paris, inspired by the extremists themselves but purporting to originate with Robespierre, which denounced the Convention and called for the establishment of a Dictatorship. At the Cordeliers Club, the Hebertists responded to this scandal of their own devising by symbolically draping - with a black velvet veil

- the panel displaying the Rights of Man. All designed, you see, to increase tension and create a feeling of imminent disaster among the people; to portray themselves as the guardians of the revolution, ready to champion the hard-won freedoms of the common folk, freedoms which at any moment might be lost under the despotic rule of Robespierre. Fate seemed to smile upon the extremists and their plans. Lindet and Couthon, two of Robespierre's most steadfast supporters, fell ill, weakening his position on the Committee. Another, Prieure de Marne, was sent unexpectedly from Paris on a mission. Hebert seized his hour and spoke openly for revolt, calling on the Commune and the Paris Sections to rise against the Jacobins.

It was a well laid plan, and by rights, it should have worked. But the earlier enthusiasms of 31st May had been blunted by four years of revolutionary turmoil, of constant shortages and incessant execution, of foreign wars and internal revolt. The people were tired, and wanted peace. Of the forty-eight Paris sections, only one responded to Hebert's call to arms. The drunken brute who commanded the National Guard, Francois Hanriot, declared against the insurrection. Even the extremists on the Committee of Public safety, Billaud-Varennes and the sanguinary Collot d'Herbois, witheld their approval. Robespierre, it was said, had worked on Collot's jealous hatred of Danton, and promised him Stentor's head in exchange for that of his ally Hebert.

Sensing failure, Hebert strove desperately to persuade his enemies that it had all been symbolic and that by revolt he had really meant "a more intimate union of the Montagnards with the Jacobins and the patriots". But it was useless. A few days later they were all behind bars, and not long after, (March 12th I think it was), Hebert and nineteen others were put into the tumbrils and made that doleful ride along the Rue Saint-Jacques (on which stood the Jacobin Club, whose members had brought him to this fate) and their appointment with Samson[11].

Hebert did not die well. One of those who watched compared his panic-stricken screams, as he was dragged bodily up the stairs to the scaffold, with those of poor Madame du Barry, whose terror-crazed shrieks were said to have been heard at Notre Dame, a full two miles distant. The crowd answered him shout for shout, and the executioner, aping the mob's festive mood, bounced the blade of the guillotine lightly on Hebert's neck, prolonging his agony, and provoking even louder terrified calls, before hauling up the axe for its final, fatal descent. All of which the crowd deemed the best sport for many a long week, and left not a few, or so I was told, weeping with laughter.

Now you may imagine the effect this news had in Fouché's office at Lyon. It was obvious he'd picked the wrong horse, and he went about for several days with a face like an undertaker at a wedding, sighing incessantly and trying desperately to convince himself that his recent spouting of Dantonist hyperbole (which he'd begun just as soon as Hebert's doom was sealed) would place him safely in the camp of Stentor. For despite this evidence of Robespierre's ruthless cunning, he remained absolutely sure that, in any contest between the brazen-voiced giant and "the petit-bourgeois mouse" as he delighted in calling Robespierre, it would be the Incorruptible's head that would part company from his body. So certain was he that Robespierre would fall, he had already decreed the dissolution of the Jacobin clubs in Lyon - which in the fraught atmosphere of those days was tantamount to an act of war.

I thought it another mistake, for with the Hebertists gone I wasn't at all sure Danton would prevail. In the bloody cut and thrust of an ordinary battlefield there would have been no contest, that much was true. Faced with the terrors of mortal combat Robespierre would simply have curled up and died - he was no warrior. But physical courage was not the way of revolutionary conflict, and when it came to cabals and conspiracies, to smooth-tongued hypocrisy and the Cornish hug, the 'petit-bourgeois mouse' had proven himself formidable. No, any fight between those two would be a damned close run bout, and only one thing was certain - with Fouché and myself ranged on opposite sides of the barricade, one or t'other of us would join the loser of this death-struggle in the tumbrils.

Or was I being too pessimistic? If Robespierrre emerged victorious there was a better than even chance (I put it no higher than that) that he'd honour our agreement and send Lucie and I back to enjoy the sights of Old London Town. But it suddenly dawned on me that, should his plans miscarry, I might find myself equally well placed. As Francois Laborde I was a simple clerk - I had hardly declared for Robespierre (nor for Danton for that matter). All the missives I sent to the Incorruptible were signed 'Chameleon', the *nom de guerre* Proteus had bestowed upon me weeks before. And there were at least three other clerks who had access to the details I was forwarding to the arch-intriguer, so even if Robespierre's ship foundered, and his papers came to light, I was still in the clear. Short of executing all four clerks (a not inconceivable outcome, I had to admit) there was no way anyone could link 'Chameleon' to the studious, faction-shunning Francois Laborde. No, despite friend Fouché's admonition to 'choose', if I kept my head down and my nose clean I could stand safely on the sidelines and watch the contestants lock horns: should Robespierre win I was no worse off and might be allowed to leave France with his blessing; were Danton to gain the laurels I would at last be free of the Incorruptible's fatal hold, and any prisoners he'd ordered held - Lucie included - would doubtless be freed automatically. In the ensuing crisis and confusion that would certainly attend the fall of such an Idol, and with all Robespierre's lackies following him to the scaffold, my incriminating links to the old order would be swept away, and we'd have a calm sea and a following wind for our flight to England! My 'chameleon' skills could only aid our chances of successful escape. It would be the best opportunity we would ever get of removing ourselves intact from *la belle France*, and I'd be damned if I couldn't bring the pair of us safe home.

Which was true enough. If we failed in the attempt, she and I would certainly be damned. I spent the next few nights tossing on my bed, cudgelling my brains and striving desperately to second guess Fate. Had I known the ghastly web of death and betrayal that the Norns, even then, were spinning for me, I think I might have done what so many Lyonnais had done before me, and thrown myself into the waters of the Rhone. But at that time I truly believed my wily brain and nimble wits could escape Destiny. Nowadays, in my dotage, I can look back and see how pointless all that scheming and planning really is - most of life is quite simply beyond our control. It's like a post-coach journey between Lyon and Paris: the carriage travels so fast you can't get off and no matter how much you shout "Slow down, please!" or "Whoa!" the blasted thing will stop only at predetermined destinations along its route. You can move about in the infernal contraption, change seats, snooze, play cards, gallop a willing trull or two, eat a sandwich - that at least is given to you. But ultimately, you and I, dear reader, are going where the carriage of life is taking us. All we can do is to try and enjoy the ride.

Chapter Eight

An apt simile really, the Coach of Life, because within five days of the Herbetists' demise I was in a *Berline à quatre*,[12] coursing through the French countryside en route to Paris and one of the most horrible episodes of my long and not always pleasant existence.   For quite out of the blue, the post had brought me word of a sudden illness afflicting my dear *Grandmère Thérèse*.

This was a prearranged signal that I was to return to Robespierre at once.   The small, apparently accidental inkblot close to the lower right hand corner of the letter told me the meeting place, a wind-ravaged copse of the edge of the Plain of Brotteaux, just outside the city. Beardie was there, with two other ruffians in tow, and I was bundled into the carriage and whisked off toward Paris without so much as a 'by your leave'.   My familiar old apparel had been considerately provided and, when I stepped out of the coach on the Rue St Honoré late next afternoon, backside benumbed with thirty hours of constant travelling, I was again clothed in the vestments and personality of Sidney Carton, lawyer.   It was odd, being myself again, and it took me all of three or four minutes to shake off the affectations of Francois Laborde as I picked my way over the planks and timbers of Duplay's woodyard to the unpretentious green door of Robespierre's lodgings.

I found him there, surrounded by his cronies - his bran-faced younger brother Augustin, thickset and ever-smiling, the very antithesis of the Incorruptible; toper Hanriot (already three sheets to the wind, as usual), Couthon the Cripple in his bathchair; and that hell-born babe St Just, tall, cool, and as elegant as ever - all of them still elated by their victory over Hebert's *Enragés*. It wasn't a pleasant thing to see, these pillars of revolutionary France crowing over the number of corpses, sniggering at Hebert's scaffold-terror, and generally gloating at the fall of their enemies - smug self-satisfied bastards, the lot of them. Their leader, the malevolent mannikin, was in a similar expansive mood, and greeted me with a great show of warmth and cordiality. He was as perfectly turned out as ever, neatly powdered hair, a pair of jonquil-coloured knee breeches, dark cravat and a silk coat of robin's-egg blue. But the man was changed from our last meeting, and not for the better . He seemed prematurely old, his face pinched and lined by the constant intrigue and as grey as a corpse beneath the powder. I'd heard that he slept only fitfully now and was prone to sudden fits of weeping. He'd fallen prey to strange worries and irrational fears too - he no longer rode horseback for fear of falling from his mount, and while he still took his habitual long walks, a deep dread of assassination prevented him from gaining the benefit he had derived from them in happier times. But within that withered face the awful fawn eyes still glittered with an undiminished fanatical gleam. He beckoned me to one side, and we retired into a quiet corner.

"Ah Carton, I trust your journey was not too unpleasant?"

"Bearable, citoyen, and much more pleasant than my stay in Lyon."

He nodded his shrunken sconce, powder flecking the air as he moved "Ah yes, a terrible business... Lyon had revolted against the revolution, it is true, and an example needed to be made.... Nevertheless, the carnage, the excess..." the sphinx-like head shook, spilling more of the white stuff over me and the carpet, "...terrible...truly terrible."

Awful, ghastly memories crowded my brain at his words, a thousand souls clamouring for vengeance. "And the murderers of all those Lyonnais" I asked quietly, holding in my fury " Collot d'Herbois and his friends, they are arrested along with the other Hebertists?"

His head came up at that, the sunken eyes burning "What? No, no! Please, I must insist you lower your voice. No, Collot is not under arrest; he has, on the contrary, been most useful to us. Thanks in part to the information you sent, we were able to, shall I say, persuade him to help our cause, or rather, not give succour to the enemy. So he is unharmed.... For the moment." I was about to speak, but he held up his hand "Fear not, more heads will roll before the Rule of Virtue is accomplished. And Collot, I fear, possesses very little Virtue..." his strange high-pitched voice trailed off and for some moments he seemed very far away, then he glanced at me enquiringly, and what I'm sure he believed was a kindly smile distorted his narrow face. "But you are not, I am certain, overly concerned with our friend Collot - another's fate doubtless agitates your heart! Dear Sir, please, do not look so worried! She is well, I assure you. Quite well, in good health, and by all accounts yearning to see the man who would have given his life for her happiness."

Now this was good hearing, though I could not help but wonder how everyone was prepared to fix on my earlier fatuous heroics and conveniently forget my chicken-hearted poltroonery on the scaffold when it had finally come to the grip. Had Lucie heard the full story? I doubted it - Froggie's penchant for romance would have turned the shameful episode into a fine saga of selfless sacrifice (well that young pedant Dickens did, so why shouldn't they?), doubtless the tale would be that I had been ready to offer myself as an oblation on the Altar of Love only to have my true identity discovered, against my will, at the last moment.

Robespierre seemed to have convinced himself of this already. Well, if Lucie had swallowed the same gammon it was all to the good, and could only aid my suit. But why had Robespierre mentioned her, apropos of nothing? Hope was suddenly revived, setting me trembling with anticipation. Was the Great Denounciateur playing me fair? Against all my doubts and fears, was he about to authorise our departure for England?

"She is lodged in a fine house at Laon in Aisne Department, about a day's travel to the north-west" Robespierre continued, gracing me with the same strangely distorted smile. "You will see her there soon."

I found I was beaming back at him, and not just because of the prospect of seeing my darling. I knew Laon, you see, had walked its streets as a young student with Stryver and our bevy of budding learned counsel. The important point was this: Laon lay not more than a hundred miles from Calais, and I knew Calais too. Or rather I knew of it. My London lawyering had brought me into contact with not a few smuggling culls, and they were a talkative bunch - especially when all my legal ploys and appeals for clemency had failed and they knew they were destined to dangle in the sheriff's window frame*₅ the following dawn. So I was well aware that there were hidden bays and coves a-plenty around Calais, and - for the right price - any number of illicit bottoms to carry a pair of fugitives across the narrow sea to the sands of Dover, no questions asked. I had an ample store of cash from my sale of *civisme* certificates, we needed only to plan our means of escape. Let me get to Laon, and see the slightest weakness in Lucie's durance, and she and I would slip the collar before they were aware we were gone. It would be French Leave with a vengeance. All this in a few seconds of joyous thought. To Robespierre: "Sir, I beg you. When can we meet? Let it be soon, *je vous en prie.*"

₅   *Hang on the gallows*

He raised a placating palm. "Yes, it will be soon, have no fear of that. You have my promise". Then, with disconcerting suddenness, he had changed the subject. "I have a question for you, my dear Carton. Do you know anything of Ireland? This was a poser. My maternal grandmother had been Connemara Irish, rest her sainted Fenian bones, and I had visited the god-forsaken place but once, many years back when I was a young stripling of ten summers. I spent a week cooped up in an earth-walled, turf-roofed hovel with three hens, a goose and a pregnant sow, trying desperately to escape the constant gale-blown deluge that fell incessantly from the heavens, gasping in the fog of peat smoke, and eating nothing but potatoes. And that was in June! Aye, I knew Ireland and wanted nothing more to do with it. Besides, the first rule in enemy waters is 'volunteer nothing', so I wasn't about to declare any of this to the Incorruptible. Instead, I drew my brows together and shook my head doubtfully.

Robespierre frowned. "I myself claim descent from Ireland" (this was news to me), "and I have always been interested in the welfare of its people. It is, so I am told, the bread-basket of Britain, and its downtrodden masses are well-disposed towards our revolutionary principles. I have often wondered if a descent upon that unhappy country with French troops would produce a double bounty, freedom for the Irish and famine in England"[13]

He eyed me quizzically and, for want of any better response I essayed a noncommittal gallic shrug. Robespierre stared briefly, then waved the idea away "It is of no moment, for the present at least. However, *mon ami*, there is just one further small service I would ask of you"

My heart sank at this, for Robespierre's 'small services' had a habit of lasting weeks and placing my poor skin in mortal jeopardy. But his request, when it came, seemed reasonable enough. Robespierre's rival, the brass-voiced George Danton, leader of the Moderates, was due to take dinner with the Incorruptible that same evening. The meal, at Danton's request, was an attempt to effect a reconciliation between the two men and their parties. Danton was tired of the incessant blood-letting and hoped to persuade Robespierre to an alliance, and an end, or at least a moderation, of the Terror. Robespierre had agreed to the meal, for Danton and he had been comrades in the early days of the revolution, and it seemed he was prepared to bury the hatchet, if the big man would come round to his way of thinking. But he still harboured strong doubts - which was why he wished me to wait at table during the dinner, suitably disguised, in order, so he said, "to familarise yourself with an individual who may, in time, prove to be an impediment to the Rule of Virtue." And we all knew where impeding the rule of virtue would lead you. Well, that was all one to me. I hardly knew Danton, though by all accounts he was one of the more likeable of the revolutionary leaders, a man given to epicurean delights and the pleasures of the flesh, not averse to a little corruption too - there was even talk that he had been in the pay of Pitt and the perfidious British for a while - but never to the detriment of the ultimate goals of the Revolution, as he saw them at least. A passionate man who could explode with anger like a volcano and yet an hour later hug you to his bosom, all laughter and ribald jests. Just the opposite of Robespierre in fact, who I never heard utter a single oath or blasphemy, and who cherished his insults like a basilisk guarding its treasure. I wished Danton well, in a vague sort of way, in his quest to patch things up with the malevolent mannikin, and it seemed a small enough thing to humour the Incorruptible with one final night's work.

Had I been thinking clearly, I might have spied the cloven hoof in this business, and asked myself why - if Robespierre were planning an early release for Lucie and myself - he should wish me to study Danton and his clique so close to the time of my departure for England. Stinking fish, you'll agree. But *Amor caecus est**[6]*, and my mind was too full

---

6   **Love is Blind*

of thoughts of Lucie and dreams of escape, so I missed its significance. Mind you, had I realised that Robespierre had no intention of honouring his promise, it would not have changed a thing - for I was as much his prisoner as I ever was, and despite his pleasant manners and his gratitude for a job well done, was well aware that I remained just a thin sheet of brown paper away from an appointment with the Revolutionary Barber. So I must smile, and endure, and await my chance for escape.

The dinner that night was an awful stilted affair, with Danton punishing the liquor and booming out bonhomie, while Robespierre ate sparingly, and sat stiff and unyielding on his chair, like a Puritan with piles. On several occasions Danton brought the conversation - it was, in truth, virtually a monologue, for Robespierre spoke but rarely - around to their common interests and the benefits of an alliance. But each time he was rebuffed. I can remember the scene as if it were yesterday, the room lit by a score of candles, their flames flickering wildly in the breeze from an open window, Danton dominating the table as much by his bulk as his great brazen voice, urging Robespierre to disown intrigue. "Let us forget our private resentments" he pleaded across the board "and think only of the country, its needs and its dangers."

Robespierre listened impassively, his face like stone, for Danton to finish. "I suppose" he answered quietly, his thin voice laced with sarcasm "that a man of your moral principles would not think that anyone deserved punishment?"

Danton's great face flushed red from his hair to his bull-like neck "I suppose *you* would be desolate if none did!" he thundered, half-rising to his feet.

"Liberty" Robespierre retorted angrily, his pinched features tighter than ever "*cannot* be secured unless criminals lose their heads."

And there it was, the huge gulf that divided them. In a way the two men personified the primary schism in the revolutionary ranks, with one side pleading enough was enough, and for the good of the revolution and the nation an end must be made of the mass executions, while the other side insisted with equal vehemence that, for the self-same reasons, it was imperative the Terror continue. And neither side willing nor able to see the other's point of view. It was bound to end in disaster, and it did.

There were more disquisitions of a similar nature, but by the time Danton made his departure, half seas over and mawkish with it, all knew that the chasm between them remained unbridged. As he reached the door Danton stopped and turned. "Maximillien" he said in a quiet sentimental whisper, so at odds with his usual voice. "do not let it end so. We were comrades once, remember how we kicked the arse of the nobles, (I saw Robespierre wince at this vulgarism, the little prig) how we humbled those royalist scum and instituted the rule of Liberty? Let us be friends, Maximillien, let it be like the old times..." and his eyes brimming with emotion, he enveloped Robespierre in a giant embrace, like a whale swallowing a shrimp. It was not returned, the Incorruptible stood straight and expressionless, cold as a block of marble.

But some of Danton's words must have struck home, for as I closed the door on the visitors, I could hear Robespierre remonstrating with St Just. "No No! Louis-Antoine" he whispered "No denunciation yet. His heart is true. He may yet be turned to the path we tread and share in the rule of Virtue."

Aha! I thought to myself as I picked up discarded bottles from the dining table, there's a spark of humanity in the cold fish yet. But then came one of those unexpected fateful moments I've seen so often in my long and chequered career, when the devil sticks his spoon in the cake-mix of human affairs and gives a little swirl. Don't be fooled by the historians and their careful logical analysis of events. It's not like that at all. Life, and history, is determined more by human moods and passions than they care to admit - for if they did, they'd be out of a job and there would go the port at high table and all that obsequious respect scholars are heir to. Take my word, more often than not the world's great events are decided by chance and caprice.

And so it was here, for as I moved to shut out the increasingly chilly breeze by closing the dining room window, Danton's booming drunken voice, borne on the cold spring air, carried faintly through the open pane as he climbed into his carriage. "Ah my friends, what a God-awful mess! Yet all would be well... yes I tell you... all would be well if only I could loan Couthon my legs and Robespierre my balls!"[14]

Another second and I should have had the casement closed - Danton's comments would have gone unheard, and history may well have run on an entirely different tack. Because Robespierre had heard it too, I'm certain, for as I turned back into the room the little man swung away, his eyes granite, his mouth a grim line in his pinched face. "That imbecile, that atheist.....that libertine!" he hissed, "I should have recognised it from the beginning, he is a danger to the Republic" and I could see he was trembling, in an absolute rage, though his fury had less to do with the republic than his own affronted dignity. "St Just - I agree. Do not delay. Act at once. Danton will be denounced."

Chapter Nine

Strangely enough, after this delightful soirée, Robespierre was very solicitous of my own needs, thanking me again for my efforts, fussing about like a hen with one chick, and finally packing me off to a not-too-seedy hotel with promises of an imminent meeting with my beloved. The accommodation was reasonably salubrious and certainly an improvement on the Conciergerie - though I'd have appreciated it more if he could have whistled up another Comtesse Beauharnais for me to oblige - but that was hardly the Virgin Inquisitor's style; I was, however, provisioned with the best of liquor and belly timber while I kicked my heels for the chief part of a week, awaiting the carriage which the Incorruptible assured me would soon arrive to whisk me off to Laon and what I hoped would be a most satisfactory and loving reunion with the widow Darnay.

The only dark side to all this was the 'companion' who Robespierre insisted accompany me - the odious Defarge. Luckily, he spent most of the day ensconced in a *fauteuil a bascule**⁷ outside my room, or patrolling the alley at the back of the hotel - doubtless in the hope that I would attempt escape and he would have the pleasure of surfeiting me with a blue plum or two.¹⁵ He almost had his chance too -

---
⁷   *Rocking Chair

though it was none of my doing.

After two days staring at the walls of my new lodgings, I had taken a stroll along the Rue Saint Antoine, to stretch my legs and take the air. As I crossed the street, heading west towards the ruins of the Bastille, a thin cribbage-faced young man in a black cape contrived to barge into me in the most artless manner possible. I stepped back, cursing, and he thrust a slip of paper in my hand, whispered in perfect English "Tonight, at that address. Seven o'clock" then span on his heels and was off the way he had came. It was a matter of seconds to realise that I was in a most devilish predicament. The young chap was obviously one of Pitt's men - a British agent operating in Paris. Word of my association with Robespierre must have reached Westminster, and Young Will and his ministers were no doubt keen to know if I might prove a useful source of information for HM Government. I might have helped too, but Defarge had been no more than twenty paces behind, and I realised the Frenchman must have seen everything; already he was racing towards me, his face grim. I knew instantly what I must do, and I pride myself that it was my prompt thinking that saved the day, and a precious life.

My own, of course. "Look here Defarge!" I cried indignantly. "That young idiot slipped me this" and I placed the note into his hand without even looking at it. "Never met the impertinent rogue in my life. Damn cheek!"

For there was nothing I could do for young cribbage-face, his own caw-handed performance had doomed him. He was seized by two of Defarge's underlings before he had made it past the Rue de Temple. *Asinus ad lyrem*₈* you see - his farcically inept attempt at communication had marked him for death no matter what I might have done. Not so much a question of 'him or me', but of 'him, or both of us', and I immediately saw the best course of action (though in either case my response would doubtless have been the same).

Defarge was even more careful of my movements after this

An Ass to the Lyre – a task beyond an individual's competence unfortunate incident. But as I had no intention of talking to anyone or making off in the night - not, at least, until I could leave with Lucie - there was nothing suspicious for his mistrustful mind to set upon. So Defarge was no real trouble, except that, there being only a single dining room in the hotel, I was obliged to take dinner with him each evening.

This was a dismal business, for the old sans cullotte remained in a towering rage over the imminent birth of his unlooked-for grandchild. He drank hugely, sometimes muttering to himself or weeping softly, and at others loudly swearing eternal vengeance on his daughter's seducer, which was deuced uncomfortable for your correspondent. "He'll beg for death" he'd call out suddenly, smashing his huge fist down on the table and setting the crockery in disorder, well-corned and brandy-faced with it. "Whichever vile son of lucifer deflowered my sweet angel will suffer all the torments of hell. Just let me lay hands on his loathesome carcase. He'll sing with the Pope's castratos before I'm done with him. I'll take his limbs off a joint at a time, then his ears and his nose...I'll cut away his bestial lips..... I'll gouge out his eyes with my bare hands and replace them with his balls! I'll....." It continued in this vein for several minutes (the threats never altered), until the feculent old sot slid from his chair, cast up his accounts on the floor and collapsed snoring beneath the table. At which point I would gently and carefully rise, spit fulsomely on his head, and retire to my rest in reasonably good humour. You must always take your pleasures where you can.

Even so, I doubt I could have lasted more than a week in the company of that hateful toad, so it was a mercy when my rattletrap finally turned up, early on the morning of the sixth day. By noon we had left the shadowed boulevards and cobbled streets of the capital, had negotiated the last of the innumerable barricades that ringed the city, had cried the inevitable 'Vive le Republique' to the last sans culotte, and were finally out into open country. I recall long lines of poplars flashing by, and beyond the verge, field after open field, just greening with the first flush of spring wheat. We made good progress despite the potholed and deeply-rutted roads that had, I marked, become noticeably worse since the revolutionary chant of *Liberté, Fraternité, Egalité* swept across the country. That's the problem with equality and the rest, you see: everyone wants his *suum cuique* and a share in the high life, but there's precious few willing to take their turn on the treadmill. Damnable, yes, but bred in the bone of humanity all the way back to Adam. And the reason, in my humble estimation - along with an unquenchable penchant for the two-backed beast - why human history comprises one unvarying tale of misery and betrayal.

It was the second of these two universal human weaknesses that occupied my thoughts as we approached the spires and smoking chimneys of Laon late that next evening. My mind was full of images of Lucie: when I first saw her at Darnay's trial; taking tea at the corner house in London; so brave and beautiful in the French courtroom, sitting by her father; and my carrying her in a swoon to the carriage, (when I had last seen her, and when I believed I was looking upon her for the last time); kissing her cheek that cold December day before my misconceived attempt to take her husband's place on the scaffold, just three months past, though the memory of it seemed like another lifetime. As indeed it was, for since then I had died, if not in the flesh then in the spirit, and I was determined that Sidney Carton would no longer play the part of reformed sot and detached altruist, consecrated to a love so high-minded it rose far above any carnal consideration. Never. Never again, by God! This love, my desire for Lucie would be consummated, not consecrated. And this very night too, if my will prevailed. I intended to lay siege to the widow Darnay, to assail her with my passion, and carry her by storm. I had waited too long.

It was in such a frenzy of emotion, caught between dreams

of desire and a wretched fear of rejection, that my memory - usually so good - simply fails me at this point. I cannot recall travelling through Laon's broad streets, or of arriving at the house in which Lucie was lodged. We must have stopped before the place, and I can only have got down from the coach and walked up the wide stone stairs which I saw later fronted the building; the door must have opened, and it's past question I entered the hallway - but I have no clear recollection of any of this. All I can remember, and this with pin-sharp clarity, is the moment when I stood before carved double-doors, which swung apart (who opened them I can't say, a maid or flunkey I suppose), and there she was, the Love of my Life, sitting in a high backed chair by the fire, working on a piece of *petit-point*, serene and intolerably beautiful in her widow's weeds.

She glanced up at the intrusion, and an expression of blank amazement swamped her lovely features; then she was standing, the sampler falling unheeded to the carpet, swaying, and at first I thought she was going to swoon. But she steadied herself against the mantle, her countenance unfathomable. For myself, I was grinning like an idiot, astounded and pleased that my memory could play me so false - I'd carried with me for the past three months an image of Lucie as a beautiful, desirable woman, which she undoubtedly was. But I'd forgotten the inexpressible glow of happiness which being in her presence evoked in me, a light that seemed to illuminate my very soul.

Still she stared. Then suddenly she was running towards me, her hands outstretched. "Sidney! Oh Sidney, You're here! At last!" And time seemed to slow as I watched this blithe golden-haired angel, this vision of womanly perfection, gliding across the room, smiling - as if in a dream my hands went out to enfold her, at last, in my arms. But at the final moment, recalling the presence of her maid in the room, she slowed her advance, and instead of the passionate embrace I craved, she took my hands in hers.

"You may go Marie." This to the gimlet-eyed Abigail,

doubtless another of Robespierre's creatures, who stood watching by the dresser, duster in hand. The maid scurried out without a word, and I had the satisfaction of seeing Defarge standing nonplussed and scowling in the hallway, as the doors shut to. Then he was gone, and there was only Lucie. She sighed deeply, squeezing my hands, then leaned back to look at me, scanning my features hungrily, her face alight with undisguised joy.

"You are looking well, sir" she offered in mock courtesy, her eyes dancing

God, how I had missed the delicious honeyed tone of that voice! "And you madam" I returned, bowing formally, " are as well favoured as ever you were." She blushed at this, she positively bushed! and encouraged, I hurried on "....which is to say, you are a Goddess of Beauty..." a coquettish toss of the head greeted this sally and I plunged on "... the more so considering your loss-".

It was a mistake. To mention Darnay was a mistake, and I could have cut off my tongue to see the way her face darkened, and all pretence of happiness fled from her. She let go my hands and turned towards the fire. "Ah yes" she breathed, staring at her fingers, head bent. "My loss. My dear Charles... indeed it is a tragedy I find difficult to bear. How I miss his presence, his protective influence..."

I found this a little hard to swallow considering his attempted flight and all, and against my better judgement I blurted out the truth. "Protection? But he fled when the coach was stopped. He abandoned you all, Mr Lorry, your father, yourself, he left everyone to their fate."

She span round on me then, eyes flashing "Silence! You presume to much Sir. He was not himself. You were not there, he was like a man possessed, as if the darkened wood had in some wise bewitched poor Charles ... Pan himself seemed suddenly to descend upon him. When they asked for his passport he uttered a cry like a wounded beast, and before I knew whither he had gone, he.... he had fled. But he was not himself..." she repeated, her voice trailing off.

God curse my wayward mouth! The last thing I desired was an argument, with Darnay's ghost standing between us, and I quickly reversed course, trying desperately to placate her anger and regain our earlier joyful intimacy "Yes, yes, quite so.... of course" I mammered, "the pressure of the moment.... Not really responsible for his actions...." I was rambling and I knew it, but for the life of me I couldn't stop and hear the awful silence that I knew would descend like an unbridgeable gulf between us "it is not to be wondered at, given the circumstances.... It could have happened to anyone..."

"No!" her voice crashed like a gunshot, echoing round the room, and I thought, Oh Sweet Jesus! What have I said now? How can I make amends..... but then I saw that she was watching me from the tail of her eye, a small, sad smile playing about her lovely lips. "No" she repeated softly, "never say it might happen to anyone. For... for it is not true. I know of one man who would never have disgraced himself in so cowardly a fashion" and she turned until I was looking directly into those wide, melting eyes. "You", she said simply, and then she was falling into my arms, her voice breaking. "You. You would never have betrayed me".

Women. How can you fathom them? One moment smiling, the next irate, an instant more and they're as soft and yielding as a lamb. Clouds before the sun. Still, I've learned over the years not to question their whimsey, and to suck the honey when it flows. And the tide did seem to be turning my way now, for she was weeping against me, and did not seem to mind in the least that my right hand had fallen to the delicious curve of her rump, or that I was kneading away gently at the mutton. Her scent was intoxicating - but this was no contrived art of the perfumier - this was essence of Lucie, a fragrance that was all her own and set my body tingling to my very toes. As I stroked her hair and squeezed her stern, she seemed to rally a little, tiny ragged sobs shaking her bosom delightfully; I kissed a golden ringlet and her head came up slowly, her expression forlorn, like a cherub that had lost its harp.

"You would never betray me" she said again.

"Never" I answered simply, kissing away the tears from her eyes. "Never!" I repeated, and at that moment I believed it. With all my heart.

"I have heard what you did for us all.... For me," she continued shyly. "They told me how you had planned everything, the drug for Charles, the exchange of clothes, and his escape from the Conciergerie, while you took his place in the tumbril, even to the very shadow of the Guillotine! I know how you were prepared to sacrifice your life for my happiness, and ... and..." she hesitated, as if reluctant to speak further, and I steeled myself for a true description of the cowardly finale (it struck me then, and I believe it still, that Darnay and I were not merely physically alike - we were of a piece temperamentally too, both cowards beneath the skin if you will, for we'd both broken at the grip).

But the shameful narration of my dastardly behaviour failed to materialise "...and I know how," she continued breathlessly, "how against your will, your noble plan was thwarted at the last minute by the French." Her arm was round my waist and with her free hand she stroked my cheek "Oh Sidney! What greater proof of fidelity could a woman wish! My Hector, my true hero! How can I ever repay your bravery, your manhood?"

Oh my manhood will devise a way, thinks I, several ways to be sure, I could think of at least four that instant. But Heaven bless the exciteable, sentimental Frenchies: for there seemed to be a conspiracy afoot throughout the Republic to forget old Sidney's poltroonery and exalt his misplaced desire for self-immolation. Well, everyone enjoys an epic tale of Love and Danger, and stories of derring-do and knight-errantry were like hen's teeth during those revolutionary times. The populace was desperate for chivalrous acts of outrageous heroism, and - for want of anything better - they'd battened on to my ill-conceived rescue attempt, and turned it, willy-nilly, into the *romance du jour*.

Well, so be it, for while not everyone might be convinced by the tale, Lucie had most certainly wolfed the legend whole, and she continued to caress my face, gazing into my eyes with undisguised admiration. It seemed the right time to kiss her, so I did. Ah, bliss was there, in that moment! For an instant she responded, and I tipped the velvet, tongue to tongue, her body arching against me as I seized hold of her bouncers, and then, just as suddenly, she was fighting against me, twisting from my embrace and pushing herself from me, trembling and gasping like a landed fish. What now? I puzzled, and tried to come to grips again, but she held up a denying hand, her face averted.

"No, please Sidney, we must not."

But why? Lucie darling, whyever not."

She took some time to answer, and her response when it came, was all I could have wished for, and damned puzzling to boot. "Because I love you."

My heart thundered in my chest, blood pounded in my head as I stepped close to her, taking her hand. This time she did not resist. "Darling. How I've longed to hear those words", I said fervently. "But then, why can't we-"

She pressed both hands against my chest, gently keeping me at bay, an action which only served to emphasise the fullness of her cleavage and set me driving forward again. "Because... No, Sidney please stop - because, dear heart, I am in mourning." She placed a finger on my lips, stilling my protests. "Listen, now, I have loved you these years past, but I dared not show it. I was a married woman, espoused to a man who, for all his faults, cared for me well and loved me dearly. The vows that bound me to Charles were sacred, made before God, surely you understand? Ah dearest, the times I have wanted to tear off the mask, to let you know, to vouchsafe some small sign or token of my affection... but I dared not! I could not bring you to temptation! I swore that I would not be the one to besmirch your honour, or make you Sin against God and his commandments!

Heavens, but I was angry then! You beautiful idiot! I wanted to shout. Lovely, stainless simpleton, to have denied both you and I such pleasures, such comfort, and all for the sake of sanctimonious words written thousands of years ago in an ancient book by some doddering old misogynist who wouldn't have known what to do with a woman if one had been pushed into his miserable monkish cell! The word of God! Where was God - where *is* God - I wanted to ask, when the Guillotine strikes, when the seamstress' head was cut from her neck, where was He during the *mitraillades* at Lyon, the *noyades* of Nice, during the tens of thousands of unrecorded acts of brutality and injustice that had seared this land since the Revolution began? Where, for that matter, was He during the whole history of mankind, the most atrocious catalogue of murder, rape and mutilation that began with Cain and shows no sign of abating? And He presumes to tell us what we can and cannot do?

But I said not a word. Nothing. I could see, past question, that she was sincere. The silly goose had denied her passion, had lived with that fop Darnay for all those years, had engaged me the while in conversation all cool and sisterly-like, when in truth she was burning with suppressed desire - and all for the sake of my good name and my immortal soul! And then, in an instant, the anger faded clean away, and it came to me that this was Love. Not the heated, lustful variety I now set such store by, but a better, a more refined and much purer conception. Yes, I had been prepared to lay down my life for Lucie in one dramatic act of self-sacrifice, (and had come within Ames' Ace of carrying through my mad scheme), but all this time, ever since her marriage, day after melancholy day, she had been silently and steadfastly giving up her own life, for me. And in that same moment it dawned on me that I should not be angry or downcast for the long wasted years - because of all men on this earth Lucie, wonderful, kind, beautiful Lucie, had bestowed this Love upon me.

"Darling" I whispered "I never knew-"

"Nor were you supposed to" she answered tartly. "At times I thought I was drawn to you because of your resemblance to Charles" she smiled then "it is a remarkable likeness, you know, two peas in a pod" the smile faded "but that was not the reason. Not at all. I came to realise that it was, in fact, quite the opposite. I have had much time to think upon this these months past, and it is all very clear to me. Charles was gay and frivolous; you, serious and grave. And deep. How I longed for you to open your heart to me, and I to you. And while I, like you, found solace in literature and the arts - oh, do you remember the long conversations we had? How I rejoiced when I heard your footsteps on the stairs and knew that I should have your company for an hour or so - but for Charles these things meant nothing. And I could see - for you do not live with a man for years without seeing his true self - that Charles was a broken reed, or rather, that he would break at the first real trial. Which he did" she said flatly, looking away. Then her eyes were on me again, eyes bright with joy and admiration. "But you, again you were his opposite, as light is to dark. A true man, doughty and valorous, like... like some royal king of honour, who fought on the banks of Troy!" she finished grandly, (and extemporising, I noted with some bemusement, on the words of an old song,).

I was about to give voice to some modest self-deprecating guff, as befits a bluff hero, but she surged on. "And so, you see we can not ... we can not - be together."

I was damned if I could see, and said so. But she had obviously thought this part over for weeks now, and had it all pat. "I am a widow, in mourning for a dead husband," she explained patiently, "and as, unsatisfactory... yes, as unsatisfactory as Charles' behaviour was, the fact remains that I should honour his memory for a decent period. It is only proper, after all. I truly feel that it would be wrong, somehow immoral, should it be known that I... that you... that is to say... oh, this is so difficult!... that we had

consummated our Love so soon after dear Charles has .....
has passed on." She stared at me imploringly "You do see
that, don't you, Sidney darling? It simply would not do if
it were to be noised abroad that you and I, that we had....
Well, I mean, it would be so dishonourable!

Ye Gods! the specious nonsense women of her class were
brought up on in those days! Didn't she know that we
were prisoners, that both our lives hung by a thread?
That Robespierre, the evil little dandyprat, could snuff
us out with a nod of his head, have us hailed away to the
Revolutionary Tribunal, and sent on to Samson the same
day for 'shortening'?   Death was smiling at us, I could
absolute hear the swish of his scythe - yet my darling
guileless ingenue remained concerned over our honour,
God help us!, over what people in polite society might say
should they get wind of any illlicit beard-splitting. (Mind
you, it's not much better nowadays, though they're a little
more direct. I tried assaulting the virtue of widowdom only
t'other day, and took a kick in the nutmegs for my pains).

But there it was, and no help for it: I had seen that
stubborn set of her rosebud lips before, and it ever boded
an unyielding attachment to Principle from which, come
fair weather or foul, she would not be prised. Besides, she
meant everything for the best, and for the honour of her
beloved, and if I was not to achieve my quest today, still I was
promised satisfaction - and lots of it - in the not too distant
future.   Hadn't she told me that her desires matched my
own, that "my heart is given over to your keeping, dearest
Sidney" and that, after the prescribed period of mourning,
she would not be averse to admitting my suit, just as soon
as we were back in England.

And so I accepted this Lenten fare, like the love-sick fool I
was, and denied more sensual pleasures chose instead to
delight in Lucie's presence, in the simple nearness of the
woman I had, for so long, loved from afar. And like all
lovers, we planned: what we would do when Robespierre
returned us to our native land, how we'd dine at the best

restaurants in Rumeville*[9], ride out in splendour each Sunday, dance at the finest balls, be seen only in the best company, and raise an enormous family - we settled on five boys and three girls in the end, I believe. All this and, just as importantly (if not more so), what was to be done if our diminutive captor reneged on his promise. I told her of my scheme to abscond and ship out to England as chance allowed. To my utter delight and pride, I found her eager and willing to undertake the hazard.

"Oh my love!" she exclaimed that first evening, her voice scarce above a whisper (for Defarge or her maid were ever at the key-hole) "it will be an adventure, like the odyssey of old, and with my Ulysses to guide me, what harm could befall?" A multitude of perils swam instantly before my eyes, but it would not do to dwell upon them, so I smiled modestly, patted her rump in answer and kept my own counsel.

The next few days were among the happiest of my life, the happiest certainly since that wretched Day of Death, so long ago in the Colonies[16]. In between scheming for escape, and our plans for a home in England once we had returned (Lucie favoured a country cottage, I remember, while my own vote was for a spacious town house - we eventually decided, with the overblown optimism of the love-sick, that we'd have both) we walked for miles on rural tracks, rode abroad on the lanes and bridle-ways of Aisne, and once we were even allowed a boating trip on the good river Oise. All with Defarge at our heels, of course, though he did have the good taste to keep a discreet distance, so we were able to enjoy some little privacy and intimate moments. Naturally, I tried at decent intervals to persuade her to renounce virtue, arguing *ad nauseam* that, as our own lives hung daily in the balance of fate, we should, perhaps, take our pleasures as we could, for we were never sure that we could enjoy them later. All this with much kissing, holding of hands and once, a most delicious squeeze of her bouncers,

---

*A cant term for London

at which she gave voice to a moan that would have done Messalina proud, which was very gratifying and boded well for the future; but then my hand was firmly removed and, with tears in her eyes, she begged me to desist, not to tempt her past endurance, for she was weak, and loved me to distraction, and if she gave way now it would spoil the magic of our wedding night and she would never forgive herself in the coming years.

The coming years! My heart soared at these words and the promised halcyon days and piping times I was sure they betokened. All my years of sorrow seemed at last to have had a purpose, to have led me home to my rightful place by Lucie's side. I doubt if anyone can ever imagine the summit of happiness to which I had flown. And I believed once more that God could be merciful.

So blithe was my mood that even the thought of parting from Lucie did not leave me utterly downcast. It was, I told myself, merely a temporary absence. Soon, if Robespierre fulfilled his promise, we would be free of the horrors of revolutionary France, and should the loathesome pigmy forswear himself, our plans were already set. Long before I left Lyon I had taken care to seek out the most skilful benfeaker*[10] I could find, a man who had already made a small fortune in supplying illicit passports to emigrés desirous of avoiding the axe by stealing furtively across the border to safety. It would cost me almost half of the gold I had stored up from my *civisme* 'commissions', but Lucie and I would have papers that would get us through every checkpoint from Laons to Calais. After that, the remainder of my hoard should see us safely home to England.

I returned to Paris still floating in a daze of happiness, a humour which even the dour presence of Defarge - grumbling into his beard and still calling down curses on the head of the demon seducer - did nothing to destroy. I found it hard to sympathise with his plight, or that of his lusty daughter, whose waist must by now be well thickened.

---

10   *A counterfeiter of passes and passports

After all, what was one bastard more or less in this horrid unfeeling world? And besides, Madamoiselle Defarge had been as avid for the game as I, with less self-control than a randy stoat, like all the other whores and dimber morts I had trodden the primrose path with these months past. Those wanton trulls, each of them so eager to buckle to - all so different from my own chaste angel, my darling Lucie.

She alone was deserving of my worship, my adoration. She was the best, the most faithful of women. While others were common as the barber's chair[17] and set their marriage vows at nought, she alone had been true to her husband, despite endless provocation and the huge attraction she now acknowledged she had felt for me over the years. Oh Fidelity personified! And even now, though chance had so cruelly shattered the solemn nuptial affirmations, still the memory of her husband held her from the pleasures that she so obviously wished to enjoy with my unworthy self. My heart swelled with pride to think that I had won the love of such a paragon of virtue and I vowed then that I would abjure fornication and loose-living forever.

I was twice-renewed: the guillotine had woken me from my introspective, self-destructive modes of thought, and Lucie's love had completed my metamorphosis, transforming me anew from selfish libertine to monogamous man of honour. When, after three glorious days, I boarded the carriage that was to carry me back to Paris and we made our parting with many a kiss and whispered endearment, my heart was fixed and my mind clear and untroubled. Whatever happened now, whatever dangers I might face, I swore that it would be Lucie's happiness, Lucie's well-being that I would keep forever to the fore.

Chapter Ten

The moment I stepped down from the coach on the Rue St Honoré I could feel it: the whole atmosphere of the capital had changed. It was in the dour, set faces of the workmen on the Pont Neuf, in the muted cries of the water sellers and road side hawkers, and the lack of urchins and bantlings on the streets and boulevards. The beggars too seemed dispirited, hardly bothering to display their withered or amputated limbs, or make their customary demands for alms. Even the animal inhabitants of the city appeared to acknowledge the change: once sprightly horses plodded disconsolately past our coach, the birds had gone and the ubiquitous curs and mongrels of the Parisian streets had ceased to bark. A funereal pall hung over everything, and the wide boulevards seemed to have shrunk to the confines of a tomb. Danton had been arrested.

It is hard to exaggerate the effect this news had on the populace. Danton was absolutely synonymous with the Revolution, from the storming of the Bastille to the formation of the Revolutionary Tribunal before which - with delicious irony - he himself was now to be arraigned. The great-voiced idol of the masses had been denounced - at the behest of Robespierre - and 'all true patriots' were now required to believe Stentor was a counter-revolutionary and traitor of the deepest dye. And it was lost on no-one that if Danton, hero and pillar of the revolution, could be accused and revealed as apostate, many more might yet be shown to be tainted. Danton's reputation and record had not been enough to save him - how much more vulnerable, then, were lesser men? I believe it was at this point that the people's eyes were finally opened to the full extent of the Terror. Before Danton they could believe that the wretches condemned to the Guillotine were supporters of the *ancien regime*, traitors to the Republic, and fully deserving of their fate. Equally, that they themselves - horny-handed sons of toil, craftsmen and labourers - were immune from the revolutionary haircut. Now, too late, they realised what a clutch of unctuous blackguards had taken power; that everyone was suddenly a potential suspect and (it was almost the same thing) a victim. Overnight, Ste Guillotine had become an altar upon which anyone might be sacrificed, and they did not take kindly to that at all. Amazing how quickly revolutionary enthusiasm wanes when your own neck could be next beneath the blade.

The tale was on everyone's lips. Danton had been taken in the early hours of 31st March. He had known he was at risk, but had believed to the last that he could manage the situation: "I will sit Robespierre on the end of my thumb and make him spin like a top" he was reputed to have answered when warned of the approaching doom. He believed, you see, that no one could send a revolutionary of his stature to the guillotine - his glorious reputation would protect him. Others said that he seemed suddenly to lose that fire in his belly, the ferocious energy that had sustained him through five years of danger and turmoil; that he had simply become sickened by the murderous politics of the revolution, worn down by events, tired of the hypocrisy that surrounded him, weary of the endless struggle for existence. Certainly he said that he was "drunk with men", and so tired of the endless bloodletting that the day before his arrest he cried

out "I would rather be guillotined than guillotine others...
besides, I am sick of the human race". Fair comment, but
he had taken a deuced long time to come to Weeping Cross,
he who had voted many a life away and was held by most to
be the prime mover of the September massacres.[18]

So, he sat in his apartment on the Rue St Germaine,
stirring his fire, meek as a lamb, until they came for him.
Delacroix, Philippeaux, and that pompous scribbler Camille
Desmoulins were detained at the same time, and joined
Herault, Chabeau and Fabre d'Eglantine - all three fervent
Danton supporters - who had been imprisoned earlier
on the standard charge of being accomplices of Orleans,
Brissot, Pitt and sundry others, as well as for "attacking the
immortality of the soul, which" the indictment added with
curious Classical irrelevance, "had been the consolation of
the dying Socrates". And this from men who daily sent
scores of victims to discover the truth, or falsehood, of
Socrates' sublime theory. Strange also, I thought, that
Robespierre, St Just and the rest should take such careful
precautions to guard their own miserable necks, if they were
so sure that Death was not the end of human existence.

But the arrest wrought an amazing change in Danton. The
very fact that his enemies had dared to move against him
seemed to breathe fire into his soul, and he became again
the fierce and boisterous Revolutionary, declaiming with
irresistible eloquence against the accusations during the
first day of his trial, carrying the public gallery with him
so that they applauded his speeches to the echo - it was
said his voice could be heard across the Seine, and having
heard the man speak I believe it - and all in all, threatening
to place the regime itself on trial, to turn the tables on his
enemies, for if Danton was acquitted then his accusers, by
the inexorable logic of the revolution, were sure to mount
the scaffold in his stead. Strangely, at one point he called
out that he wanted to talk about "the three rascals who had
deceived Robsepierre" - he still believed, mark you, that
Robespierre was blameless, and that St Just, Couthon and

Hanriot were to blame for his arraignment. Well, he was soon shorn of that illusion; and much else besides.

All this but yesterday: the trial continued and all now hung on the outcome of the second day's debate. I conferred heatedly with Defarge, demanding that we make straight for the Palais de Justice, but if I expected an argument I didn't get one. The old sot was nothing loathe, for while Danton might be ignorant of Robespierre's part in the arrests, Defarge was not, and he realised full well that his own fate must hang upon the verdict. Should Danton succeed in demolishing his accusers, the Incorruptible would certainly fall, and Defarge would be called to account for all the atrocities and devilry committed under Robespierre's tutelage.

What my own fate would be I didn't care to contemplate - I might be free of the weasel-faced homunculus or I could just as easily be lumped together with the rest and guillotined. Which was why I was in such a froth to see the trial's outcome. I had to admit that, on balance, and despite my earlier belief that I might safely observe the conflict from the sidelines, I was with Defarge on this one - I wanted Danton dead. At least with Robespierre I knew where I stood, more or less. And I had already laid plans with Lucie to counter any treachery on his part. But if Danton won everything was back in the melting pot, you see, and life was chancy enough already. So, although I liked the man, it was best for all concerned - especially me - if he were forced to take a peek through *la lunette revolutionaire*. We hurried through the gardens of the Louvre together, Defarge and I, pushing through the crowds on the Pont Neuf, and made across the courtyard to the Palais de Justice. Even before we entered the courtroom Danton's voice could be heard booming out over the hubbub.

The place was packed, but we shouldered our way inside, to stand with the mob at the very back of the hall. I can see it still: high on a dais, behind a long wooden desk in the centre of the chamber, sat Herman the president, and the other two judges, all wearing tricolor scarves, black turned-up hats and ostrich feathers *à la* Henri IV. Beneath these august personages was a sturdy olive-skinned figure with piercing collied eyes, pock-marked aquiline nose, and thick dark hair swept back in a prominent widow's peak. He was dressed top to toe in sombre black like an undertaker; which was, indeed, his job, in a manner of speaking: for this was Fouquier-Tinville, the infamous *accusateur publique*. He was conferring animatedly with one of two scribes sitting next to him, each bending low over his inkpot and quill. Above all this, with unconscious irony, towered a statue of Justice, scales in one hand and sword in t'other, with the sacred book of Law by her side. The blindfold round her eyes seemed apt enough, as if the perpetrators of this travesty did not wish the goddess to witness the crimes committed here daily in her name.

To the right of the judges, ranked on a narrow stepped bench, perched the rows of accused, fourteen in all, Danton's huge frame dominating the group, flanked on either side by a slovenly squad of gendarmes with carbines and fixed bayonets. I noted with no surprise that Danton and his friends were being tried alongside the Compagnie des Indes swindlers Chabot, Delaunay and Basire[19], and a clutch of four assorted villains described by the *accusateur* as "foreign agents". An old trick, this, to lump your political adversaries with men of a different kidney, criminals, mountebanks and fraudsters, and to demand from the jury a single verdict for all, and so make a conviction surer.

A glance to the left confirmed the expedient. Here, on benches, sat the jury, and I saw at once that these 'good men and true' had been whittled down from the normal twelve to a mere seven, all place-men of Robespierre who could be counted on to deliver the verdict required.

It seemed as if Danton had just made some *outré* jest as we entered, for the public gallery was in tears of laughter and calling encouragement to the accused. Even the jurymen were smiling, though not Herman, or his creature

Fouquier-Tinville who, I noted, was pressing a small note on his scribe, his eyes darting continually towards Danton, who had remained standing to accept the approbation of the masses. As I watched, the clerk rose and scurried from the building. A trivial incident and I doubt many in the court marked his departure - but it was Danton's nemesis all the same.

The big man was in fine form, smiling indulgently, his coarse shaggy hair and piercing eyes lending him a ferocious appearance as he towered above his guards and fellow prisoners, more a prosecuting attorney than a defendant, casting calumny and scorn on his accusers:

"Danton an aristocrat?" he asked theatrically, raising his great bushy eyebrows "France will not believe that tale for long!..... I have sold myself?" and here he pounded that great barrel chest "No money can buy Danton! My name is associated with every revolutionary institution - the levy, the revolutionary army, the revolutionary committees, the Committee of Public Safety, even the Revolutionary Tribunal! And I am accused of being a moderate?" He turned to Cambon, a breathless Robespierrist who was in the process of giving evidence against him: "Do you take us for conspirators?" he demanded and, despite himself Cambon smiled at the absurdity of the suggestion. "See!" roared Danton triumphantly. "See. He laughs! Citizen secretary, write down that he laughed! Small wonder - this whole sorry mess is a farce, a gigantic joke perpetrated on the People!"

And much more from the same sack. The mob loved it and lapped up his oratory like cats in a creamery. His performance alone seemed sufficient to secure an acquittal, but Danton now declared he had witnesses for the defence that would absolutely prove his innocence, and demanded they be heard forthwith. Tumultuous acclaim followed this announcement. He was utterly dominating the courtroom, bestriding the Revolutionary Tribunal like the colossus he was, ridiculing the prosecution, disparaging his opponents, demolishing their accusations with magnificent jaw-breaking eloquence.

And all the while Fouquier-Tinville's little scribe was scurrying about his fatal business. The note he carried to St Just at the Convention can still be seen, with the public prosecutor's desperation evident in every hurried, jagged line. The accused, writes Fouquier, are dangerous ruffians "whose observations disturb the tribunal." Danton, he continues, has the effrontery to demand that his witnesses be brought to speak for the defence - and (the noble prosecutor is obviously scandalised by the thought) there is absolutely nothing, in law, that a public prosecutor can do to prevent this happening. Fouquier pleads despairingly to St Just for the passing of a new decree to somehow silence their rebuttals.

When he received this desperate missive, St Just must have known that he had no reason, no pretext even, to demand such a decree from the National Convention. So, quite shamelessly, he invented one. Even as Danton's eloquence drove all before him at the Tribunal, St Just was rushing to the podium of the Convention and, before the astonished gaze of the delegates, brazenly declaring the existence of a new plot "to murder the patriots and the tribunal", a conspiracy launched - unbelievably - from *prison,* by a captive army officer, General Dillon. It was a lie, plain and simple, but none dared gainsay it. Raising objections invited denunciation and death, so nothing was said as St Just elaborated on his monstrous falsehood. Other conspirators were named, apparently at random, including Lucille Desmoulins, the frail and harmless wife of Danton's friend and co-accused, Camille. It was all of a piece for the implacable Angel of Death. "Liberty is a bitch who must be bedded on a mattress of corpses" he had said - and he meant every word.

This sudden treachery, declared St Just, demanded a new decree to deal with the emergency - nothing less than the severest draconian measures would suffice, enacted immediately. And the Convention, cowed as always by their terror of Robespierre's vengeance, sought no corroboration of these outlandish fantasies and passed the required legislation on the spot. The new decree was voted into law in a matter of minutes. It sounded the death knell for Danton, and for not a few of the delegates themselves later, for it removed from all judicial proceedings the last vestiges of a fair hearing. This pernicious piece of legislation declared that "any prisoner who resists or insults national justice" - that is, mark you, any person who spoke out in their own defence - was to lose any right to a defence! No chance to call witnesses or even to rebut the accusers. Arrest was now tantamount to guilt. And this, passed unanimously, at the heart of a nation sworn to Freedom, Equality and Liberty.

Carrying the new decree, Fouquier's scribe scurried back to his master at the Palais de Justice, well pleased with his errand. I watched the public prosecutor snatch at the paper he was handed and scan the document quickly. The deep etches on his face lightened, his shoulders relaxed; he looked over at Danton and smiled wolfishly across the courtroom. Then he was standing and proclaiming the new law, reading it aloud in court to a stunned silence.

At a stroke, Danton was disarmed, and his foes rushed in for the kill. Immediately after the decree was read Herman closed the trial for that day, to stifle any dissent, but all knew that we were hurtling towards a final inevitable conclusion. On the morrow, almost as soon as the trial resumed, the foreman of the jury, lickspittle Trinchard, rose to declare in obsequious tones that he and his peers required no further evidence. Their minds were unanimously settled on a verdict. To no-one's surprise all defendants were declared guilty. The sentence - death by beheading - to be carried out immediately, that same day. Speed was essential, you see; Robespierre and his cronies dared give no time for a coherent opposition to form around Stentor. Danton had to die at once.

Along with the other thirteen defendants he was bundled from the court and taken down immediately for the 'toilette' of the condemned - the same indignities I had suffered not four months before - hands bound, collars cut and hair roughly shorn at the nape. I watched them depart with mixed feelings - it was better so, for me at least, but I could not escape the feeling that I was witnessing the end of the best of the revolutionaries, and that only God could help France now. I left the tribunal with the rest of the silent, shocked citizenry and took my way to the courtyard where three tumbrils had already foregathered, rigged to carry the condemned men to the Place de la Revolution. Danton was the first to emerge and take his place in the carts. It took over an hour for the rest to embark - Camille Desmoulins delayed the whole business, refusing to have his hair cut or his hands tied, and fighting with such vehemence he twice knocked Samson to the floor. It was only with the help of three burly gendarmes that he was eventually persuaded to take his toilette and join his friends. During this commotion Danton seemed in great spirits, laughing and joking with everyone, his friends and the guards. The rest did not share his good humour and I heard Fabre, the poet and playwright, bitterly lamenting that his work, *L'Orange de Naples,* had been confiscated. It was a fine play, he lamented, in splendid verse. Verse, you must know, is *vers* in French, and the same word also designates 'worms'. "Yes" repeated Fabre, his head in his hands "such splendid vers."

"Vers?" jeered Danton across the cart "Vers? Don't worry, Fabre. Eight days from now you'll be making splendid vers!" and he laughed heartily at his own sally, his great voice carrying easily to the watching crowds. Camille Desmoulins appeared a moment later, lungs heaving, his shirt in ribbons, screaming imprecations at Robespierre, the Committees, and the Tribunal as they loaded him into the cart.

I didn't follow the tumbrils as they left the courtyard, though many of the crowd did. I did not want to see the end of this great patriot. I'm told that the route was thronged with spectators and that, as he passed Robespierre's lodgings on the Rue St Honoré, Danton cried out to the shuttered windows "Vile Robspierre. You will follow us!" Many people regard that outburst as prophetic, in view of what happened later. I doubt it myself - just wishful thinking on Danton's part, if you ask me - he was ever a bad loser. It's said that further along the road a watching citizeness, possibly seeing the noted revolutionary at close quarters for the first time, exclaimed "How ugly he is!" "No point telling me that now" Danton shouted back, smiling good-naturedly as the cortege moved on, "I shan't be ugly much longer".

Some report that the Abbé de Kéravenan, a priest who had blessed Danton's marriage just a few months earlier, followed the tumbrils all the way to the Guillotine, silently pronouncing the absolution. I can't vouch for that, but tell the tale for completeness. Mind you, it wouldn't have been the first time a blackfly risked his own neck to give one of his sheep this final comfort.[20] It was growing dark by the time the cortege reached the scaffold through the press of bodies, and Samson was in a hurry to finish his day's work. Herault was the first to die. As went forward to the knife, he tried to embrace Danton, but the executioner would brook no delay and rushed him on. "Fool!" Danton was heard to say "you won't prevent our heads kissing in the basket!"

He was the last of the prisoners to die. As his name was called out he bellowed "My turn now!" in a strong voice and quickly mounted the fatal steps. Only then did his courage seem to waver. He was newly married: "My beloved" he was heard to murmur "shall I never see thee more?" Then he rallied, whispering "Come Danton! No weakness!", and turning to the Executioner exclaimed in that brazen voice so all could hear "Show my head to the people. It is worth it!" Then he calmly allowed his great frame to be tied to that hideous wooden runner, still hot and reeking with the blood of his friends.   They say his final words were "It's just a sabre cut", a phrase Camille Desmoulins had used many years before, when enthusing on the humanitarian swiftness of the new method of execution. The axe rose and fell, and the best of the revolutionaries was no more. They showed his head, holding it up to stare sightlessly over the crowd. The mob remained deathly still all the while - no one cheered. The last compassionate light of the Revolution had been snuffed out.

Which was just as well for me. I lamented his death, of course, but one must be practical about these things. My own chance of survival (already lamentably low under Robespierre) would have been vanishingly small had Danton triumphed.   Not that I felt too sanguine about a future untrammelled reign of Robespierre; all that I had seen of the loathsome homunculus promised that, if the situation was bad now, it could only get worse under the Incorruptible's beneficent Rule of Virtue. I planned an ordered retreat to Lyon, as quickly as possible, there to wait out the inevitable round of blood-letting that was sure to follow Danton's demise. *Vae Victis* indeed - I didn't hold out much hope for any delegate of the Convention who so much as sniffed of an association with Danton. Or Hebert for that matter. The final time of reckoning was at hand, and I wanted to be well out of it.

I was given leave to return to Lyon the following day, and hurriedly made my preparations. So keen was my unease, I was in a carriage just after dawn, and had already taken on the persona and vestments of Francois Laborde, when word came - via messenger Defarge, of course - that Robespierre required a final word. Immediately. Defarge would permit no delay and hustled me out of the coach there and then. I shook him off and stormed ahead down the Rue St Florentin, disappointed and angry - God knew what new schemes and disasters the Incorruptible had planned for me now. So angry was I that, as I stepped into the alley from the Rue St Honoré, I collided with another fellow who was just leaving

Robespierre's lodgings. I begged his pardon peremptorily, then stepped back, aghast. It was Fouché.

He seemed just as surprised to see me, but recovered his poise almost immediately. "Francois!" he said, wringing my hand. "How good to see you. And how is your grandmother, well I hope?"

I stood gaping like a landlocked cod for a moment, paralysed by fear and quite unable to make head nor tail of his question. My mind was impaled on the hideous, inescapable fact that Fouché had seen his clerk Laborde about to enter Robespierre's private rooms. And my grandmother? Why ask about her? She was in East Cheam cemetery, dead these twelve years. Then a small voice called faintly from the back of my head *your French grandmother is ill!* and my brain slipped back once more into its familiar duplicitous track. "She's.... she's... dead" I gasped, my mind racing "A lung fever, carried her off not four days since. It's why I've been so long away, why I've overstayed the time you allowed me. I'm sorry, I'll make up the time, I'll-"

"Softly, softly", Fouché said gently, and for the first time I noticed the worry and fatigue that etched his tired face. "I am sorry for your loss, Francois. But you must not worry about Lyon, and you may take all the time you wish, as far as I am concerned. I am no longer your master there".

"What? I don't.... how-" I began, but he cut me short with a single word:

"Robespierre".

He might well have said 'merde'. I looked at him blankly "I am recalled" he continued, fingering his walking cane and speaking in something like his normal voice, "by order of the Incorruptible. I have just been in to see him, my second visit, by heaven, and as productive as the first. He will not even deign to speak to me, but stands there, staring his venom while I act the supplicant. Psha!" and Fouché's cane rang down on the cobbles as if he was crushing a serpent's head. "He washed his teeth in a basin as I asked his pardon, making no sign that he heard me, then gargled and spat on the ground by my feet! What a monster! I have never seen anything so impassive as his expression, not even in the faces of the dead." He controlled himself with an effort, and gave me a wan smile. "Such was my interview with Robespierre. I can hardly call it a conversation, for his lips never parted. No words will move him, he is implacably resolved on my demotion. Fortunately, I remain a member of the Convention still."

Some of my funk was abating at this news. Fouché no longer had the power to harm me, thank God, so this chance meeting was not as great a calamity as I had first thought. But removed! We both knew what that boded, and I could not believe that Fouché's membership of the National Convention would provide much protection if Robespierre had decided on his removal, permanently, from the *mise en scène*.

"But tell me, Francois," he asked suddenly and I thought I saw suspicion glow briefly in his eyes "why are you here? What business have you with Robespierre?"

My brain had been busily turning over all this while and I was ready for the question "Clemency" I said simply "I seek clemency for a friend who has fallen foul of the revolution.".

"Clemency!" Fouché positively snorted. "Like most things in France today, you will find that commodity in short supply, especially within those hallowed portals." and he gestured with his head towards the door to Robespierre's rooms. "The temple of Virtue is not known for its compassion".

"But still, I must try" I said gently, as one fulfilling a duty he knows must fail.

An expressive gallic shrug from Fouché. He looked more despondent than I had ever seen him "Yes, we must try", he agreed sadly "Even sheep and oxen, knowing themselves doomed, will attempt to escape the encroaching wolf pack." He was given to these poetic flights of speech from time to time, you know. But the image stirred a memory in my head, and for no good reason that I can think of, even now, I suddenly blurted out " I travelled with the *voyageurs* in

Canada, in my youth, and the oxen there stand together in a circle when danger threatens, facing the pack - no wolf can touch 'em" It's true, the great shaggy musk-ox of the north, with their recurved horns and massive bulk can face off any number of wolves - I've seen it often enough. I thought it a stupid banal comment, even as I spoke, but the words had a most remarkable effect on Fouché and, I believe, changed the course of French, and probably world, history. Without that trite comment we'd have had no Napoleon, no invasion of Russia, no Nelson or Wellington, no Trafalgar or Waterloo. Aye me, I've a lot to answer for.

For there was a light now in Fouché's eyes, and he was smiling as broadly as Archimedes stepping from his bath. "You are right Francois!" He looked around to ensure he was not overheard. "It seems, my friend, that I have been wrong on two occasions" he whispered, stepping closer. "Like Hebert and Danton I have underestimated the cunning and determination, the ruthless ambition, of the wolf. But we oxen have power still!" He clapped me on the shoulder (and I silently praised God that Defarge was not around to see that incriminating gesture). "Thank you, dear friend, thank you for your counsel. I see my way clearly now. This third throw of the dice will determine all. *Adieu* Francois, we may meet later, in happier times - or we may not meet again." And he brushed passed me and was off into the street, his head high and his step spritely.

I listened until the tap-tap of his cane receded into silence, then continued down the shadowed alley into the brightly lit timber yard. Mother Duplay sat on a stool in the spring sunshine between a pail and a salad bowl, busily cleaning herbs. Two gendarme guards squatted nearby, helping with this homely occupation, and chatting away happily with the lady of the house. They sprang to on seeing my arrival, one covering me with musket and bayonet while the other rapped tentatively on their master's door. Peg-leg Duplay appeared at once, he must have been dozing in the hallway; the young man recognised me instantly and I was led upstairs to Robespierre's cabinet. I found the great man wrapped in a sort of chemise peignoir; he had just left the hands of his hairdresser who had combed and powdered his hair and his face, so that he looked like some effeminate clown who had lost his way from the circus. A clown who now held all of France in his implacable grip, and possessed the power of life and death over yours truly. I was suitably obsequious.

Robespierre turned his awful feline eyes upon me and asked coldly if I had seen Fouché. I answered that I had but that I had fobbed off his questions with plausible excuses. "Nevertheless, it is unfortunate that he saw you, as Francois his clerk, in Paris. It may complicate matters". The Incorruptible's lips tightened and he seemed to lose himself in thought for a moment, but at the end he waved a dismissive hand ."It is of no matter" he said airily in his piping tones "we have drawn Fouché's teeth. That atheist will not walk this earth much longer. By what right does he inform the populace that the Deity does not exist? That death is merely an eternal sleep? What right has he to snatch from innocent people the sceptre of Reason and give it to the hands of Crime? He will pay for this affrontery!"

This was a new Robespierre I was seeing. I would never have credited him with such strong religious convictions. But I was wrong, as events were to prove, for now that he had vanquished his most potent enemies he was ready to put in place a scheme to restore religion - or his own version of religion - to the country as a whole.[21] But all this was in the future . For the moment he continued to pour out his spleen on Fouché and his 'co-conspirators', an invective which turned slowly but quite perceptibly into a paeon of praise for his own work, and the dangers he braved in restoring Virtue to his beloved fatherland.

This was the worst of Robespierre's many annoying traits. Most people prefer speaking of themselves to any other topic, but in him the propensity seemed irresistible. And while praise acts as a cordial on most people's spirits, it is the praise they have from others which provides a balm to their soul. What set Robespierre apart, and confirmed his sublime egotism, was that he seemed as much enlivened by the eulogies he bestowed on himself, as others are by the applause of their fellow citizens.

The panegyric he pronounced on his own virtues must have lasted all of half an hour, but evidently it raised his spirits, for at the end he turned to me, breathless but smiling. "And you sir" he said, making a small bow in my direction "have done the work asked of you most splendidly. Splendidly. Nor have your actions in Laon gone unnoticed, for I am informed that you conducted yourself most admirably with the Widow Darnay. That there was no attempt at..." he turned quickly towards the window, embarrassment clouding his sunken features "...at... indelicacy."

Well, it wasn't for the want of trying. But I inclined my head sagely, and attempted to hoist a suitably chaste and noble expression onto my face. Evidently it worked; he turned back to me beaming broadly and revealing mis-shapen teeth made all the more yellow by contrast with his grotesque, lead-white powdered face. "Yes, yes. Such chaste behaviour deserves its reward. You are revealed as a true man of virtue, sir, as I knew from the first you must be - no, no, please, your modesty is misplaced here, Citoyen Carton. Your first act of self sacrifice at the Guillotine can not be gainsaid. You are English, but Revolutionary Ideals are not limited to France. I felt you should know, therefore, before you left for Lyon..." he paused "... that I have ordered that your love be removed from Laon. The journey to that city is long and tiresome. So...." And again he dragged out his words, for all the world like some indulgent uncle revealing a surprise present to a favourite nephew, "....she will be brought to Paris tomorrow, and housed with all honour in the Rue Mont Martre!"

The room seemed suddenly to take on a scarlet hue, the air stifling, and it required all my self-control not to seize the little runt by his scrawny neck and wring the life from him. This unlooked-for 'reward' set my schemes in ruins! Paris was further yet from Calais. A longer journey with additional checkpoints and more chance of being revealed as fugitives from revolutionary justice. It would be that much more difficult to fly the coop when chance offered.

But no matter, I told myself, striving to be calm, swallowing my rage and disappointment, and attempting at the same time to mould my features into a suitably grateful expression. No matter, Lucie and I would revise our schemes and plan our flight homeward just as soon as we could meet again. All would still be well - aye, that was the point I must hold to. I gave the odious dwarf my finest bow (officially frowned upon, of course, but he smiled nonetheless at the courtesy, as I knew he would) "You are kindness itself, Citoyen Robespierre, and have my heartfelt gratitude. But, if I may be so bold, when might it be possible to see the lady again?" "Soon, soon" he nodded placatingly, "but Virtue is patient, sir" he added portentously. (and desire fervent, I wanted to add, but it was bootless - all longing was beyond Robespierre's ken - except of course his lust for power) "You will see your lady again, I promise you. But first..." and here his eyes frosted over once more ".... first we must root out the enemies of the revolution. And for that, my dear sir, I may be forced once more to use your unique talents. You may be needed at a moment's notice, to infiltrate the traitors in Paris and elsewhere."

I began to say that, while I was of course at his disposable, considering the urgency of the moment, perhaps it might be best if I remained in Paris, but he cut me short "No, no sir. That is why I send you to Lyon, to avoid your exposure as a very special - I might say an exceptional - agent of the Republic. We want no repetition of the deplorable Fouché incident this morning. I wish there to be no possibility of your true identity becoming known. Your service will prove invaluable, I have no doubt, and soon, for there are many who name me tyrant and wish to earn for themselves the acclaim of Brutus!" he shook his head in what appeared to be genuine sorrow and puzzlement. "They say I am a tyrant, Monsieur Carton - rather I am a slave, a slave of Liberty, a living Martyr to the Republic!" he intoned, his hands clasping spasmodically "But I have promised to leave a redoubtable testimony to the oppressors of the People. And I will not be foresworn. I shall leave them the terrible truth - and Death".[22]

Bully for you, my lad, thinks I - nodding like a good flunky should - provided I'm well out o' the firing line. I was expecting more sermonising, for he seemed in full flow, but there was nothing more. The months of constant fear and agitation were taking their toll y'see, the little man wasn't as young as he had been, and he simply wasn't up to the daily three hour harangues he'd been wont to foist upon his underlings. I can't say I was disappointed, but somehow it wasn't what you expect of a blood-drinking dictator. Indeed, Robespierre seemed utterly spent after his outburst and collapsed into a chair, trembling slightly and merely nodding to me with a whispered *bonne chance*", as I took the opportunity and quickly made my adieus.

I hated leaving, knowing that Lucie would be in the city the following day, but another part of me was happy to get back to Lyon; happy too, that Lucie and I remained under the protection of the most powerful man in France, for tired and exhausted though he might be, Robespierre was doubtless the master of the country. He was a chancy cove, past question, but you must understand that France at that time was a place of suspicion and death where we daily supped on perils. If I could remain useful to Robespierre - exceptional he had called me - I and my love stood a reasonable chance of coming through the Terror unscathed. Mind you, it was obvious now that I would never be granted leave to return to England. The more exceptional my skills, the less likely Robespierre would wish to lose them. No, escape was the only option now. But I must bide my time and await my next recall to Paris.

The days hung heavy on my hands in Lyon. For one thing, I seemed to be in a state of constant agitation over Lucie. I worried ceaselessly: had she been brought to Paris? Was she well? How was she coping with her confinement in that Terror-ridden city? When would bastard Robespierre allow us to meet again? And for another, there was very little to do, the Lyon trials and executions having dried to a trickle after the destruction of Hebert and Danton, and the recall of Fouché. Even the demand for *civismes* had collapsed, a pitiable state indeed, as a little light diversion with any reasonably personable female supplicant would have done wonders for my morale.

The news from Paris was equally bleak - the whole of the capital seemed to have been marked for sacrifice, which was not surprising with Robespierre in the ascendant. The Incorruptible had denounced Fouché by name in early May, but instead of quietly resigning himself for death, my former master had refused to accept his fate and struck back at his enemy. Within a month he had somehow got himself elected as president of the Paris Jacobin Club, an organisation which, until then, everyone had regarded as Robespierre's private fiefdom. The Great Denounciateur was livid, and quickly mounted his own counterattack. I was ordered to rustle up the Lyon Jacobins and send them all to Paris *toute de suite*. I complied with alacrity, and on June 11th they testified against Fouché's conduct in Lyon, backing up an outpouring of invective from Robespierre which ended with poor Joseph being unanimously expelled from membership of the Jacobins. "Vile Imposter" Robespierre had called him, hurling his abuse from the podium with twisted, froth-speckled lips "Despicable Intriguer! A man whose hands are stained with loot and dripping with blood and crime!" His speech was cheered 'til the rafters shook, and all were now agreed that Joseph Fouché was marked for the Guillotine as the corn is marked for the scythe.

But the man himself was not there to witness his own condemnation. Fouché had disappeared into the shadowy underworld of Paris, there to do what he did best - to plot mischief, against Robespierre and his murderous intimates. Wherever one turned there were tales and rumours of a half-glimpsed Fouché, of clandestine meetings at dead of night with those most at risk from Robespierre's despotic regime. The ox was seeking allies against the wolf.

Amid all this cheerless political gossip, a single bright episode illuminated the gloom of exile - news of the Glorious First of June took a full week to reach me in Lyon, and if this great British naval victory left the snail-eaters mopish, it did much to help me keep my sanity.[23] The triumph set me thinking too, and my ruminations culminated in the discovery of an inviolable Law of History I've named "Carton's Minimal Syllable Rule", and which provides a cogent and logical reason for the undoubted fact that throughout the history of Anglo-French conflict, Britain usually gives Monsieur Crapaud a jolly good thrashing

Wisdom is a capricious mistress, and never reveals her secrets lightly. It took me many years of living with the froggies to understand why the garlic guzzlers never seem able to best the British Lion when it comes to fisticuffs. Certainly they've had some successes, (the Maid of Orleans for example), but only when they are particularly well led, and when our hearts aren't really in it; or when they cheat, as they did at Formigny, unsportingly using firearms against our longbows. But take a comprehensive look at the record and the truth's obvious: Agincourt, Crècy, Poitiers, The Battle of the Spurs, Oudenarde, Malplaquet, our signal victories against them in the Americas, the Battle of the Nile, Trafalgar, (both of which I witnessed first-hand) and the triumph of Waterloo, since when they've wisely kept their heads well beneath the parapet. Consider too, the relative success and failure of the two nations in the race to plant colonies around an unwilling world - Union Jack has beat the Tricolor into second place just about everywhere that Jacques and John Bull have fought it out.

Now, I ask you, why should that be? Patriotic men of our

island race will, of course, speak of it all being in the blood, of stronger Anglo-Saxon stock and other such rubbish, while Monsieur Crapaud - when given the chance, (so don't) - will croak on interminably about lack of honour, treachery, and Perfidious Albion. Also nonsense, in my humble.

Because you don't need a bushel of brains to realise that France has thrown up as many strong, brave, resolute heroes as we have here across the Channel; and from my experience of the Gallic nation - not inconsiderable, you'll grant - they're second to none in the falsehood stakes, arch-deceivers, scoundrels, world-class liars and schemers (much like ourselves, in fact). You could argue all day over specifics, but man to man (or man to woman for that matter) there's really nothing to choose between the two nations. This talk of moral or physical superiority is the most utter tosh, all of it. And why? Because the true reason for our French friends' abysmal showing over the centuries lies somewhere else entirely.

Language. That's the real answer to poor Froggie's problems. And not a thing he can do about it. Look'ee, I have before me a copy of an enormous tome by that new Russian chap - Tolstoy's his name - some sort of Ruskie nobleman apparently, but that's by the by; *War and Society*, it's called.[24] Absolutely gigantic piece of work, as I say, runs to 442 pages, full of unrequited love, untimely deaths, moral and spiritual decay, and other such worthy and for the most part sleep-inducing topics (though he does give an excellent feel of the French retreat from Moscow, and I should know because I was there and walked every frozen, tormented, death-strewn mile). But that's another tale we'll come to presently, if God spares me.

However, the important thing to remember is the number of pages, because I happen to have another copy of the same opus, sent me by an old friend I still correspond with in France. Now the two books are twins for size, and they are both printed in an almost identical font, with (give or take) the same number of words on each page. So, peas in a pod, to all appearances, and there's the rub. The Frog version runs to 663 pages. It's what set me thinking. Translated from the same Russian original, in an identical style, but a full 121 pages longer in French.

Plain as a pike, what? No? Well then, imagine the scene, Napoleon in his tent before Waterloo, or Montcalme at his Quebec headquarters, studying the disposition of the hostile English troops. Imagine too, a similar scene in the opposing British forces, with old Hook-Nose or the boy Wolfe busily assessing the strength of the French troops they face. Suddenly - and simultaneously - French and British gallopers arrive at their respective headquarters with dispatches carrying identical information, details vital to the success of the campaign, and demanding immediate action or the battle will be lost. Union Jack and Tricolor both read the despatches but, because of their incomprehensible obsession with using four syllables where one would do, the French message is longer! So while Froggie is still perusing the manuscript, the British bulldog gains a few vital seconds and is already on the march ahead of them. Important messages that require discussion (and which does not?) simply compound the problem. French may be the language of love (and as an aid to seduction I'm the first to celebrate its sonorous, mellifluous tones - absolutely nothing like it for making the ladies melt). But when bullets fly and the cavalry's charging and there's a square to form lickety split, there is no contest - when every second counts, give me English every time.

It's so obvious once pointed out: we say "stop"!, they say "a-rret-ez" - and take three times as long to say it; 'help' and 'aid-ez moi', (or "m'aidez" if you want to be scrupulously fair, but still twice as long). 'Gunshot' is 'coup de feu', while 'at gunpoint' is 'sous la menace du pistolet' , a full five syllables longer, God help us (or rather God help the poor froggies, for with a language like theirs they're most certainly in need of Divine Assistance). The list goes on forever, and I dare say you can think of other examples yourself, because it's certain sure: every sentence in any conversation merely serves to magnify the time advantage, and to place the Lion's paw more firmly on the Cockerel's throat. Damned if they speak, and damned if they don't.

Note too, that Frenchie's message would have taken longer to write in the first place, and you can see the extent of the handicap our Gallic friends labour under. A sad truth (or a blessing - it depends which side of the Channel you're on), but poor Jean-Pierre simply cannot pass information as quickly as the hated *Rosbif*. It is just an unfortunate fact of life for Jacques, like a woman with a flat chest - they're both automatically at a disadvantage in the struggle for existence. No, the French aren't stupid, cowards or weaklings - far from it - they keep losing to us because they have a surfeit of syllables. Simple as that. Not so much long-winded as long-worded. The poor snail-snafflers are stuck with this huge disadvantage, fed to them with their mother's milk, and not a damn thing they can do about it. Except learn English.

Chapter Eleven

Not that these profound insights into the linguistic weakness of the French made a ha'pence o' difference to my own hapless position – Lucie was still in Paris, pinned beneath Robespierre's panoptic gaze, and I remained kicking my heels in Lyon, effectively imprisoned in that city, spying and doubtless spied upon, and ever at the Incorruptible's capricious beck and call.

When his summons finally came, four long months after Danton's murder, I hardly noticed that the dispatch was delivered, not by old Beardie, my usual contact, but by a thin, maggot-pated catchfart of Defarge, a one-finned fellow whom I mistrusted from the first. I asked him where Beardie was; I'd grown accustomed to that gross-bellied Babbletongue who, for the charge of a glass or two of purl, kept me well informed of the intrigues and gossip of the capital. "He's been trimmed", says this one-armed Death's Head. "He was accused." And so strange were the times I accepted this as a complete explanation for Beardie's passing Everyone knew then, you see, that to be accused was the end. There were no acquittals at the Revolutionary Tribunal.

Still, I did find it strange that Robespierre's crab-like signature was missing from the note; instead, attached to the parchment was an enamel cufflink - which I immediately identified as belonging to the dandified Denonciateur – in lieu of his moniker, I supposed. That, and the message itself, greatly allayed my fears, for the note was characteristically imperious and succinct – *Return at Once.*

I could have bellowed aloud in relief and exultation. At last! At long last! Back to Paris and a meeting with Lucie! So transported was I at the prospect of seeing my beloved all natural caution evaporated. I thought only of those sea-blue eyes, those soft lips and welcoming arms. Had I known then the horrifying outcome of obeying Robespierre's call, I would have tried for England that very day, and left Lucie to hazard his wrath. I couldn't fathom it at the time, but Robespierre's note was a call to Disaster. For everyone.

I spent the whole carriage journey to Paris in a fever and not simply because of the weather, which was intolerable, the hottest in living memory and becoming more close and humid the nearer we got to the Capital. No, the political situation in Paris was also at fever pitch. The Terror's grip on the city had tightened; everyone was suspect; most foreigners, especially Britons, were in gaol; and so great was the tide of blood that now flowed daily from Madame Guillotine, there were plans afoot for a specially constructed *sangueduct* to drain the gory stream into the Seine. Fastidious people, those French revolutionaries – quite at ease beheading a hundred people every afternoon, but sully their fine cobbles with these innocents' blood? *Quelle Horreur!* Something must be done!

Robespierre's new messenger remained tight-lipped throughout our progress north, evading my eyes and rarely answering questions. Not that I spoke much myself. I was in a lather to arrive, to see what Robespierre desired of me and, most importantly, to persuade him to allow an immediate visit to Lucie. In the lining of my coat I had secreted our two counterfeit passports, and enough gold to carry us safely to England. Pray God she had escaped any purge or accusation and still lived safe at Rue Mont Martre. Should chance present us with the opportunity, I was as primed as I'd ever be to fly this revolutionary bedlam with my love.

The journey was an ordeal; the heat was bad enough, but the force of Phoebus' unremitting ardour had sucked all moisture from the land and our passage was an interminable jostling, jerking torment as the driver tried, as best he could, to negotiate our way over the iron-hard ruts and potholes. It was an impossible task - French roads are insufferable at the best of times, but this pilgrimage was a nightmare. We travelled in the early morning and late evening to avoid the worst of the sun, but on the morrow of our final day, as we approached Paris, the constant jolting proved too much for our old rattlebones, and we lost a wheel. It took another two and a half hours to locate a wheelwright and effect a repair, so it was at half-past ten instead of the tabled eight o'clock that we finally arrived, travel-worn and weary, in a narrow alley running north to south, that gave out onto the Avenue des Tuileries, hard by the Place de la Revolution. It was the 9th Thermidor Year II (the 27th July 1794 to you) and as hot as Satan's kitchen.

The cobbles shimmered in the heat as I heaved my weary frame from the coach and scanned the sky. It was a dull, stifling day, threatening storm, clouds like lead, and thunder rumbling away somewhere over the horizon. Rain would be a blessing, anything to chase away the cloying, almost tropical atmosphere. Old lanksleeve followed behind me, and I was just setting my hat on my head when I scried, from the crook of my eye, two figures emerging from the shadows on my left. Chosen Pells as ever was, dressed alike in Highwayman's rig, riding coat and billycock hat, though I noted the shorter of the two sported a blue cockade in his hatband. Both were well set up with sword and pistol. Before me, another Damme Boy had appeared, blocking my passage north with an unsheathed hanger in his hand. Sidney my son, thinks I, this is distinctly unhealthy, and acting immediately on the thought I turned to flee.

It was my white liver that saved me, for as I span round to make my escape, Lanksleeves' cudgel, intended for the back of my sconce took me a glancing blow on the shoulder. Stunned, I lashed out wildly and by good fortune caught the deceiving bastard across the nose with my fist. He sprang back, snarling, his nostrils spurting blood, still barring my escape south, and giving me no choice but to drag out my *espadin**[11] and prepare to defend myself.

I backed smartly against the coach to prevent an attack from the rear, feverishly doubling my cloak over my forearm, and trying to show a confidence I did not feel while simultaneously puzzling out the reason for this ambush. These men were nothing to do with Robespierre, that much was certain. Enemies of the Incorruptible, then, but who? Danton's friends wishing to wreak vengeance? Not bully-boys of Fouché, surely? But then - why not? If he knew how I had played him false at Lyon he was the very man to exact such retribution. But why this elaborate ambuscade, when a simple accusation would have been enough to send me to the tumbrils? Then again, did it really matter – I was attacked and unless I could win free, questions of 'Who? and Why? were no more than piss in the wind. I flourished my sword "Come! Lay on, you bastards!" I yelled, scowling manfully, while terror did its best to devour me body and soul. Combat is dreadful, and I speak as one who has unwillingly seen more than most. For one, it is such a horribly chancy affair. Oh, training is a fine thing, and will certainly see you through dangers that would kill an untried novice. But I've lost count of the mighty men of valour I've seen, Paladins to a man, striding through the battlefield careless of both friend and foe, invincible one moment, and the next laid low by a stray musket ball that no amount of training could foresee or avoid. No, a damned

---

[11] * *Spanish short rapier*

dicey business, an affray, and best avoided.

But while all murder and mayhem should be shunned like the plague, it has allowed me to discover one thing about myself. I may be full of terrors before an encounter and, if chance serves, more willing than most to show my opponent a clean pair of heels, but once it's come to the grip I'm glad to say I don't panic. When bloodletting is inevitable, it's my fears that flee, and my mind suddenly becomes crystal clear, detailed and defined, with everything seen in sharp relief. I take no credit for this, it's a gift, inborn, and I thank God for the boon, for it's meant the difference, on more occasions than I'd like to remember, between survival and being put to bed with a mattock and spade. It's failed me only on the steps of the guillotine, as I've explained earlier in this history, and I hold that even then there's few men who would have had the presence of mind to call out to Defarge in such a situation. Besides which, as I think I've demonstrated full well, *omnis amans amens**[12].

So, as I watched my four assailants move cautiously towards me my mind was suddenly calm and I took in their every aspect of their approach, watching for strengths and flaws. I can see them still, sixty years on and as clear as day: the Chosen Pells calm and business-like on my left, each with a falchion in their right hands; Lanksleeve cradling his cudgel in the centre, the blood beginning to dry on his beard, while to the right my fourth opponent looked for all the world like an angry undertaker, dressed *cap à pie* in black, very formal in frock-coat and tricorn, cack-handed and carrying a wicked-looking rapier. And suddenly the years had dropped away and I was back in Madrid, with Don Anselmo my fencing master, teacher of *La Destreza* in lineal descent from its originator, the illustrious Don Jeronimo de Carranza.[25] "Keep your diameter perfect, and remember *señor* Carton, the circle is always inferior to the straight line"; by which he meant that, other things being equal, a thrust will always beat a cut. The style he taught

---

12   **Every lover is demented*

was outmoded even then, and I took to its study because I knew the value of learning techniques that one's opponent had not seen before - and it appealed also to my sense of symmetry and beauty. *La Destreza*, you must know, is based on mathematics, geometry and an intimate knowledge of the Classics, with a careful study of angles, distances and sword lengths. But much of it was plain Common Sense really. Take that phrase of Don Anselmo's: 'the circle is always inferior to the straight line'. When you consider swordplay seriously (as you must), then to strike a blow a cutlass-man or bold *sabreur* must first pull back his weapon and then swing the blade forward at his opponent. All this takes time. The swordsman must also raise his arm while attacking with a faulchion or cutlass, and during this span his chest is unprotected and can be easily penetrated by a thrusting sword, which needs to travel only a short distance to its target. And, mark you, an attack with a thrusting sword, such as a rapier, does not leave that swordsman's chest unprotected, the weapon is lighter and therefore faster, and since the hit comes straight from the shoulder, less force is required for a thrust than a cut.

But enough pedantry. What all this theory told me was that I could discount the cudgel- and faulchion-men. All slashers you see. The real danger came from my left-handed friend with the rapier. He had to be laid by the heels first, or any thrust I made at the rest would quickly see me spitted on his blade. They were still advancing, almost completing the diameter, leering now, confident in their superior numbers. This would require finesse.

With a wild bellow I took a reckless swinging slash at the three men to my left, forcing them back by the brute ferocity of my attack. Don Anselmo would be grave-spinning at my lack of subtlety, but I meant to redeem myself quickly. The left-to-right cut ended with the point of my sword facing cack-hander, just as I had intended. He had already moved forward in the approved French stance and was just beginning his thrust his rapier towards my exposed right side. French and Italian schools would have demanded I retire (impossible with the coach at my back) or move into the oncoming assault with parry and counterattack. I did neither. Instead, using the imaginary circle that had been imprinted on my brain from hours and hours of practice under Don Anselmo's unrelenting gaze, I swung away to one side, like a toreador side-stepping a charging bull, and allowed the deadly thrust to spend itself on the air. Only then did I close with my opponent, elbowing him smartly in the eye, and bringing my knee up hard into his unprotected crotch. There was a satisfying crunch, he screamed, and I was springing back, taking guard as he slumped unconscious to the ground. Finesse you see. It's all you ever need.

My first instinct was to run him through as he lay there, to "mak siccar" as The Bruce had it, but there was no time. The other three were closing on me, more heedful now, and the leers had gone, but still resolute. It was clear they intended to come at me in a rush. Lanksleeves risked a look at his fellows "Careful now. Remember. He's to be taken alive".

Alive? The news froze the very marrow of my bones . There is only one reason a foe is taken alive - information. And that meant torture. I had to get away! Even though, if captured, I'd have happily vomited forth every secret I was privy to (and whatever else my fevered brain could come up with to appease their curiosity) I knew as sure as night follows day that playing the nightingale would avail me nothing. Such men as these always believe their prisoner knows more, that he's holding something back, and they're never satisfied until his fingernails are out or he's been broken on the rack and lies a bloody bundle on the floor before them. It was sport for them, like a prize fight or bull-bait; they enjoy the gory game for its own sake. And after all the torment, at the end, whether you've spilled your guts or bravely held your tongue (presuming they haven't already cut it out), there's just the knife or garotte for your *quietus.* That knowledge steeled me for the fight, and I knew I'd die before they put me in fetters.

They came on suddenly, and I stopped one falchion blow to my head on the forte of my blade, trapping the second, a chest-high stroke from blue cockade, with my cloak. The cloak spread most of the force of the cut, but I took a sound buffeting in the ribs, which quite took the breath from my lungs. Seeing his chance Lanksleeve rushed forward his cudgel ready, but I recovered quickly and sent him reeling away, his cheek opened to the teeth. Still trapping friend cockade's sword in the folds of my cloak I rammed the hilt of my sword into his face, then span him round to my front as his companion came to the attack again, faulchion aloft. I should have liked to have finished him with a classic thrust to the heart – in honour of Don Anselmo, but the angles were wrong and all I could manage was a disabling thrust, pinking his sword arm through the wrist. Time to decamp Sidney my lad, thinks I, throwing my cloak over both Gentlemen of the Scamp, and making off hobbledegee down the alley. As I ran I saw a movement in a doorway to my right, but I was stretching almost full tilt now, haring away, ignoring the pain in my ribs, impossible to catch.

The cobblestone caught me squarely on the back of my head. White spots exploded in my eyes, my vision sliding slowly upwards as I crashed heavily to my knees and fell forwards onto my hands. I remember thinking how hot the roadstones felt against my palms. From the crook of my eye I realized a figure was approaching. Slowly, gasping for breath, I turned my head. My vision steadied and I noted dully that it was Defarge. Then the full meaning of the image flashed into my brain. Defarge - Robespierre's man Defarge! Thank God! Salvation, at the eleventh hour! I was saved.

But something was amiss. At first I couldn't put my finger on it, the blow from that beggar's bullet had disordered my wits in fine style, but gradually it dawned on me - his expression was wrong. Defarge should show some satisfaction at this rescue, surely, perhaps even smile a little? I knew him of old for a Friday-faced mar-all, but this was different. Why was his face set like stone, his eyes staring hatred? And why, I asked myself dully, had he not sheathed the foot-long knife he still held in his hand. He was pointing it at me now and screaming, though I realized I could not hear his words - I wondered about that for what seemed an age – had the cobble-blow made me deaf?

Rough hands were suddenly grasping me from behind. I was pulled upright by my armpits and held fast, all in perfect silence. Someone was prying open my jaws, none too gently either. I resisted, but there were far too many of them, and they were too strong; besides I still felt strangely divorced from the whole proceeding, like a spectator watching a play, and soon it just seemed easier to accept the inevitable. A hand passed across my gaze bearing some grey and bulbous object and suddenly I was struggling madly again as what felt like a cannonball was pushed by main force between my teeth. It filled my mouth, a hideous metallic taste against my tongue. I could hardly breathe for the size of it, nor close my lips together. Then the hands receded - except for one, which made a single twisting motion and suddenly my mouth was on fire as a dozen barbs impaled themselves on my tongue and cheeks and I knew in an instant the horror of my predicament - I'd been fed a choak-pear.

This pleasant little toy is rarely seen these days, so perhaps an explanation is in order. It was never a British custom, more continental, and the Hollanders brought the beastly thing to a fine state of perfection. The choak pear was made of iron and shaped like a fruit of the same name. Forced into the mouth, the simple turning of a key caused certain interior springs to thrust forth a number of points in all directions, enlarging its dimensions so that it could not be removed; neither could the iron - case-hardened as it was - be filed away. There were only two methods of ridding yourself of this unsavoury mouthful: either cutting the cheek open (sometimes a number of teeth had to be removed as well) or by advertising a reward for the key, which was normally forthcoming, once a price could be agreed. A pretty thing, the choak pear.

Defarge's face suddenly appeared before my own, demented, mottled with fury. He was yelling at me, screaming his rage, his eyes staring, specks of spittle flying as he mouthed away in arm-flailing silence. There was no sound at all and it was quite the most eerie thing I'd ever experienced. What the hell was happening? What-

Then my hearing came back with a vengeance and in one terrible, fearful moment I understood and my bowels dissolved in terror. "-ye English bastard. She's gone, d'ye hear? My beautiful, sweet angel, gone. I lost my wife because of ye and your filthy friends, my dear wife, so gentle and compassionate" and he broke off for a quiet sob.

I calmed a little at this. For one horrifying moment I'd believed Suzanne Defarge had unburdened her soul to dear Papa. But that had been my guilty conscience at work, stirring up a fear that always lurked just beneath the surface of my mind. No, matters were not in so bad a case - Defarge was merely bemoaning the loss of his wife which, while sad, of course, was hardly a concern of mine. For one, I'd had nothing to do with the demise of Mrs Defarge, and for a second anyone who had known the cold-eyed, implacable, bloodthirsty harpy would certainly not have recognized the baleful old hag from her husband's tearful encomium. Still, grief does strange things to people. I was sure I could explain things to his satisfaction, if only he'd remove this infernal gobfiller.

But Defarge had not finished. "Losing a wife is a tragedy..." sniffs this dyed-in-the-wool sansculotte, this monster who had happily watched families torn apart, and chanted *vive la revolution* with the rest of them as the heads of a hundred wives and husbands fell beneath the glaive. "... a tragedy, but t' lose a child, an only child..... It is past bearing!" and all at once his face was against mine, froth on his lips and I was in an agony of terror, all my fears returning. "She bled t'death, ye foresworn pimping curler! Bled away her life when the bastard she bore miscarried, *your* bastard, ye lying fornicating whoremonger-"

Your bastard! The words were a knife in my belly. Oh Christ, he knew, he absolutely knew! But how?

"- told me all, every detail ye seducing son of whore! How she... that night at Citizen Robespierre's... Then she begged me t'spare your life, absolutely begged, even as she lay there in the blood-sodden sheets, paler and paler she grew, my lovely girl, weaker and weaker as her life ebbed away. And always pleading with me, begging me t' leave ye your miserable life-"

Hope welled within me at these words. Surely even a cross-grained mulligrubs like Defarge would not refuse the dying wish of his only daughter. Sweet Suzanne: to look so pretty and go so ill. But surely-

"How could I say her nay? Is my heart made of stone? She was dying, my poor angel, there was nothing the doctors could do, and still her heart was full of compassion". He struck me suddenly, a back-handed blow across the face and my mouth exploded with pain as the spines of the choak-pear tore into my cheek. "Compassion for a whoremongering rake-hell like you." And on a sudden, quite unexpectedly, when I was steeled for a second swipe, his hands fell to his sides and all the life seemed to go out of him. "Ah, it was past all bearing, but I could not deny her! And devil take me, I agreed" he intoned quietly, his eyes on the ground, his massive frame seeming to shrink before my eyes. "She prayed for your miserable life and t' calm her, t' please her, t' grant her peace in her final moments, I promised that ye would not die by my hands".

Relief swept over me like a golden wave. Saved, saved by God! Sweet, kind Suzanne! So I had been more than a glorious gallop for her after all. She had been genuinely smitten by my 'bravery', and my manly charms too, doubtless (many have y'know, I've a genius for bewitching the fair sex – it's a fact). Even *in extremis* she had borne

me no ill will, and I blessed her memory then, and swore I'd
pray every night for her soul, at the same time attempting
to gargle my commiseration to her bereaved father through
the choak-pear. No easy task, I may tell you.
But Defarge had not finished. His eyes slid upwards to
meet mine and I froze in horror at the look of malicious,
demonic joy they held. He was smiling now, his yellow,
broken fangs exposed, the smile of a wolf scenting prey.
"And believe me, Monsieur Carton, ye'll not die. Though
for the rest of your days ye'll wish that ye had".
He took me by the throat then; I can still feel those calloused
fingers, the cracked nails pressing into my skin "Hark'ee
now. I will geld ye, y'bastard. Dock ye smack-smooth. But
only this-" and his hand was down under my breeches
while I shrieked aloud through the monstrous obstacle in
my mouth. "Just your *arbor vitae,* eh? I'll leave the trinkets
intact. So ye'll ever have the desire but lack the means of
discharge, *hein?*" And around him his devil's crew cackled
away, well pleased with the jest. "Lots of powder, but no
cannon, see? That's the way of it" He paused, and released
his foul grip. "Not that you'll have the chance to ogle another
pretty maid. For I'll have your eyes on my blade like two
fresh plums long before we move lower. I mean to blind ye,
Monsieur Carton, and hock and hamstring ye, and sever
the ligaments in both your elbows. And we'll have your
thumbs too, for luck eh?" he spat in my face "You'll crawl
in the dirt like the worm ye are, and eat whatever food is
thrown in your way without the aid of hands, sniffing it out,
pressing your face into the dirt for every morsel. And ye'll
not bless your benefactor – for we'll leave that wholesome
fruit to rot in y'mouth" And with a careless swing he had
thrown the choak-pear key into the dust of the street! "Ah
yes, clever Mr Carton, seducer of the innocent, I will keep
my pledge. I'll not take your life, though by the time I've
finished. ye'll beg me to destroy you."
He bent closer his lips touching my ear, his foul breath
stinking of onion and garlic. "Think of it, ye whoremongering

son of a bitch. "Unmanned. Crawling on your belly in perpetual darkness, dumb, your four limbs useless, an object of pity and derision for year upon useless, pointless year, until Old Age takes ye in - what? Thirty, Forty years?" "Ohgskierre! Ohggskierre!" I screamed madly. It was all I could think of to stop this mad man and the horrors that awaited me. "Ohggskierre!"

Defarge stepped back and viewed me with a sardonic smile. "What? Oh I see, Robespierre!" he chuckled malevolently. "Y'think Citizen Robespierre will save ye? But he doesn't even know you're 'ere," and he waved a cufflink before me, the twin of that I still carried in my pocket with the accursed letter. "borrowed these y'see, to bait a trap for vermin. I'll return 'em later." Then his face was in mine again "Fool! Have ye not heard? The Incorruptible has no need of your sort now. Y've served your purpose, and he's ready to strike. Neither will he recognize ye later, when begging your bread, another noseless, blind beggar among many.... Y're shocked I see.. I'd not mentioned it? How remiss! Then, listen, scum! I intend to be thorough – I will have your nose, and your ears too. And your glims. Now, to begin..." and he waved the knife before my face, its point almost touching my right eye. "Take your last look on the light, ye filthy murdering bastard. And know that this very day your protector, Robespierre, will cleanse the Assembly of scum like y'self and begin the Rule of the People...."

In terror I screwed up my eyes, knowing it was useless, yet unable to accept the ghastly inevitability of empty eye sockets and hideous mutilation. The point pushed slowly at the lids and I felt the skin breaking. I pushed my head back, shaking it violently, but strong hands seized my ears, my hair, and held me still. Oh Jesu, if only I could speak; I had no chance to beg or plead (and I can plead most convincingly when need arise). I could hear nothing over the hollow formless cry of despair that issued involuntarily from my mouth. Then, through the all-embracing panic that consumed me, I realized that the knife had not pushed

home. Christ, had he no pity? He was waiting, the bastard, taunting me, waiting 'til hope returned before-
But no. I must have stopped screaming for suddenly I could hear voices, or rather one voice, talking earnestly with Defarge. Hardly daring to hope, I risked a squinny with one eye, and to my inexpressible joy, beheld the Undertaker in fervent conversation with my tormentor.

"Do him later, I sez." my black-clad friend was saying. "We're running behind time, what with his coach being late an' all. Robespierre's due to denounce the traitors today at the Assembly, and the sitting begins at eleven, not ten minutes hence. What a sight that will be, eh? All the enemies of the people, destroyed at one blow." He looked at me contemptuously, nursing his eye which showed signs of producing a fine bruiser. "Christ knows I've reason enough mesel' to want him hurt. But if we gelds him now, we'll have to be quick about it, or we'll miss the fun at the Convention. And that'd be a waste, I sez. He's sure to be interested in what Robespierre has to say about his girl and the 'discussions' at the Rue Mont Martre, eh?" General laughter ensued at this incomprehensible comment. "And so will a certain delegate, I'll be bound. He's secure enough now, so why hurry things? When we can take our time with him, crimp him[26] at our leisure? *After* he's heard the good news about his whore!"

I was too numb to understand what was being said at the time. My whole being was concentrated on Defarge's lined, implacable face, on the desperate hope that he might relent. Oh Sweet Jesus , let him relent if only for a day, an hour, a minute! My blood froze as I saw him shake his head "No. I don't like it. Having to wait an' all" and I knew it was the end, all hope gone. I hardly heard the rest as I slipped away into a blessed faint "But you're right, curse it. Maybe he will keep 'til after......"

Chapter Twelve

I have no recollection of moving from that cobbled alley.
But Defarge must have managed to control his desire for
mutilation, as the next thing I remember is coming to, held
securely between two of Defarge's strongest buckos, in the
public gallery of the Assembly, a knife at my spine, and
a scarf tied securely around my mouth to hide the choak
pear. "Toothache" was their excuse, I remember. A good
choice, for the pain from that hideous contraption, and the
evil strait in which I found myself, had me rolling my head
and groaning aloud.   And yet, all the while another part of
me was trying to think aright, to take stock and divine a
route, any route, from this sudden nightmare.
There was no doubt this was but a short respite. I knew,
as certain as the sun rises, that should I fail to devise a
means of escape soon then, come the dawn, I would be that
misshapen, mutilated half-man that Defarge intended.
The thought alone was sufficient to burst any man's heart.
But as if this was not enough, the Undertaker's mention of
Lucie had my innards in further turmoil. What were these
'discussions'? And the 'delegate' – what of him? One thing
was certain, it had to be ill news – Defarge had been too
pleased.

Below us, as I contemplated my own sad fate, the floor of the Convention was filling up. Intrigue was rife in every corner, etched on the tired faces of the members, most of whom had been up all night. Knots of worried-looking delegates were scattered about, with messengers moving between them - "a volcano with a boiling crater" someone called it later – all of them whispering intently or gesticulating wildly as they threw insults and imprecations towards their foes or tried desperately to bring a waverer into their camp. The gallery itself seethed with men and women, restive and ill-at-ease as the crisis approached. Many were armed, there were short pikes, pistols and swords everywhere. But not all the gallery crowd, I noted, were of Robespierre's faction. I saw veteran Hebertists, and a few old Cordeliers, friends of Danton, on the benches, looking sullen and dispirited. Why should they be here, I wondered, to watch Robespierre's apotheosis and the final destruction of all their hopes? Like most people, you see, I simply could not imagine anyone, or any group, besting the arch-intriguer. I'd forgotten Fouché and my 'wolf and oxen' talk, or rather I'd discounted the possibility of my former employer orchestrating any sort of effective attack on Robespierre and his ghastly crew.

In fact, Robespierre's continued grasp on power had become vital to the desperate plan I had been forming to escape the clutches of Defarge and his gelding knife. For I had resolved to await the very moment of the Incorruptible's victory, when he had swept away his foes, (a time I judged Defarge and his friends most likely to be off-guard, carried away by the triumph of their hero) and to break free from my captors and throw myself from the gallery onto the floor of the Assembly. I was quite calm about this admittedly desperate act. It might mean a broken leg, perhaps a broken neck, but any fate was better than that planned for me by Defarge and his crew. If I survived the fall (and I would leap where the crowd below was thickest - a bed of fat, overfed delegates being my best guarantee of safety) there was no doubt in my mind that Robespierre would succour me. Even if Defarge brought the whole sordid business of his daughter into the open - though I would doubtless lose much esteem in the prudish eyes of the Incorruptible - I was still, surely, too valuable to be repudiated by the master and left to the tender mercies of his servant. At worst, it would mean the Guillotine again, and in my present predicament even Samson's ministrations were preferable to those Defarge had in mind for my poor body.

A wave of anticipation rippled through the great room, and moments later Robespierre appeared, smiling and confident, backed by his wolfpack of St Just, Couthon, Lebas and the rest. A wild outburst of applause greeted his arrival and I noted that at least three-quarters of the public gallery were of his faction. He was dressed in his favourite coat of robin's-egg blue with jonquil-coloured breeches and white stockings. His hair, as ever, was powdered and immaculate. St Just followed on his heels, cool and impeccable in chamois coat, white waistcoat and dove-grey breeches, looking the very Angel of Death and carrying in his right hand the fatal papers of accusation; then my eyes were back on Robespierre, silently willing him to get on with the business – my mouth was on fire, the spines from the choak-pear were like so many hornets against my cheeks and tongue – once he had done away with his rivals I could begin. That was when I saw him falter; for the briefest moment his confident mien slipped and I discerned the tired frightened man behind the public mask. St Just seemed out of countenance too, and as I followed their gaze I realised the source of their anxiety.

Seated in the President's chair was one whom they had already marked for death – that erstwhile patron from my barbering days in Lyon – Collot d'Herbois. This was undoubtedly a check, for the President, could, in theory, bar any delegate from taking the rostrum and addressing the Assembly. But against the tide of sentiment from the gallery and pusillanimous craven instincts of the mass of delegates that made up the Convention, it was but a minor setback, and I saw Robespierre quickly recover his poise and make his way confidently towards the benches.

For the rest, the Assembly looked much as always. The wide spacious hall had been the old theatre of the King's Palace in the days before Virtue ruled. The president sat enthroned above the rest now, close to one wall, under the somewhat romanticised gaze of two canvases representing the murdered deputies Marat and Lepelletier. Below was the speaker's rostrum, facing a wide wooden writing table and stretched out in an arc around this centre were the benches of the delegates, the right much depleted by Robespierre's earlier depredations, with a yawning gap on the Mountain made by the execution of Danton, Hebert, and their followers. Only the toadying Marsh, the mute, supine Plain in the centre, were without defects in their ranks, and it was here that the Incorruptible seated himself, with many a nod and smiling acknowledgement, both to be near the rostrum when his turn came to speak but also, I suspected, as a compliment to the men of the Plain, to reassure these spineless creatures that they were safe and that, for today, he did not intend to vent his spleen in their direction. Few, I suspect, believed him.

I learned later that, in a speech the day before, he had spoken darkly of his intention to accuse "the conspirators". That was his style, spreading fear and dismay with opaque phrases and vague accusations, keeping the Assembly in a continual state of Terror, and therefore impotent. But on this occasion the delegates had demanded the names of Robespierre's 'conspirators' and, in a rare error of judgment, he had refused to name any of them. Had he called the roll on ten of their number, the remaining three hundred delegates would have sighed their relief and let him have his sacrificial victims. But with no-one named, every deputy in the Assembly now feared he might be numbered among the accused. And fear can make men bold.

In keeping with his cautious character, Robespierre had deputed St Just to make the accusatory announcement.

With confident step the Angel of Death strode to the rostrum and a great silence fell over the hall. St Just looked around him, savouring his power, his face cold and impersonal. He cleared his throat. "The course of events" he began "has indicated that this rostrum may be the Tarpeian Rock for the man who-"

He got no further, for this time Fouché's oxen were ready, and the trap was sprung. Tallien, one of those marked for death, rushed to the rostrum crying "I demand to be heard" and as St Just opened his mouth to protest Collot d'Herbois drowned out his voice with the clangour of the President's bell. St Just was pushed bodily aside, the bell quietened and before its echoes had faded Tallien was calling out to the delegates. "I demand that the curtain be torn away".

A score of voices responded in chorus "It must be! It must be!" It was then that I realised Fouché had been busy. The unified response was too perfect, too pat. This had all been planned.

Tallien gave space to another delegate, I forget whom, but I do remember this worthy giving a graphic account of a meeting the previous evening at the Jacobin Club, at which Robespierre had presided.[27] "We will perish if we show weakness" he bellowed. "These people are planning to murder the Convention". A gasp of horror attended his words as he pointed towards the gallery. "I see one of those men who dared menace the Convention sitting among us now"

A dozen voices barked in unison "Arrest him! Arrest him!"

At first I thought they meant Defarge and my heart soared, but the gendarmes moved swiftly to seize another man seated close by, a burly, bearded cove with a red pyrric cap, bundling him smartly out through the side door. I looked at Defarge and the shock was plain on his face, and on all the Jacobin supporters. They had come to see another performance of the spectacle they had enjoyed these three years past – the denunciation and destruction of their enemies. But something had gone badly awry. One of their own number was now on his way to the summary justice of the Tribunal and an assignation with Madame Guillotine. They did not care for that at all, for what might it betoken? I noticed the surreptitious removal of red caps amongst several of the crowd; some Jacobins were, even now, reassessing their allegiances.

The same tune was being played on the floor of the Assembly. With each strike against Castle Robespierre, with each stone knocked from the wall, the men of the Plain grew less complaisant. I heard, unbelievably, the cry *Vive le Convention* from the throats of more than one of their number. Could the worm be turning?

Robespierre's ally Lebas made a rush for the rostrum, only to be pressed back by force of numbers. Tallien returned to his theme "I asked a moment ago that the veil be torn aside" he thundered "It is now ripped asunder! The conspirators are soon to be unmasked and annihilated. Liberty will triumph!"

Cheering erupted from left and right, throwing Robespierre's partisans into further dismay and confusion. And where they might have hoped for leadership, they saw only apathy. St Just appeared stunned by this sudden twist of Fortune and stood mute and marmorean among his foes, arms hanging limply, his feared accusation slipping page by page from his lifeless fingers, not even attempting to protest. The great Robespierre sat quaking in his seat, his face congested and twitching uncontrollably. He was, as I have said, no man of action, and now, when a physical assault might well have carried the day and brought him to the rostrum to scatter his foes, he simply froze before the challenge.

Tallien was speaking again. "I too was at last night's meeting of the Jacobin Club. I saw the army of a new Cromwell being formed!" And suddenly there was a poignard in his hand - Therezia's no doubt[28] - and he was thundering on, waving the weapon above his head with unconscious melodrama, "I have armed myself with a dagger which shall pierce this man's breast if the Convention does not have the courage to decree his arrest".

A bas le tyran! Someone called and the cry was taken up sporadically around the Assemby. On my left the Hebertists in the gallery were chanting in unison "Liberty! Liberty!" But note, no one had yet summoned up the courage to *name* the Tyrant. The malign aura of Robespierre still stopped the mouths of even the bravest.

The unnamed object of all this invective now rose, his face livid with anger (and, it seemed to me, not a little fear) and strove like a madman to reach the rostrum, calling out God knew what, for his voice was drowned by the constant ringing of the President's bell whenever he tried to speak. Fouché's squadrons, bunched around the speaker's place, held him in check, and he finally fell back, his carefully coiffured hair awry, his hand against his chest, breathing hard.

"I demand the arrest...." Uproar, Tallien strove to make himself heard above the din, many on the right of the Assembly were howling like wolves. Behind me, I felt my captors stiffen. I too, was holding my breath. Could it be that the Tyrant would be named at last ? "I demand... demand the arrest of Hanriot and Dumas!"

At my back one of Defarge's crew groaned aloud. Small wonder, it was a masterful stroke, worthy of the arch intriguer himself . He had ever isolated his main foe before striking the fatal blow. The Assembly erupted with cries of assent, the warrants were made out, and with those arrests Robespierre must have heard the sound of the axe being sharpened. Toper Hanriot was the Jacobin 'general', you see, and for all that he was drunk as David's Sow morn, noon and even, Hanriot controlled the puissant forces of the Commune, Jacobins to a man. Dumas, of course, was President of the Revolutionary Tribunal and ready, at Robespierre's bidding, to send the world and his wife for a revolutionary haircut.

At one stroke the Incorruptible had been shorn of his

army and control of the Courts. One by one, the props underpinning Robespierre's carefully constructed rule of terror were being razed. The good ship *Jacobin* had lost its topsails and was heading rudderless for the rocks. It was impossible, but all could see now that the Great Denounciateur was vulnerable. He rose again to speak, desperation plain in every line of his face, but a tumult of angry voices obliterated his words.

Collot d'Herbois handed over the Chair to Thuriot, Danton's old friend. Robespierre made a third attempt on the rostrum, gesticulating wildly, speaking as he went. He was rebuffed once more, and with Thuriot wildly ringing the Presidential Bell, not a word he spoke was heard in the gallery. As he gave back, great beads of sweat running down his mottled face, his eyes starting from his head, a minor deputy, Louchet by name, reached the rostrum and dared to say what, just ten minutes before would have been both unthinkable and suicidal. I heard his voice, shrill with fear, above the hubbub; somehow we all did: "I demand the arrest of Robespierre".

The hair rose up all over my scalp. Finally, the word had been spoken! A single word *Robespierre*, yet it tore to shreds the web of impotence and fear in which the Incorruptible had so skilfully ensnared the Assembly. There was an instant of silence, then pandemonium. Now that the word of condemnation had been voiced, Robespierre's carefully woven tapestry of fear swiftly began to unravel. The mountain rang with applause, hats were waved and the cry of 'Down with the Tyrant" resounded again and again against the walls of the Assembly.

Then, at that moment of crisis, when Robespierre fate appeared sealed, I saw something new to me, something I have seen but rarely in my long eventful life: an act of true, selfless devotion. Augustin Robespierre, the Incorruptible's fresh-faced younger brother, rose to his feet, as solemn as death, and cried above the hubbub "I am as guilty as my brother. I share his virtues. Decree my arrest with his".

Utterly brave, you see, and utterly, totally unnecessary. I remember thinking, even then: you bloody fool. I think it still.

Augustin's self-sacrificing demand quietened them a little, and Robespierre took this opportunity rush the rostrum, demanding a hearing. "For the last time" he screamed at Thuriot, his voice shaking with a mixture of fear and barely suppressed rage "will you give me leave to speak, you President of Assassins".

Now, as a town lawyer in Arras, the young Robespierre would have endlessly advised his clients to avoid gratuitous insults during any legal dispute (I have done so myself in London, scores of times). He should have heeded his own advice at this court of Life and Death. *President of Assassins* was a mistake, and one which Tallien, a one-time lawyer's clerk, seized upon gladly. "The monster has insulted the Convention" he declared indignantly. Another delegate, Duval, stepped forward "Is this man to be the master of the Convention? Let us put the arrest of the two brothers to the vote."

Encircled by foes, Robespierre turned from the rostrum and rushed towards his accustomed place on the Mountain. "Begone!" someone called "The ghosts of Danton and Camille Desmoulins reject you!" He tried to speak, but no words came. "The blood of Danton chokes you!" called another. Spurned, Robespierre ran from right to left repeating "Death! Death!". "Yes" came the reply "you have deserved it a thousand times."

I saw him turn and make towards the men of the Plain, the Marsh as he had called them in prouder days, most of whom still sat silent, watching events unfold. "Men of Virtue! Men of Purity!" he gasped, holding out his hands imploringly "I appeal to you. Give me the leave to speak which these assassins refuse me!"

But the Toads of the Marsh were playing their accustomed game. They had already totted up the hands raised on the Right and Left against this battered creature - and seen that he was doomed. As ever, they were immune to pity. "Out! Out!" they croaked, and Robespierre span again, a look of panic on his stricken face, and scrabbled his way over the empty seats of the right to collapse gasping on an vacant bench.

Even here there was no respite. One of the remnant of the right, who had escaped the earlier purges spat at him. "Monster!" he called out. "You are sitting where Condercet and Vergniaud once sat!" Robespierre staggered on, coming to rest on a bench and gazing imploringly towards the gallery, as if the People, that abstract concept he had so stirringly invoked in happier times, would somehow fly to his rescue.

Unfortunately, almost all the red caps had mysteriously disappeared by now, and many of the whilom Jacobins were now chanting 'Liberty' alongside the Hebertists. Robespierre's idealised 'People' were more concerned with saving their own precious pelts, and the few loyal Jacobins in the gallery had suddenly become as much an object of hatred as the isolated wretch panting alone on his bench below.

So compelling was the drama acted out on the floor of the Convention that I had, for a space, quite forgotten my own predicament. Now it returned with a vengeance and I readied myself for a desperate break from my captors. For me, nothing had really changed. A disaster, I reasoned, should make Defarge and his crew quite as unwary as the triumph they had looked for. I was shaking with fear and anticipation. It only lacked the right moment and I would act.

By now the arrest of Robespierre, his brother, Couthon and St Just had all been decreed. An usher took the document up to Robespierre, but he made no acknowledgement; to me he seemed quite overwhelmed by events, his mind numb with shock. Others were less charitable.

"He refuses to obey the Convention's decree!" Tallien announced indignantly "carry him down to the bar".

And so it was done. Robespierre was pushed and carried to stand before the bar with St Just and the rest. The Decree of arrest was read to them. It was only then that Robespierre seemed to come to himself. "Hypocrites! Assassins! Scoundrels!" he suddenly called out, and again, as he was led away "The Brigands have triumphed!".

This admission of defeat wrought the final change in my captors. The fickle mob in the gallery began chanting for Robespierre's death, and they were swift to turn their new-found hatred against any Robespierre loyalists, by which I mean those too deeply implicated in his affairs to turn their own coats. Defarge and his bully boys were suddenly on the defensive, thunderstruck by this rapid change of fortune, and I felt their restraining hands slacken as, beset about with enemies, they sought desperately for a way to safety. There was no thought now for the pleasures of a torture bout with Sidney – for Defarge's cronies it was each for himself and the fiend take the hindmost.

In his panic, the Undertaker drew out a dagger and brandished it towards the threatening mob, relinquishing for a moment his hold on my arm. I seized my chance, and for the second time that day my black clad opponent received an elbow in his eye. Then I had grabbed the pistol from his belt and smashed its hilt into the face of my other captor, leaping across the seats towards the gallery rail from whence I fully intended to cast myself into the mass below. In my frantic, panic-stricken haste I did not realise how close safety lay, and had I not caught my foot on a carelessly laid pike staff I dare say I would even yet be walking with crutches. As it was, I stumbled on the damned thing and crashed all of a heap in a tangle of benches, winded, and unable to move.

I've said that the Robespierrists were concerned only with their own safety. And so they were, with one exception. Defarge. The hatred that he had conceived for me was so overwhelming it blotted out all other mentation. Bellowing like a bull he came rushing forwards, knife out, unstoppable, throwing aside seats as if they were kindling, consumed by his dreadful need to maim and kill my unworthy self. Winded as I was, I tried to rise, to escape this awful, garlic-breathing nemesis, but my limbs would not serve and as I fell back I remember thinking 'well, at least it will be quick'. Then a series of long, thin shadows slid across the floor in front of me and I saw Defarge check his headlong rush, staring beyond me, while anger and frustration played in equal measure upon his gargoyle features. Looking skywards, I saw four long wooden shafts just a foot above my head, pointing towards my nemesis, and each topped with a needle sharp pike head. The Dantonists! Defarge was a known supporter of the Incorruptible, and relying on that old maxim "my enemy's enemy is my friend", the supporter's of our late-lamented Stentor had leapt to my aid in the nick of time, and were even now forming a solid protective phalanx around me.

But Defarge was not to be denied his revenge. Beside himself with rage, his arm went back and an instant later he had cast the dagger straight towards me. Shrieking, I drew up my knees for protection and howled with pain as the weapon struck home. But by good fortune the knife struck the heel of my boot, embedding itself more than inch into the wood and pricking the skin most damnably. I grabbed the hilt and prised the weapon clear, readying myself lest his red-eyed fury sent him headlong at the pikes. But even immersed in his frenzy of hatred Defarge could see it would be a futile sacrifice. Tearing tufts from his beard he screamed the most vile curses and imprecations in my direction, while, I was pleased to note, slowly backing towards the exit as the Dantonists gave him curse for curse, and moved their schiltron of pikes inexorably forward, leaving me gasping on the floor.

"Here now dearie, what did that bearded bastard want with you?" I looked up into the rheumy eyes of an old *tricoteuse*, smiling toothlessly. "What had y'done to make him so angry?

I began to explain my innocence of all wrongdoing, only to realise that naught but strange mumblings sounds were issuing from my mouth, which ached abominably. The choak-pear! Desperately, I indicated the source of my discomfort with both hands.

"What's that now, dearie? Pointing to y'mouth are ye?" the old fool asked, all gummy sympathy. "Have you no tongue then, my lamb? Did – oh, Holy Mary Mother of God!" she took a step back, shock drawing from her a forbidden pre-revolutionary oath. "A pear! Friends, comrades, gather round! The poor citoyen - we must do all in our power to help him".

Most of the rest ignored the old hag, following the Jacobins in their eagerness to settle accounts with the Robespierrists. But one or two foregathered, most of them, I thought, more concerned to see the results of a choak pear than to bring succour to its poor unfortunate victim. My mouth was prised open a score of times; I was prodded and poked; they turned my head this way and that ignoring my screams of protest and my desperate attempts to explain that, short of surgery, the best thing they could do was help me find the key – or leave me be. But no, the French are as long-tongued as Granny, they must discuss everything: one talked of carrying me to the surgeon, another of calling a locksmith, everyone had their own idea and everyone agreed something must be done. Then, quite suddenly, it was.

Without warning, a burly bearded cove had me by the sconce and had jammed my head between his knees, while a herring-gutted knave was drawing out a clasp knife with what appeared to be a very blunt blade. "Better do it now friend" says he "Cut it out. I'm as good as any barber and it'll not cost ye a sou" He moved forward, his eyes gleaming wildly "Brace y'self now."

It wouldn't do. The devil would be blind before these idiots fathomed the meaning of my grunts and mumblings - I must charge this shot alone. I relaxed suddenly, slumping down in feigned acquiescence; then, giving my Samaritans no warning, I swiftly drove a stiffened right thumb into my bearded captor's adam's apple, hearing the ghastly wheeze as his grip weakened. At the same time I kicked wildly at the knife in the 'surgeon's' hand. A moment more and I was on my feet, barging through them, sending old granny arse over wizened dugs among the benches, rushing harum scarum for the exit, hearing their cries of remonstrance but noting too that they were not attempting to follow. Glad to be rid of me, probably.

I heard something else too, an announcement I am loth to report for fear that you, my gentle reader, will misdoubt my sanity. I still find the tale incredible myself, but I know what I heard. As God's my witness, having just arrested the most powerful man in France, a man whose followers numbered thousands and whose partisans still controlled much of the army and militia, those misbegotten fools of the Assembly announced that, as they had over-run their allotted working period by thirty minutes, they would now suspend the Convention for two hours - and take Dinner! No further proof of the French obsession with food need be given. Absolutely typical Froggies, you see, their bellies always come first. No doubt they'd have been incensed to come to table and find the wine hadn't been allowed to breathe.

My mind registered astonishment at the time, and I remember thinking 'you'll rue that meal my lads', but it was a passing thought, for I had other more pressing concerns just then. I was cursing the hideous object that filled my mouth, but there was still hope, a slim chance I could free myself of its swollen presence. I'd be damned if I was going to allow some sawbones to slit my cheek just yet. I had to find the choak-pear key!

I pressed forward through the thronging multitude, weaving my way along the seething corridors and running out into the Paris sunshine, my mouth on fire. No one was the least interested in my progress; they were too stunned, all of them, by the news of Robespierre's arrest, more and more of the population converging on the Assembly in search of confirmation and further news. That was all to the good; the more people, the harder it would be for Defarge and his merry men to spy my escape, or if they did, to follow my route through the crowds. I remained terrified by the thought of that odious sanscullotte, you see, that he was still intent on seeking me out for murder and mutilation. I could not know that he, his crew, and the rest of the surviving Jacobins, had already taken flight, scuttling off with their tails between their legs, rushing pell-mell for the Hotel de Ville and the safety of the Commune, there to plot revenge.

I was almost at the place I'd been ambushed – God's blood, could that have been just this morning? The fight, my capture, it all felt like a lifetime ago. I turned the corner into the alley and realised with a sinking heart that the thronging multitudes I had blessed for their anonymity were now more hindrance than help. There were scores of people in the alley, kicking up the dust and horse-manure, and obliterating all signs of my earlier struggle – I found it hard to even locate the place our carriage had stopped. There was nothing to see, nothing to- No, wait, what was that? A formless dark brown stain in the dust – blood? Yes, yes, it was blood. Here then, here was where we had fought. The blessed key was somewhere close. Desperately I tried to place myself with my back to an imaginary coach. I got some strange looks from passers-by as I danced a broken choreography of the morning's combat: here the wild slash, there where I finessed the Undertaker, then Lanksleeves, the cloak over the Chosen Pells and then the run down the alley – how many steps? Oh God, let me remember! Ten? Eleven? Here! It must be here. Struck down. Then hauled up again. Defarge. And he threw the key- where? Over his shoulder, yes! And I was running, crashing down on my knees where the key landed, where it must, where it *had* to have landed, scrabbling in the dirt, pressing my fingers into the cracks between the cobbles, all the while looking desperately over my shoulder for signs of Defarge, searching, searching and finding – nothing!

I howled my frustration to the leaden skies and slammed my fists against the uncaring cobbles, close to tears, cursing Defarge, Robespierre, damning Darnay, the Revolution and the day I was birthed. How long I ranted and blasphemed against my fate I'm not sure but I remember I was huddled head down into the ground, weeping with rage, when I suddenly became aware of two small bare feet just inches from my face. I followed the feet up stick-thin calves, ragged breeches and filthy, torn shirt and found myself looking into the eyes of a curly-mopped, snot-nosed kinchen of perhaps 8 years.

"Los' somefing Mistah?" he asked, head to one side and a strange knowing glint in his eye.

I pointed despairingly at the Pear of Agony, pantomiming the unlocking of the infernal machine, making what I hoped were pitiful pleading noises. The bantling frowned his puzzlement, so I repeated my charade with heightened dactylogy and even more grossly extravagant symbolism before gesturing to the surrounding area, shrugging expressively and making my eyebrows leap heavenwards in exaggerated puzzlement. Surely he would understand? He must!

"Ye'll be wanting this then" says this blasted canary bird. And there, lying in the palm of his small scruffy paw, was my salvation – the key!

"Mmmm Mmm!" I scrabbled forwards on my knees, hands outstretched but his fist closed like a gin and he leapt backwards. "Money. Ye wants it, ye pays."

"Mmmm" I stuck my hands in my pockets, finding only a ten sou piece. Those sanscullotte bastards had robbed as well as kidnapped me! I offered the coin and it was snatched from my hands.

"Not enough Mistah. Gimme more! More or I'll cut!

I held up my hands, shaking my head, mutely pleading for him to wait, then inspiration dawned, and with as close an approximation to a smile as I could manage with a ball of iron stuck in my mouth I dived for my pocket again. The passports and gold I'd sewed into my coat lining hadn't been touched by Defarge or his men, thanks be to God, but I'd be damned to perdition if I'd give our passage money to England to some bastardly gullion of a daggletail whore. There was, however, one other item I'd discovered in my desperate search for pelf; it lay snugly in my right pocket and might well persuade this greedy guttersnipe to see reason. I fished about, holding one hand up, palm-foremost, as if the say 'hold' but in truth to prevent him seeing too clearly what I was about. I made great show of searching as I readied myself, then in a trice I had pulled out the barker I'd taken at the Assembly from the Undertaker and pushed it in his arrogant little face, cocking the flint as I went. He went white as a winding sheet, all his bravado leaking from him like water from a collander

"Here, here" he says, all smiles now, tears streaming down his grubby cheeks "Ah wuz on'y jokin', honest. Jokin' see? Takes it, please Mistah, please" and his scrawny paw was over mine and I almost fainted with relief as his fingers opened and the blessed, the wonderful, sacred key was dropped into my outstretched hand.

Chapter Thirteen

Moments later I was running from the Pont Royal, my mouth clear, the ghastly mechanism cast into the Seine. I tore along the Quai de Tuilleries, keeping to the river, passing the Pont Neuf at full pelt, the Palais de Justice looming to my right, then swinging left into a side alley, making with all haste for the Rue Mont Martre and the house where Lucie lodged. As soon as that iron pear had left my mouth all those horrifying, gut-wrenching fears for Lucie's safety had come flooding back. I was desperate to know she was safe, desperate also to know what Defarge's comrade had meant about Lucie and 'the good news' . What 'discussions' had he meant, and which Delegate was involved? It had sounded serious, had to be, if Robespierre had planned to use the matter today in his speech – that devious bastard spoke only to the point.

Yet strangely, despite all my anxieties I felt curiously elated. It's something I've seen often enough in folk who, through bravery, foresight, or sheer blind chance, have escaped the cramp word and come to safe harbour, if only for a while. There may be horrors ahead, but the very fact of dodging a trip to Peg Tantrum's can do wonders for the spirits – you've bilked Death of his winnings, you walk and think and plan on God's good earth - what could be better? There was another reason to rejoice. The fall of Robespierre (which I was by no means certain was permanent) had set the world on its edge. Paris would be in turmoil, the revolutionary government's authority in tatters, and the ensuing mayhem offered me the perfect opportunity to seize Lucie and flee. *Periculum in mova**[13], by God! I fairly sped along the alleys and by-ways. There could be no better time. I debouched from a passageway onto the Rue Mont Martre about fifty yards from Lucie's apartment, huffing and puffing and just in time to see two men descending from a coach hard by my love's house. It was obvious at once they were up to no good. The first to alight was a cove of medium height, wrapped in a all-enveloping cloak that masked his features and rank, while the second was obviously a body-guard of some kind, thick-set and massive, looking suspiciously up and down the street as the cloaked figure made his furtive way, with many a backward glance - to Lucie's door!

My heart was against my teeth as I watched him produce a key – a *passe-partout* doubtless – from the folds of his cloak. A moment more and the door was open and he had disappeared inside, his Myrmidon defending the entrance with his sword unsheathed and held inconspicuously against his thigh. Lucie was in danger, no question, deadly danger, and only I could save her.

As I've told you, "Dishonour Before Death' is the precept I've kept ever before my eyes during a long and mostly terrified life – if the Carton Family had a crest it would undoubtedly display the tail of a snake disappearing into a thorn bush, with the stirring motto *Fugo* writ in gold beneath. Normally I'm the first to seek safety in flight, no shameful act is impossible in pursuit of that most worthy aim of saving my own precious life. But Lucie *was* my life – bereft of her wondrous sweet presence, my existence would return to the bleak, pointless monotony I had endured in

---

13   * *Danger in delay*

the Colonies. And that decided me.

I moved almost without thinking, crossing the road and moving haltingly along the sidewalk with the air of a man, ignorant of the area he finds himself in, who seeks an address. It was a living torture, moving so slowly, stopping to check a door number, shaking my head in sham puzzlement, all the time knowing that, even as I acted my part, that grim cloaked figure might be shedding the blood of the only soul I cared for in this world. After what seemed an age I was facing Lucie's door, my heart hammering in my chest, my right hand in my pocket, clutching Defarge's poignard, and with the huge bulk of the bodyguard barring my passage.

But my pretence had worked. Goliath took a pace towards me "What house d'ye seek, Citoyen?" he asked. One more step and I could act. I feigned confusion, searching in my pocket . "It's here somewhere" I said frowning, "on this paper here, look..."

He was cautious, this one. "Your pardon citoyen", his sword was up now, "Come no closer, *je vous en prie*", and there was nothing slipshod in his movements as he stepped forwards to take the note. But step forward he did-

There are many ways to kill a man with a knife: in the neck, through the eye, cutting the artery of the inner thigh, striking to the heart. But apart from heart and eye, all of them are very messy – you'd be astounded how much blood there is in a body, and I speak as one who knows, having seen more than my fair share of battle, not to mention the shambles of the Guillotine. And most deaths are lengthy too. These days, the audience smile at Shakespearean heroes who, stabbed by a foe, clasp their chest with a cry of "I die!" - and then proceed to hold forth in blank verse for another ten minutes or so. But that, in truth, is the nature of most knife and sword wounds: they are overly sanguinous and they don't back the opponent swiftly or silently enough; I couldn't have Goliath screaming like a stuck pig and alerting our cloaked friend or the worthy burghers of the Rue Mont Martre. No, for swiftness it has to be the eye or heart.

Here you face two difficulties. The eye is a small object and trying to achieve a solid straight thrust through it to the brain, when the opponent is bobbing about all over the place, is next to impossible – try throwing a potato in the air and skewering it with a carver next time you're in the scullery, and you'll see what I mean. Which leaves the heart. Unfortunately, you can't simply stab a man in the heart and hope to strike home. There's ribs, you see, and while the gods might smile on your endeavours and let the iron slip all the way in, you're more likely to find your dagger bouncing off a bone or getting jammed between two ribs before its done more than nicked the opponent. Happens all the time, especially if you hold the blade vertical, as most tyros do, thank God. I speak from experience. I have a chest scar, a souvenir of Ama, an Ashanti priestess who loved me, after a fashion, and took exception to my roving eye. She left me for dead with a dagger protruding from my heart - but the knife was just an inch in my beef, lodged between two ribs and did me no lasting hurt. But that's another tale, and one song I'll sing presently, God willing. The solution to this impasse was taught me by the pagan priest who sewed up Ama's parting gift. Savage he may have been, but he knew his anatomy better than any of those butchers at Lincoln's Inn Fields[29].

Goliath had made his, I hoped fatal, step forward, sword horizontal in his right hand, six inches from my chest, his other paw extended to receive the note. In one fluid movement I parried his weapon with my left hand, slipped inside his guard and delivered an upward, diagonal stroke which started at my left hip and entered his body just below his sternum, missing the shield of his ribs as it travelled through his diaphragm and spitted his heart from base to peak. I continued to push him backwards, holding the knife in place with my left hand beneath my right elbow, twisting the blade to increase the damage. We ended up against the door stenchion and for a moment there was a look of absolute surprise in his eyes, which were light blue, I remember. Then they clouded over in the familiar green mist of death; I felt his body go slack, took his pistol from his belt and lowered him quietly to the step; no easy task, for he must have weighed close on half a ton. It had taken perhaps 15 seconds: swift, silent and not a trace of blood anywhere. I left him sitting there by the door – any passer-by might think him asleep – and entered the dark passage before me.

Out of the sun the corridor was as black as Satan's crotch and I had to feel my way gingerly past several doors, checking each room for signs of occupancy. Nothing. I inched forward again, the guard's barker held in front of me, and as my eyes adjusted to the shadows I suddenly realised I was approaching the end of the passageway. There was a wide panelled door and beyond... a muffled noise! My ear was on the wood panelling in an instant. Tumult behind the door - gasping, groaning, Lucie's voice crying out! My worst fears were realised – she was being attacked! Murdered!

I burst through the door like the avenging harpies and the first thing I saw was a naked male backside pumping manfully away between two graceful female legs. I recognised the back of the man's head too – a barber always does you know, and I would have known those bat-ears anywhere – the odious Collot d'Herbois, as I lived and breathed, working out his lust on some poor doxy. By God, he had been fast. A prime mover in the disposal of Robespierre, then into the carriage and off for a celebratory gallop with his whore: one could not help but admire his style.

I covered my face and was about to retire with some suitable apology when I noticed the lady's shoe buckles, silver with the tiniest Cupid's bow in the centre, just like Lucie's. And in an instant the floor had fallen away and the room was spinning around me. God have mercy, they *were* Lucie's shoes! These were Lucie's apartments. And none of the other rooms were occupied – hadn't I checked them all myself? It was then I believe my heart died. It had been cruelly broken in the Americas, and all but frozen during my life in London, but now it simply stopped, stone dead. Lucie, my Only Love, and the murderous Collot-d' Herbois, *in flagrante!* Buckled to. Rattling like stoats. Oh God, it couldn't be true! please, for the Love of Christ, let it not be true!.

But there was no answer to my prayer. Collot had noticed the interruption by this time and was trying extricate himself, swearing like a Billingsgate porter at my intervention and promising a painful death to the interloper. As he tried to raise his body off Lucie's supine form, and before he could get even a glimpse of me, I struck him full across the side of the head with the pistol barrel. He went down like poleaxed bullock, rolling onto the carpet without even a groan. And there she was. My angel, my fallen angel, her lovely blonde hair in disarray. Lucie - a naked, spread, sweating Lucie! On her back, like the meanest Covent Garden Nun! It was a nightmare, it had to be, one of those horrific dreams where everything suddenly slows and you cannot turn away and must behold every horror in appalling detail. She looked ashamed, fearful, her beautiful blue eyes brimful with tears. Moving at a snail's pace, I watch her draw the bedclothes around her body, hold out her hand towards me: "Sidney, please, it's not -"

But all I can see now is Lucie at Laon, so chastely refusing my advances, telling me I must wait, it wouldn't be seemly, that she could not bring me to temptation! Besmirch my honour, make me Sin against God and the commandments! Oh Fidelity personified - and now this! Dancing moll pratley's jig with Collot d'Herbois! The lascivious lying bitch!

The recoil from the barker brought me to my senses, and suddenly everything was moving swiftly once more. I had not realised I'd pulled the trigger, or that the muzzle was pointed straight towards her. I saw the force of the ball drive her backwards, twisting her body as she smashed against the bedhead. Then, mercifully, the acrid smoke from the shot obscured the sight of Lucie dying, and I had cast the pistol down and turned towards the door, gasping for breath. Away! Away! I had to flee this place. Christ, it was worse, much worse, than before! My beautiful golden-haired doll - the infamous two-faced whore! Sweet Jesus, Lucie was dead! Dead! And I had killed her!

Chapter Fourteen

Whether it works me weal or woe, I've chosen to write nothing but the unadorned truth in these pages. Very noble, you're doubtless thinking, but in truth it's less laudable an attitude than it appears - after all, at 98 I can't have that many seasons left me, and the place I've chosen to seal up my history will keep it from prying eyes for a good few years after I'm in the ground and wearing the green gown. Who knows? It may have mouldered away to dust long before it ever sees the light of day. So the story will either come out long after I've gone to join the majority, or it will never come out. Either way, it will be no concern of mine.

And yet I am loath to dwell too deeply on the events of those doleful hours. Even today, seventy years on, palsied of limb, bald, weak of eye and weaker still of bladder, and with all passion spent these long years past, even now, the memories gnaw at the very roots of my soul, and despite the intervening years, contemplating the tragedy of that moment, the utter ruin of all my youthful hopes, still risks my spiralling down into black despair. Ah, dear God, how different it might have been! I have hidden my feelings for such a long, long time, especially from myself, I am reluctant to marshal my own dark thoughts, as I should, before I set pen to paper.

Suffice to say, I was in the deepest circle of hell, humiliated, betrayed, and now bereft – by mine own hand! – of the one kind spirit that made life tolerable. It was unbearable.

I stumbled along the corridor and out into the street, intent on one thing only, my own annihilation. Strange.... to feel so certain that life was unendurable and then, by chance or fate, to live, laugh and cry for another seventy-odd years, and never seriously contemplate suicide again. Fickle things, emotions, and not to be trusted. But back then, at that nadir of all my hopes, everything seemed crystal clear: every second I breathed brought only unremitting insufferable anguish. I wanted to die. I would run to the Seine, cast myself in and snuff out my bright flame of life in its dark cold waters. I was tearing for the river before the thought had formed into words. How long I ran I can't remember, only that I became dimly aware of something bouncing in my coat pocket, striking my hip and disturbing my stride. I stopped, breathless, and drew the offending object out. It was a barker. For a moment I believed I was going mad – I had cast the weapon from me after I had- Oh God, Lucie! – Lucie and d'Herbois! It was true, true, just as Defarge's man had said! But the pistol, I'd thrown it aside, how could I hold it in my hand? I found myself wondering if the barker was real or, like MacBeth's dagger, a mirage of my overheated brain. And with that conceit came the blissful thought that perhaps this truly was a dream, that I should wake in Lyon and all would be tolerably well. I seized on this idea like a drowning man grasping at a straw, then groaned aloud as I suddenly realised my error: this wasn't the weapon I'd taken from d'Herbois' bodyguard – it was the pistol I'd had from the Undertaker, in the gallery of the Covention. It was no vision, but as solid as the ground I stood upon, as real as Lucie's death . That was when I thought: why wait until the river? Do it now. Use the pistol! I'd murdered her with a barker, it was only fitting I should die by powder and ball. And there was but a gnat's breath between the thought and the deed. The barrel was in my mouth, I absolutely longed for death, and God's damnation on them all: Darnay, Defarge, Fouché, Robespierre-

And then it came to me, with irresistible certainty – Robespierre was to blame!

Robespierre! If he had let Lucie and I go free, had let us return to England, none of this would ever have happened. Instead he had made me his cat's paw, using Lucie as a hostage to my continued obedience. Slowly, I drew the barrel of the pistol from my mouth as another realisation struck home. He had known! What was it Defarge's man had said? *"He's sure to be interested in what Robespierre has to say about his girl and the 'discussions' at the Rue Mont Martre, eh? And so will a certain delegate, I'll be bound"*. So he had known, absolutely known, and had allowed the sordid affair to continue when it was in his power to prevent it; this self-proclaimed champion of Virtue had let Vice flourish, to serve his own megalomaniac ambitions.

Slowly, I uncocked the barker and pushed it once again into my pocket. I still sought annihilation, but before that happy release, I would have vengeance on the source and origin of all my woes. *Vile Robespierre!* Danton had called him from the tumbrils. *Anguis in herba*[14] indeed, but I would not allow the earth to suffer the presence of this serpent for another day. As dearly as Defarge had desired my own mutilation and death, I now sought to see Robespierre suffer. I would seek the execrable dwarf out in his cave and kill him; but slowly - a belly wound that would have him lingering in agony for days. And after, *ruat caelum!*[15] I cared little for what they might do to me once the deed was done: the knife, the gun, the guillotine- Yes, of course, the Guillotine! To my disordered wits the Guillotine appeared a fitting, even a poetic end to my sad life. Had I persevered in my subterfuge nine months before, and taken Darnay's place beneath the glaive, Lucie would still be alive today. And I would not have murdered her.

---

14   *Snake in the grass
15   *Let the Heavens Fall!

I hurried back towards the Tuilleries, where Robespierre must lie imprisoned, the pistol warm and snug in my pocket. No amount of bars and locks would keep the dissembling hypocrite from my vengeance. I was hardly aware of it at the time, but there were areas of the city where news of the arrests had not yet run: the lights still shone at the Opéra-Comique – it was showing *Paul et Virginie,* I remember - and I learned later that *Armide* had been sung at the Opera. But it was dark at the Théatre Des Sansculottes, with a note posted on the doors saying "No Performance". In my distracted state, it seemed like an omen.

I've noticed over the years that most of humanity shares a common failing: when we are buffeted by tragedy or disaster in our personal life, and while our minds are full of our own selfish misery, we tend to believe that the rest of existence is somehow frozen in time, set in aspic, as it were. And it comes as a great surprise to discover that, despite our woes, the old world has been turning still. And so it was with me, that hot summer evening, for I arrived at the Tuilleries to discover that much had happened in a short space.

Robespierre was free.

It had taken just one shrewd and doughty fighter to turn the tables. When the Incorruptible's arrest had been noised abroad, that staunch Jacobin, the Mayor Fleuriot, had not lost heart, but had immediately ordered the gates of the city closed and the Tocsin rung. He knew that his own fate hung with Robespierre's, and he had summoned a meeting of the Council General of the Commune, who speedily declared the three hundred delegates of the Assembly 'rebels', and themselves the true Provisional Government of France. Immediately, Fleuriot had sent written orders to all Paris gaols, forbidding them to accept any new prisoners. Then, at the same time that those fools at the National Assembly were sitting down to their victory dinner, the Mayor dispatched a courier to the Jacobin Club, requesting that a posse of brawny arms, "including women" be assembled outside his residence at the Hotel-de-Ville. They complied immediately, their numbers swelling the formidable mob that, summoned by the tocsin, were gathering at the Place de Grève. A good hand at a dead lift, that Fleuriot. Thanks solely to his efforts the rebels now had a government and an army. All they lacked was Robespierre, and their military commander, General Hanriot.

This brave Paladin had been in his cups since morning and, pot-valiant, had compounded the Commune's troubles by contriving to have himself captured after riding off alone in a drunken attempt to rescue Robespierre. He was pulled from his horse at the Place du Palais-Royal by gendarmes loyal to the Convention, trussed up like a chicken, carried to the Tuilleries, and locked away in the offices of the Committee. Another client for Jourdan Coup-Tête.

But if Hanriot was immured within the Tuilleries, Robespierre was, unbelievably, still free. Fleuriot's letter forbidding the acceptance of new prisoners meant that he had been refused entry at the Luxembourg prison, where the Convention had sent him. Nonplussed, his captors had actually asked their prisoner where he wished to be taken! The cowardly hop-o'er-my-thumb plumped for the *Mairie* on the Quai des Orfèvres – a choice which says much about his scheming character. The calculating manikin knew, you see, that plans were afoot to raise insurrection, and this white-hearted go-by-the-ground wished to be well out of it. The *Mairie* was about half way between the Convention and the Hotel-de-Ville, exactly where Robespierre wanted to position himself, politically: should Fleuriot and the mob succeed he could join them quickly enough, and seize his share of glory; but if the delegates of the Assembly triumphed he could claim that he had remained obedient to their wishes and so avoid the condign punishment that was sure to be meted out to the rebels. This was the measure of the man – always hanging fire, watching and waiting, letting braver souls risk their lives while he schemed what benefit he could garner from their courage.

Fleuriot was having none of it. Robespierre's presence would invincibly boost the morale of the rebels – especially as word had now reached the Hotel-de-Ville of Hanriot's capture - and the Mayor sent an urgent appeal to the Incorruptible, asking that he join his friends and put himself at the head of the insurrection. Robespierre demurred. An hour later a second message arrived. "You no longer belong to yourself" Fleuriot wrote "You belong now to your country". Robespierre again prevaricated, continuing to cling stubbornly to the relative safety of the *Mairie*.

Outside the Hotel-de-Ville, the crowd of willing patriots were growing impatient, waiting for leadership. God knows what the Mayor thought of his erstwhile hero, but the die was cast – rebellion was proclaimed and he could not turn back. In despair, Fleuriot underpinned his third message with armed troops, who shepherded our reluctant hero to rebel headquarters at the point of the bayonet. Robespierre arrived there at eleven o'clock, just as I tooled up, more than half out of my mind with grief and bent solely on his murder. I saw the diminutive figure walking hesitantly up the stairs to the entrance and bounded forwards, my hand on the barker. But the press of people was too great and, try as I might, he had disappeared into the building long before I was within pistol-shot.

Had I only walked a little faster, had he delayed a moment longer at the *Mairie*, and history might well have been different. As it was, cheated of my quarry, I moved close to the entrance, under an arch, and set my back against its cold stones, lost as much in hate as in the shadows, and determined to wait on his reappearance. St Just, Lebas, Couthon and Robespierre's brother, Augustin, arrived a little later, but I was not tempted to make an onslaught against any of them. There was one ball in my barker - and it was Robespierre's.

I did not know it then, but even as Robespierre had equivocated and I had stalked the streets towards the Hotel de Ville, the Assembly itself was in mortal peril. Coffinhall, vice-president of the Revolutionary Tribunal and a Jacobin to the bone, had led two hundred stout gunners to the Tuilleries and set Hanriot at liberty. Imagine the scene: the delegates, stomachs bloated as they return from their insane dinner, are faced with two hundred well-armed 'rebels' on their doorstep. The Committees of Public Safety and of General Security barely escape capture and flee white-faced into the Convention, compounding the terror. The delegates are without bodyguards, alone, milling about the Convention Hall in panic-stricken terror, unable to resist even the lightest assault. And Coffinhall is urging Hanriot to attack, to wipe out all these traitors to liberty.

I'm told the delegates believed themselves lost. Certainly, Collot d'Herbois, who must have recovered from the blow I'd given him and returned post-haste to the Assembly, announced to his peers that "The moment to die has come". Quite so, the sooner the better, and I wish I'd been there to see that fornicating bastard given the old *mitraillade*. I'd have happily pulled a trigger or two myself.

But it seems imprisonment had disordered Hanriot's wits. Instead of bursting into the hall with his two hundred bully boys and putting volley after volley into his enemy, the drunken sot inexplicably ordered an about face and took his heroes back to the Hotel de Ville. This unlooked for reprieve gave the Assembly new heart and the time it needed to muster their own small army. In less than two hours they had raised a troop of some two hundred men. As very few of the delegates had seen active service, (and fewer still of those cowards, I dare say, wished to see it), Paul Barras, who had served briefly in the army, was appointed commander and reluctantly took his merry men off to the east to confront the rebels.

All this unknown to my good self. I sat there beneath the arch, a rigid mass of congealed hatred, oblivious to everything, brooding on my vengeance and hardly noticing that the mob before the Hotel-de-Ville was slowly melting away. I discovered later that word had reached them that most of the Paris Sections were going over to the Assembly. A good commander would have addressed his troops and steadied them in the face of this worrying setback, but the time slipped by, and no one came from the building to inform this loyal mass of supporters what they must do. Leaderless, they muttered and grumbled among themselves. Then the thunderstorm that had been threatening all that long day finally broke; the heavens opened, the rain crashed down, and in the downpour the remainder of Robespierre's supporters dispersed, slipping away silently in ones and twos. Even Hanriot's gunners gave up on their drunken commander and disappeared into the warren of alleys surrounding the Place de Grève.

The rain seemed to break my trance. I looked around, suddenly aware that the square was empty and silent as the tomb. This was my chance. I could slip into the building unseen and work my vengeance on that vile duplicitous scheming dwarf! But just as I moved from the archway, I saw the light of flambeaux, and the Convention's 'army' of hastily gathered supporters, as rag-tag a battalion of fly-slicers as I've ever struck, marched into view swearing vengeance on Robespierre and all Jacobins. I recall that moment so clearly: an incredible gallimaufry of artisans, labourers and down-at-heel street-sweepings, standing shoulder to shoulder in the flickering light of the torches with clerks and well-to-do lawyers; all of them clutching some implement of war, pike, musket, pistol or sabre; the whole boastful yet strangely fearful, their collective backboned stiffened only, (or so it seemed to me) by a peppering of national guard in their faded blue and white uniforms, their hobnails ringing on the wet cobbles. And far in the rear, the hero of the hour - the fat and hesitant figure of Barras, red-faced and sweating with fear - leading from behind as usual.

I remember feeling unreasonably angry watching them approach. Those bastards would try to seize Robespierre and carry him off to execution - and I'd be damned to hell if they'd cheat me of my prey. As the mass of men flowed past I stepped smartly from the shadows and attached myself to their vanguard – they hardly noticed me, so flown were they with their own fear and bravado. We mustered by the gate of the Hotel de Ville. The order was given: strictly no shooting unless the rebels fired first – the blood-drinkers must all be taken alive, and made an example of at the Place de Trône.

As silently as possible, we mounted the steps, I recall the wet footprints left by the men in front of me as we massed in front of the door of Egalité Hall, hearing a low murmur of voices behind the flimsy wooden barrier. We could not know it, but Barras's little army had arrived at the very moment Fleuriot and the rest had finally persuaded Robespierre to sign an appeal asking the Army and the Sections to come to their aid. I was told later he had spent precious time asking "In whose name do I sign it?" and disputing the answers of his colleagues, as if such legal niceties mattered in a revolution. At such times an oaken club is a better argument than an Act of parliament. But Robespierre seemed incapable of understanding this simple fact, or of coping with the enormity of the crisis he faced, Ever the legalist, he fell back on splitting judicial hairs.

The little army of the Convention had no such qualms. We were bunched at the doorway, a mass of tense faces, pikes, muskets, daggers and pistols at the ready. A whispered command from the sergeant-at-arms: "Remember, no shooting", then the door was breached and we crashed through into the hall. The scene before us is etched in my mind, all movement stilled like a tableau: Couthon in his bath chair, his face a mask of fear, his hand frozen in the act of stroking his pet spaniel; Augustin frowning by the window, sabre at the ready, and beside him Coffinhall, his head in his hands; St Just and Lebas were standing by the fireplace, craning their necks to see the source of the commotion, eyes widening in sudden consternation;

and toper Hanriot, lying sprawled across the table in a puddle of *vin ordinaire*, slowly looking up, his drink-sodden face filled only with a tolerant, bemused interest at the interruption. All this at a moment's glance, for I had eyes only for Robespierre, who was sitting at a table on the point of signing some document. At the sight of that diminutive figure, the inspiration of all my afflictions, a flood of rage and hatred, the like of which I had never imagined, consumed me utterly. I wanted him dead. I raised my pistol, took aim, and fired. The ball took the little dandyprat in the head, the impact snapping his face to one side and sending the quill flying from his hand. Vengeance!

Then all hell broke loose. As the Convention's men poured into Egalite Hall, Augustin Robespierre, so calm and heroic at the Convention, flung down his sabre, pushed open a window and fled with unseemly haste along the cornice. I heard St Just plead with Lebas to shoot him. "Fool!" Lebas thundered "I have more important things to do!" and, raising the pistol to his own head, he fired, scattering his brains across the far wall. St Just surrendered quietly to his foes. But Coffinhall, the hero of Hanriot's rescue, turned on the man he had succoured, and cursing Hanriot for a drunken sot who'd brought them all to ruin, seized him by the shoulders and cast him bodily from the window into the courtyard below. I rushed to the sill, pushing passed angry, swearing soldiers, already busy binding their prisoners, and was just in time to spy Augustin as he lost his footing on the cornice and plunged three stories to the pavement. He survived, but I could see by his pathetic attempts to crawl away that every limb was shattered. Hanriot had fared better: his descent was broken by a dungheap, but the fall knocked his right eye from its socket so that it lay grotesquely on his cheek. Not that the bold general cared. He lay spread-eagled over the horse-shit, stinking, snoring, blind drunk and oblivious to any calamity.

I turned back into the room as the last of the rebels was discovered. In the uproar, Couthon the cripple had fled his wheelchair and crawled to a hiding place beneath the table. He was dragged, pleading his injuries, from his funk-hole by three gendarmes and thrown bodily down the staircase, when his piteous cries ceased abruptly. His spaniel had disappeared; they told me later the poor dumb creature had been put to the sword as soon as the attack commenced. It too, went out by the window, to join Hanriot on the dungheap.

Robespierre was not dead, more's the pity. He still sat his chair, his body slumped across the table so that the injured head lay on the paper he had been about to sign. Blood was staining its pristine surface. I would have taken my knife to him then, and slit his scrawny gizzard on the instant, but it was impossible to get near - by this time there were guards all around his broken figure.

My ball had struck the left side of his face and shattered the jaw; there were tooth fragments mixed with the blood on the table. He was moaning with pain. Good. An infinity of pain would not cancel out the agony and suffering he had caused – I meant to me, of course. Filled, utterly consumed by my own misery I wanted only to see the author of my woes atone in blood for his crimes. But then, looking at him, it crossed my mind that I had, perhaps, already achieved my aim. Yes, it could be better this way, I told myself as I sank in a heap in the corner, suddenly very tired, my hands and knees shaking with reaction. Let the bastard suffer for a space. Then let him face the axe in the very place he had sent so many others to their doom.

I leaned and hid my face in my hands, despair gnawing at my thoughts, despite the pleasant prospect of seeing my enemy on the scaffold. Robespierre would die, but was I to go on living? Enduring, day upon pointless day, the doleful outcome of his evil designs? Had my aim been true I would be arrested by now, my own fate decided and nothing to do but compose myself for a welcome death. As it was, I was ignored and another of the Assembly's men was already boasting he had taken the shot that laid the Dictator low.[30]

Around me, men were busy disputing the source of his injury, some saying he was shot, others claiming he had turned the gun on himself in a craven attempt to escape justice. The fact he had a jaw-wound should have stifled that idea at birth – even the bedlam-born know a brainshot is needed, and whatever else he was, the Incorruptible was no fool. I've known men blind or cripple themselves with misaimed pistol shots designed to escape this life, but not one, never a one, with a jaw wound. Robespierre a suicide? How could anyone credit that tale? The man hadn't the courage to do anything so cowardly.

By four o'clock that morning I'd discovered he wasn't the only craven spirit in the place. I had managed to beg ball and powder from one of the guards, and retired to a quiet room (there were many at hand – *mirabile dictu,* there were suddenly no Jacobins to be found anywhere in Paris) with the firm intention of sending myself heavenwards. I was finished with the Incorruptible now, finished with the lot of them. Robespierre was doomed, past question; all the leading lights of the Jacobins were now dead or in chains and I knew that before the day was out the head of every man-jack of them would be adorning the pikes of the populace, in whose name they had delighted in shedding so much blood.

I had no desire to see their end, only for peace, an end to my agony of mind and a swift cessation of existence. No more pain, no more sadness, no more despair. I laid the barrel gently against my temple, cautioning myself against hurried movements (that's how mistakes happen – you angle the gun in your haste and the shot goes awry), closed my eyes, and began a gentle squeeze on the trigger....

At that moment a bird, a thrush it was, decided to greet the dawn with a full-throated song, and with notes of such surpassing beauty I found my hand benumbed, as if by a spell. I would listen, I told myself, until the song ended before cutting the thread. But the blessed bird would not stop. Its liquid, piping tones fled skywards, on and on and on, trilling and warbling in an ecstasy until it broke upon my mind that this was no simple song, but a joyous celebration of Life. And no sooner had the thought arisen than the dawn light broke through the window into my room in a glorious golden cascade. I could see its bright splendour behind my closed lids, feel the delightful warmth on my skin like a caress. And just as a dying man is said to see his whole life pass before his eyes, so I was suddenly aware, in a torrent of broken images, of the best, the most meaningful parts of my life rushing one after the other through my mind: my father kissing me goodnight as a child; playing ring-a-roses in the hay meadow with my sister and cousins; travelling with the *voyageurs* on the lakes of Canada, the sun going down like molten fire behind the mountains; my marriage; Jane and the baby, new-born, my darling Nathan, smiling up at me from the rocking chair, eyes alight with joy and love; Lucie-

That last, bittersweet memory brought me to myself once more. I opened my eyes and everything, the room, my hands, my clothes, the world beyond the window and the thrush - that blithe speckle-breasted bird, still giving voice to the world - everything seemed touched with the Divine, preternaturally sharp, indescribably beautiful. And I was changed.

'It's a good world yet'

The thought came from nowhere, unasked and, in my present state, unwanted. Yet I brought the pistol slowly from my head and laid it gently on a table. It wasn't that I was healed, or suddenly ecstatic, or filled with the spirit of forgiveness – nothing of the sort. My heart remained a wasteland; I was desolate, a shell, dead to all joy. But now, instead of a pitch-dark void I could at least contemplate a future, because I saw there, faintly, indistinct as a mirage, the *possibility* of happiness. After all, I told myself, this was not the first time Fate had spat in my face; the dreadful events in the Americas had left me quite as wretched as my present situation. Perhaps more so, if truth be told, for time's a great healer. And yet I had found Lucie and, for a while at least, been blessed beyond my dreams. It could happen again, surely?

It will happen again came the reply. *But everything your love touches is destroyed.* I squeezed my eyes shut against the dismal thought, fighting down the hopeless melancholy that bid fair to swallow me whole and turn my hand once more to the pistol. Perhaps it was true. Then again.... In the grounds the thrush still sang, and other birds had now taken up his canticle of joy. Mayhap I could too. Eventually. I stood up slowly, blinking away the tears, and walked from the room.

By five o'clock the torn rags of humanity who, just the day before had made all France tremble, were carried, none too gently, to the Assembly. I saw Barras, who had quaked in the centre of his men, named hero, and heard his dramatic announcement to the assembled delegates: "The coward Robespierre is outside, do you wish him to enter?" And that august assemblage, who the previous evening had put their bellies before the safety of the state, and not two days before had applauded Robespierre's speech to the echo, and voted that it be published *pro bono publico*, refused to admit him to its presence. It was Talien, I think, the primping, vainglorious prig, who answered for the delegates. He stood there in the doorway, the picture of arrogance, dressed in a dark mixture, a scarlet waistcoat, lead-coloured kerseymore breeches and brilliant white stockings "To bring a man covered in crime into our hall would be to diminish the glory of this great day" says this pompous humbug, "The body of a tyrant can only bring contagion with it. The proper place for Robespierre and his accomplices in the Place de la Revolution!"

They carried his broken body off on a plank to the audience chamber of the Committee of Public Safety, and cast him unceremoniously upon a table where, just days before, he had disdainfully heard the pleas of a multitude of supplicants.

Someone thrust a white wooden box of munitions beneath his injured head for a pillow. That green room, which had ever witnessed him neat, haughty and merciless, saw him now abased, his once-perfect hair clotted and dishevelled, his robin's-blue coat and jonquil-coloured breeches torn and stained with mud; he had lost his cravat and his bloodstained shirt lay open on his thin chest; I saw that his shoes had gone too, and his fine stockings were filthy and dropping about his ankles. He seemed no more than semi-conscious, moaning softly, his eyes closed.

Within a short space a crowd had gathered to view the fallen dictator. They shuffled by the table, jeering and gloating, and I noted most of them belonged to the lower classes, the poor, the workers, to The People, that idealised gaggle of humanity Robespierre had always believed he represented and served. Ironic, ain't it? I remember one thin-gambed cove - who, by his uncombed hair, ragged linen and mean attire I knew for a sansculotte - offering an ironic bow to the piteous wretch on the table. "Sire" he sneered sarcastically "Your Majesty seems to be suffering". Another crashed his fist against Robespierre's improvised couch. "Tyrant!" he screamed "the Republic wasn't big enough for you, but you've wound up with only the two foot width of this little table."

And similar jests; the taunts were almost continuous and the onlookers found it good sport. That's the lower orders for you – forever pleading poverty and begging Charity of their betters, fawning and toadying when they find themselves beneath the axe, but as ready as a shark shoal to fillet their fallen leaders. It disgusted me, I can tell you. Robespierre was for the Revolutionary Haircut, past question, and no man deserved the honour more. I had helped compass his destruction, and there were few with so great a desire to see an end to his miserable existence, he who had been the agent of so much misery. But this baiting, by those who, had he triumphed in the Assembly, would even now be fawning upon him as *Flambeau, Colonne, et Pierre Angulaire de* *l'edifice de la Republique**[16], well, it fair sickened me. So much so that when, in the midst of the endless taunting, he silently gathered up a few sheets of paper on the table and used them to try to staunch the wound in his cheek, I took pity on the poor wretch and brought a bowl of water to bathe his wound.[31]

He seemed hardly to notice at first. Then he murmured "Thank you monsieur" (lapsing back, you'll note, into a pre-Republican courtesy), his lids flickered open for a moment, looked towards me, and to my horror I saw his pupils contract as recognition flared, and in a shocked whisper he gasped "Chameleon! Chameleon!". I stared back, terror-stricken. Surely everyone had heard him (his voice sounded like the crack o'doom to me, you may be sure). I was exposed, revealed as an acquaintance of the Incorruptible - accusation enough to send me with him to the glaive. Then suddenly, mercifully, I was being pushed away by new arrivals eager to see the humbled dictator, forced willingly along the table edge with Robespierre's eyes - those hideous fawn-coloured eyes – following me in that expressionless, ravaged face until he disappeared behind a sea of jostling, jeering figures. I looked about me, shaken to the roots of my soul. No one was taking the slightest notice of my presence, and I thanked God for it – his words of recognition must have been lost in the general hubbub, or misinterpreted. Whatever the reason, I had escaped the after-clap I believed his outburst must bring down upon my head. I stood for a space contemplating the injured man and his awful fate, and the High Ideals towards which he had climbed, step by step, through a tide of blood, to Infamy. *Nemo repente fuit turpissimus**[17]. Then again, if you sup with wolves.... And I turned and made my way, a little unsteadily, towards the door.

"Hello Francois". There was hand on my shoulder and for a moment I could not place the voice. Then I was turning and the smile froze upon my lips. There he was before me,

16   *Light, Column and Keystone of the Republic*
17   *No man becomes a villain all at once*

as large as life and beaming benevolently. Robespierre's nemesis, and my erstwhile employer, Joseph Fouché. "I thought it was you at Robespierre's table" he said blandly, while I gawked like a constipated chicken. "I was standing just to your right but we were separated in the crush... but my dear fellow, are you well?"

Indeed I was extremely indisposed, sick with unspeakable fear - but I had to mask my feelings, and for my very life. I cleared my face, hoisted a friendly smile upon my features and grasped him warmly by the hand, one hand over the other, pumping it up and down, but not yet able to speak. For my head rang with a single ominous question: *had he heard?* Dear Christ in Heaven, had Fouché heard Robespierre name me Chameleon?

Chapter Fifteen

It was a while before I could regain mastery of my tongue, but Fouché seemed not to notice. Indeed, he was so flown with the success of his *coup* against Robespierre "and those vile Jacobins" that he spoke without ceasing as we made our way down the stairs and out into the clear morning air of a beautiful day, informing me of his clandestine machinations, of his endless nocturnal discussions with those delegates who had finally rebelled against the rule of the Incorruptible, and generally taking me completely into his confidence.

Which was all very reassuring. Of the recent incident with Robespierre he made not a mention, except to compliment me on my humanity in bringing the injured man water. I took this praise with a diffident shrug and a few choice, self-effacing phrases while my twisted innards gradually unwound. God be praised, the man was all smiles, he could never have heard what Robespierre had whispered! "No false modesty Francois" Fouché returned "for if I, Joseph Fouché, was the author of the Dictator's downfall – and I tell you candidly and immodestly, I was - then you have been my muse". Seeing my puzzled face he continued "had I not met you that happy day outside Robespierre's apartment – you sought clemency for a friend, if I'm not mistaken; you were successful? No? No, I thought as much. But if our paths had not crossed that morning I would never have heard your advice - stop gawking man! You remember surely? The wolf and the oxen, *hein*? Yes, I see you recall the moment, as I will until the very hour I step down into the grave. Ah Francois, without you I would that day have attempted flight, perhaps even suicide. But your words armoured my soul, put mettle in my heart, they rekindled hope, and stiffened my resolution to succeed. And now the wolf lies bleeding and awaiting his *coup de grâce!* That talk, brief as it was, proved crucial in our struggle against the Dictator, and has led to this most felicitous outcome." He smiled then, and placed a thin brotherly arm around my shoulder. "Come man, cheer up! We will have a pleasant lunch together, you and I. And afterwards you will ride in my carriage to the Place de la Revolution where we will see a sight that I'll wager will gladden both our hearts, and set our minds at ease."

His mind perhaps, my own was still too conscious of the danger in which I stood. What cruel fate had joined me with the only man in France who might have reason to wish me ill. (Defarge excepted of course; Collot d'Herbois too. And the Undertaker, I suppose, and Lanksleeves.... Oh Christ, the bloody place was teeming with enemies. The sooner I was back in England the better!).

But I could not say him nay, and while the unfortunate Robespierre and his crew were being arraigned before the Revolutionary Tribunal, Fouché and I were taking luncheon together. And a fine celebratory meal it was, I recall: soup, roast fowl (pheasant if memory serves), fried carp, salads of two kinds, bread, a bottle of good burgundy, with coffee and liqueur to end. Excellent cauliflower in sauce too, I seem to remember.

Before we'd even finished the pheasant, Robespierre's own goose was well and truly cooked; we'd been at table for just an hour or so, which was as long as it took for the Revolutionary Tribunal to process and condemn all twenty-two accused. The Convention had declared them *hors de loi*, Outlaws, and a simple confirmation of their identity was all that was required to ensure that they climbed the fatal ladder to bed. No trial, no cross examination, no witnesses were needed. Fouquier-Tinville oversaw the destruction of his allies, as he had so many others; they say his face was convulsed and his complexion livid, as well it might be: Tinville was Robespierre's creature and without the Incorruptible's protection, he too was ineradicably marked for the glaive. The final irony was that it had been St Just and Robespierre that had framed the legislation. The wheel had come full circle, y'see. Those who had devised the 'laws' for the swift processing of suspects were themselves now subject to its arbitrary mercies. "The time taken to punish the enemies of the fatherland should only be the time taken to recognise them", as St Just had so succinctly put it. Quite so. All twenty-two were found guilty and condemned to death.

Fouché and I saw nothing of this, of course, and spent most of the afternoon in pleasant conversation, lingering over our repast. Word had arrived that the condemned were not to be executed immediately. The Convention had decreed that such a momentous event required that the Guillotine be restored to its traditional site in the Place de la Revolution.[32] I remember hearing the carpenter's hammers booming faintly through the restaurant window, reassembling that fell contraption, as we settled down with our Mohametan gruel*[18].

It wasn't until around five in the afternoon that three tumbrils carried the condemned along the *via dolorosa* of the Rue St Honoré. And while we had missed the arraignment and condemnation of the prisoners, Fouché's new-found authority, and the height of his coach, gave us an excellent vantage point for the execution. Through the curtained windows I watched the doleful procession pass by not ten feet distant, appalled, despite myself, at the change

---

18   *Coffee*

that had been visited upon these men who, not two days past, had caused all France to tremble. I can see it still, clear as day:

Robespierre's brother, Augustin, lay half-dead on the floor of the first cart, his clothes in tatters and his broken limbs asprawl; beside him, a crumpled mass of humanity, was Hanriot, caked with manure, and a hideous sight with one eye swaying to and fro on his cheek. Robespierre himself lay propped against a plank in the second cart, his fractured jaw supported by a most undignified bandage that went under his chin and was tied at the top of his head. The mob were having splendid fun following along, poking and prodding his inert figure with umbrellas and broom shanks, screeching imprecations. At one point, as the procession slowed for a moment, an old woman, hysterical with grief, half-climbed onto Robespierre's tumbril "Monster!" she screamed "I am drunk with joy to see you suffer. You are going to Hell with the curses of all wives and mothers following you!" Robespierre did not even stir.

Of them all, only St Just retained possession of his dignity. He had surrendered without demur and so had been spared the affronts heaped upon his colleagues. His chamois coat, white waistcoat and dove-grey breeches were unstained and without a crease, and he himself sat straight and elegant, viewing the chanting plebs with cool disdain. An odd fish that - a lad of just twenty-seven summers, you would have thought he would have been the first to lose his nerve at the approaching doom. But I saw him look towards Madame with about as much interest as he might have regarded a fly.

It was a beautiful day, the sun shining on the broad boulevards, Paris at its most beautiful, the sky cloudless after the night's storm. A carnival atmosphere prevailed among the crowd, groups of citizens leaned from every window, cheering and laughing, people were singing, some dancing rondés. They were intoxicated, you see, drunk with the freedom they believed Robespierre's fall would bring.

While Danton had ridden to death in silence, Robespierre was fated to depart this earth to the sound of a vast mob screaming curses, or singing in jubilation at the downfall of the tyrant.

Robespierre was the twenty-first victim that day. I can't recall the names of the first four, but I do know Couthon died fifth – and it was a terrible business. The cripple was carried, pale as death on to the scaffold, but his twisted body could not be made to assume the required position on the plank. Samson and his minions spent nearly ten minutes trying to prise him into shape, with Couthon groaning piteously throughout their rough handling. Eventually, they gave up, and he was guillotined lying on his side. Samson could have saved himself a deal of trouble, for the device seemed to work just as efficiently with a sideways cut, and Couthon's head came away very neatly, I remember. I think Hanriot was next, though I doubt the pitiful winebarrel knew much of what was happening; when they dragged him to the plank he appeared somnolent – probably still drunk – but a grotesque sight nevertheless with a gaping wound on his forehead and his loose eye swinging like a cherry on a stalk about his cheek. They strapped him down, slid him in, and it was *bon nuit, Hanriot.* Samson was a fast worker, I'll give him that - mind you, he'd had much practice over the past few months - the bodies seemed to come up the fatal stairs at least once every minute, laid down, pushed in, and whist! the head in the basket and the still-bleeding trunk pushed off into the waiting, red-painted cart.

Just one other victim stands out in my memory – the tall and handsome St Just, who insisted on walking to the scaffold unaided. "Those who would make a revolution in this world" he had said in happier times, "must sleep only in the tomb." Well, he had made his revolution, and it led him to the tomb far earlier than he imagined. There were no last words or telling phrase from this curious, passionless young man, by far the youngest of the revolutionaries who had held France in thrall these three years past; the Angel of Death never lost his sang-froid for a moment, and looked about him, calm and self-assured, while the crowd raged and they tied him to the slide, cold as marble to the end.

When Robespierre's turn finally came the little man was dragged up the stairs between Samson's burly assistants, the ridiculous bandage round his jaw removing all vestiges of dignity. He was tied to the wooden runner already sodden with the blood of his friends, and a hush like death fell over the square. It seemed as if the World itself was holding its breath. Then, just before he was pushed forward under the axe, and for no good reason that I could see, Samson leaned across and roughly ripped away the bandage supporting his shattered jaw. Robespierre let out a scream of pain, "like that of a dying tiger" they'll tell you in the history books. But in truth – for I was not a furlong from the scaffold and heard it plain - it was more the high-pitched squeal of a rabbit with a stoat at its neck, a haunting wavering screech of pain and fear and despair that rang across the silent square, then ended abruptly as the fatal axe descended, and the Incorruptible's shattered head fell into the basket. Samson held it up for public gaze, as he had done with those of Dumas and Hanriot - the Dictator, his Judge and his General. It was as if to say: "Look! They are no more. It is finished". The effect was spoiled with Robespierre, at least for those close enough to see: the Incorruptible's eyes flickered to and fro, and his lips continued to mouth soundlessly in that severed visage, as if silently formulating some new denunciation.

But few saw this gristly coda to the execution, and an exultant yell of triumph broke simultaneously from a hundred thousand throats. A vast sea of humanity swaying in waves of joy at the death of the Tyrant. The hats were in the air again, hundreds of them, people were throwing themselves on each other's necks, weeping with joy, kissing cheeks with wild abandon, hugging perfect strangers in a frenzy of relief. The Thermidorean Reaction they call it now, when the Terror's sanguinary deluge finally ran its course, and swept its creator to his doom .

I found that both Fouché and I were from our seats, leaning half out of the coach, our white-knuckled hands rigid on the woodwork. I relaxed my grip and sat back against the fine leather, grimly satisfied. It was done. It was over. All that remained was for me to pass some pleasant hours with Fouché and after a decent interval, make my excuses, promising perhaps to meet with him again on the morrow. After which, I'd slip quietly away from this froggy Bedlam, and make my escape to boring, sensible old England. Then we would see. Perhaps, despite all that had happened, I could still make a life that was worth living. I had friends in London, they could speak for me, perhaps procure me a position at-

Fouché's voice cut across my thoughts. I knew he had spoken but I'd devil an idea what he'd said. He was sitting opposite me, fully composed once more, his face as bland and demure as a whore's at a wedding. "Your pardon" I spluttered, afraid those quiet eyes had read my most secret thoughts, "my mind was elsewhere."

"Perhaps you wish yourself elsewhere, Francois."

I was suddenly on my guard. That comment had a distinctly ominous note, despite the placid smile wreathing Fouché's face. I began to answer, but he held up a restraining hand. "No matter, my friend, no matter". He paused, and from outside there came a grinding thump and another great roar from the crowd. Fleuriot the Mayor, the last and probably most competent of the condemned Jacobins, had taken his last look through the revolutionary window. I hardly noticed, but Fouché seemed absorbed in contemplation of the scene about the Guillotine, and sat staring out the carriage window for an indifferent long time (or so it seemed to me) while I attempted to paint a neutral expression on my face, my innards squirming like a nest of snakes, hands clasped tightly together to mask their shaking. After what seemed an age of meditation, he turned his gaze back to me, smiling benignly "That's the

last of them. Those that matter, anyway. The runt of the Commune have already been rounded and up, some sixty souls in all; they'll be despatched tomorrow". I nodded, smiling at him appreciatively, not yet trusting my voice but comforted by his smiling countenance, and beginning once again to relax. All was bob now - the danger seemed to have passed. "Yes" Fouché continued, studying his hands. "They present no true danger, these others, but prudence is in order, yes? Barère was right" and he leant forward and gave me a sudden fist on the knee: "*Frappons! Il n'ya que les morts qui ne revient pas.*"*[19].

"Yes. Yes, quite so" I returned as Fouché sat back beaming. My mind seemed to have gone blank, For the life of me I couldn't think of what else to say "Better safe than sorry... Any old port-"

"So then" says he, abruptly ending one topic and obviously beginning another. "It is over. What will you do now, Francois?" and suddenly the face before me was as still as a snake's, the eyes flat and calculating. "Or should I call you.... *Chameleon?*"

The world seemed to shrink in that moment, to narrow to the compass of Fouché's pale blue eyes. It was the end, I was sure. Fouché would call for his guards and have me dragged up the scaffold to make the twenty-third victim. The crowd would not mind one jot if a spy of Robespierre was led out to the slaughter. It would prolong the entertainment.

"I- please, it is not how it seems... I was-, Lucie and I... we wanted only.... how can I explain?" I began, stumbling over my words, unsure where to start, or how to couch my story to produce the desired effect – freedom from pain and death. "It was Robespierre, you see..." Yes! Yes, that was it, I must blame the Incorruptible! "Robespierre! That dastard. He plotted and schemed abominably and I, I-"

"Peace, Peace" says Fouché. "I have already had the opportunity of scanning the Dictator's private

---

19   *Let us strike: the dead alone never return

correspondence. I know that a spy, with the *nom de guerre* 'Chameleon', was working for the Incorruptible in Lyon. Someone who reported neither to the Committtee of Public Safety, nor to the Committee of General Security, but directly to Robespierre alone. His very private eyes and ears, *hein?*" I stared back, my bowels churning as Fouché paused, holding my eyes with his, before continuing "I had suspected as much, for many weeks. Friend Robespierre always knew too much, too soon...nothing in Lyon escaped his notice; but I was not sure - until this morning". A long, horrible pause ensued. I said nothing; because there was nothing to say. But I was thinking like blazes, puzzling how best to phrase my confession. For a confession there must needs be: Fouché knew too much. The question was – how much? Please God the trail stopped with Francois Laborde. But my companion was speaking again. "Robespierre recognised you today, did he not? When you ministered to him? I heard him speak. He called you Chameleon. But you are no lizard – a snake in the grass strikes nearer the mark!" His voice was cold as ice, implacable. "You were the viper in my bosom, those long months past, keeping your secret, smiling me fair and feeding my enemy details while we drank and talked and joked together." He sighed deeply, pulling at his chin, like Jove in Judgement; then he cast his thunderbolt. "But it appears you harbour even deeper mysteries, for you are neither Chameleon nor Francois. Are you - Monsieur Carton!"

My last shred of hope had been torn in tatters; Oh sweet Jesus, he knew everything. Everything! I was trapped, exposed and most assuredly damned. They'd try me as an English spy! There was no way on God's earth I could escape the pit that now yawned before me. Unless. Unless I could stir some feeling of compassion in Fouché's calm, indifferent mind. Desperately, I tried to explain myself but Fouché silenced me with a peremptory flick of his hand, and I leaned forward, my head in my hands. Another longeur ensued, a silence I gainfully employed in composing various pleas for clemency for the Tribunal I knew I must now face. I was half way through a touching disquisition on my aged grey-haired mother, sick of the palsy and like to die without the constant presence of her beloved son to ease her bed of pain, when Fouché's words broke in upon my thoughts, and I found his voice had taken on an unexpected, and much lighter tone.

"I have studied Chameleon's reports carefully" he had been saying "and I note that while he makes much of Collot-d'Herbois' crimes and wrongdoings, the reports show no mention of my own actions, some of which, I own, were at least as bestial as my brother *représentant-en-mission*. I risked a squint from the tail of my eye and discovered he had quite regained his former good humour. "That was kind of you Francois, or may I now call you Sidney ?" he asked, smiling towards me. Please, forgive my little masquerade. I confess I do so enjoy making others squirm for a while. It's a failing of mine. Unforgivable, but amusing nonetheless. Come, 'chin up' you English say, yes? That's right man, smile, be of good cheer. No harm will befall you. Here, take my flask, restore yourself with some good French brandy. There. That's better, no?"

And it was, the fiery liquid went some little way to calming my shattered nerves. I took another long pull as Fouché sat back, steepling his fingers. "I think, perhaps," says he thoughtfully "that in Lyon you have been in much the same position as I. Forced to do something which you found abhorrent, no? But which your own survival required you to do? Yes, I thought as much.... It is written in your face. Very well, that being so, we will draw a veil over Lyon, for both our sakes." He paused, and a well rehearsed look of counterfeit puzzlement crept slowly across his smooth features. "Well then, that is settled. But the question remains - what can we do with you now...?" Put me on a boat to England was my first thought, but I was wise enough to bite my tongue. Fouché held all the cards; I was completely in his power and he knew it. I would accept any suggestion he made. It was enough for now that I was allowed to live. He paused theatrically, then snapped his fingers as if just realising the answer to the problem. "Why of course, that's it! Why don't you continue to do... what you have been doing for Robespierre - for me? A Chameleon could be a very useful animal to have in my menagerie."

And I listened, helpless, speechless, sick with fear, as Fouché unconsciously parroted Robespierre's earlier query, the horribly familiar words echoing in my brain

"What then, Monsieur, is your answer? Are you willing to aid the Republic? It will not be for long".

Chapter Sixteen

If I had been deceived in believing Robespierre's removal would bring a swift end to my woes then I was, at least, in good company. No sooner had the Incorruptible's head been shorn from his narrow shoulders than a sudden, spontaneous outbreak of popular rejoicing swept all France. Everywhere, in village, town and hamlet, in all the great cities, people flocked together singing, dancing, clasping and kissing each other in transports of joy. For, to their simple minds, the long-sought deliverance had at last come to pass. The Terror was at an end. How could it be otherwise? For them, Robespierre was the Dictator of the loathesome Committee of Public Safety – it was he who had controlled the revolutionary tribunal, he who had approved the warrants that marked priest and potter, duke and dairymaid alike for death. And Robespierre was dead. *Ergo,* the Terror was no more. Those who had engineered the monster's fall, Fouché, Tallien, Barras and the rest, were unanimously acclaimed heroes of the Nation, brave stalwart souls who, disgusted and repelled by the continuous bloodletting, had bravely risked their own lives to conspire against the *Denounciateur's* vile clique and bring the Terror to a close.

Which was news to Tallien and Fouché, I may tell you. For

the conspirators, the disposal of Robespierre had been just another political adjustment; he had sought their deaths and they had outmanoeuvred him. It was the revolutionary way, had happened before, a score of times, and it would no doubt happen again. I was at the Tuilleries the day after Robespierre's execution when Barère said openly that what had come to pass was of little import "a mere difference of opinion within the Committee" was the phrase he used, I remember, "which will have no noticeable sequel." Nothing had changed, you see; so soon do some men look on horror with familiarity. For the victors of Thermidor, it was to be business as usual at the Revolutionary Tribunal and the blood-washed steps of the Place du Trône.

Then they noticed the people, and to their utter surprise and consternation, found themselves cheered as liberators, saw crowds mass in the streets wherever they went, back-slapping, hand-pumping crowds who hailed them as heroes, and called down God's blessing for their selfless act of liberation. Police reports from across the country spoke of similar astonishing demonstrations, of an unstoppable, irrepressible exaltation that the killings, the arbitrary arrests, the mock trials, were finally at an end - and that friend Fouché and the rest were to be thanked for this fatal stroke against the Tyrant. And being good politicians, they stopped, listened, and swiftly trimmed their sails to this new wind.

They knew, of course, how little cause the common people had to be grateful for their self-serving acts, but if the hoi polloi wanted to make heroes of them, then so much the better. An attitude not unlike my own, you might say, after my near-immolation on the steps of the Guillotine, and you'd be right. Shrewd fellows these revolutionaries. It never does to have scruples over what is needful for one's survival, and these men knew they were playing for their very lives. They had intended to use the Terror to remain in power, for only when they held the reins of government could they prevent retribution for all their past crimes against the very people who were now – for the moment - paying tribute to their heroism. But if they must yield up the Guillotine the better to survive, then so be it. So they hid their astonishment, smiled at the cheering masses, waved, blew kisses and prepared to play the part that had been so unexpectedly thrust upon them.

It could not last, of course. There were too many bodies, too many ghosts. The blood of thousands cried out for vengeance. Within days, prisoners had been released from the Conciergerie and a score of other prisons and were regaling the crowds with hideous tales of privation and death. And then from the provinces, from Nantes, Arras, Nîmes, and aye, from Lyon of blessed memory, deputations arrived to describe the scenes of butchery, eye witnesses to the noyades and mitrillades, to atrocities that had been fostered and nurtured by the agents of the Committee, some of the very men now hailed as saviours! The fiction that Robespierre was solely to blame for the conflagration that had engulfed all France became impossible to sustain. The People's love turned swiftly to hate, and a clamorous call for vengeance.

I understood very little of this at the time, and cared less. The initial flush of vengeful excitement that had sustained me through Robespierre's capture and execution was soon spent, and I lapsed into a hateful, depressive stupor as the full realisation of Lucie's betrayal with the bestial Collot d'Herbois - and the part I had played in her death – began to cast its gloom about me. Few noticed the change; they were all too busy saving their own miserable necks from *Jourdan Coup-Tête* – but Fouché kept me close and always seemed to have some task for me to perform; looking back, I suspect that he knew more of my sorry tale than I imagined, and tried to keep me busy for my own sake. As I say, he always had a soft spot for me. Heaven knows why.

I took note, mind you, when Collot was denounced, and the prospect arose of a vicarious vengeance on that poisonous toad. Not that he was accused of any crime against my person, nor anyone else for that. No, the proceedings were, once more, entirely political. With the populace in arms and screaming for the blood of all prominent revolutionaries, the saner heads amongst them realised the game was up, and that their only means of safety lay in deflecting the people's spleen onto other victims. The role of Liberator was swiftly changed to that of Avenger of the People, and France was treated to the elevating spectacle of the Butcher of Marseilles, Louis-Marie Freron, pointing the finger of accusation at the equally guilty Fouquier-Tinville, public prosecutor of the Revolutionary Tribunal; of Tallien, terrorist *extraordinaire*, demanding the head of his erstwhile ally Billaud-Varenne; and of my own master Fouché, *confrère* of the Lyon massacres denouncing, in words dripping with pathos and righteous anger, the shameful atrocities committed by Carrier in Nantes. And they called me Chameleon!

Then again, the ruse worked. People wanted scapegoats, and the crimes of whoever obligingly rustled up a steady flow of victims were all miraculously forgotten. Two days after the execution of Robespierre, the whole of the Paris Commune, 60 men in all, were guillotined in less than an hour and a half (one every 90 seconds, which I thought damned efficient of Samson, and proved the old maxim 'practise makes perfect') and though I was standing above 100 paces from the place of execution, so fast did the blade descend the blood of the victims streamed under my feet. Nor were they the last. In vain did Fouquier protest that he was "the head of a conspiracy I have never been aware of, and accused by those always eager to find others responsible." The people required a sin-offering, and he too went to the glaive with 15 other 'co-conspirators' sometime in early May. It wasn't that the scheming bastard didn't deserve it – the guillotine was the least of the punishments I'd have visited upon his sallow, greasy head. Nor that his whole trial was a travesty of justice from beginning to end (which it was): Fouquier had presided over enough of *those* in his time, and happily sent better men than he – I think of Danton - along the road that he was now finally to wend himself. No, it was the sublime hypocrisy of it all that stuck in my craw – Moloch denouncing Beelzebub and prodding his hell-spawned compeer gleefully into the flames.

Collot d'Herbois escaped the guillotine, along with Barère and Billaud, but they were spared only for a more sombre fate. The new rulers of France knew that the popularity of these three with their sansculotte supporters precluded any staged, public execution. But there was more than one way to bake a revolutionary and they were soon about it. Collot and his friends were marinated, sentenced to perpetual exile in the foul hell of Cayenne, in the Guianas, a steaming cess-pit on the western shoulder of South America, a land full of miasmatic air, blood-drinking bats and venomous snakes, and a bewildering variety of noxious fevers that would have you carried off on six men's shoulders before the sun had run its course. I speak from bitter experience, for I spent more time than was good for me on that pitiless, benighted continent – a tale I'll rehearse presently, God willing.

So fatal was Guiana's reputation, exile there was called the Dry Guillotine; not so messy as the original, y'see, but just as sure. I was well pleased by the verdict, but many thought otherwise. The Paris sections seethed with indignation when news of Collot, Billaud and Barère's deportation spread through the capital. The sansculottes massed in the streets on the day of their departure, intending rescue, and had it not been for the work of General Pichégru in directing his men to use main force in dispersing the would-be rescuers, the odious Collot would undoubtedly have escaped a much deserved requital. Ironic too; poor old Pichégru was deported thence soon after, and never lived to louse his own grey hair, perishing horribly within weeks of exhaustion and disease.

So too, I'm delighted to report, did d'Herbois. I'm not normally a vindictive man (leastways not overmuch) but even after all these years it still gives me a warm feeling of satisfaction to know the squat swaggering bastard languished in that tropical netherworld for almost a year, forced to slave through the unremitting heat, tormented by unrelenting clouds of insects, and tortured by thirst and lack of food, the *buveur de sang*'s own blood quaffed by an army of leeches and mosquitoes, sleeping where he fell only to be awoken at daybreak to another intolerable, interminable day of misery; until in March 1796, he finally succumbed in an agony of bloody flux and vomit to the worst of all contagions that Hell-hole has to offer - Yellow Fever. To remember all that, and then to know I am still on my pins - shaky as they are, still among the thrice blessed[33] - and still gloating. Aye, as those brave black lads of Asante have it: there is nothing so sweet in life as to vanquish your enemy.

Satisfying as this was for me personally, following Robespierre's fall the continued in-fighting among the members of the Convention made for a catastrophic lack of firm government. As you'd expect, the plebs had the worst of it. The winter of '94 was unusually hard, and many perished of cold and want. I remember hard frosts and snow piled up along the boulevards; scores of corpses, bright and icy, frozen in the most grotesque positions half-hidden in the alleyways; the Paris poor, standing in lines for a miserable pound of flour, or a few sticks of firewood, swathed in whatever clothes they could find so that only their eyes were visible, their looks brimful of anger and resentment.

They felt cheated, you see, all the heady revolutionary dreams of *Liberté, Fraternité, Egalité* driven from them by years of fear and privation. In place of Liberty they had seen the democratic Constitution of '93 withheld and justice corrupted by a pack of self-seeking unscrupulous adventurers. Fraternity had been pledged, but how could universal brotherhood prevail where spies and informers prospered? In theory there was Equality, but in practice a new privileged class had simply replaced the hated nobility. Speculators, embezzlers and profiteers made fat and proud on ill-gotten gain, lorded it in the streets or sped by in covered carriages with their painted jades, making for yet another dazzling ball or sumptuous banquet while the common folk starved. It was this, and this alone that ate the Revolution from within, hollowing it out until just the slogan-chanting husk remained. Y'see, while all had suffered equally the people were willing to abide any privation to preserve their dream of the Rights of Man. But had they swept away the Nobles, killed a King and endured years of Terror merely to see a corrupt race of politicians seize the place and privileges of the *ancien regime*? No by Christ, they would not abide it.

The year turned in bitterness and as the early months of 1795 wore on there were murmurings along the Rue de Lappe, resentful meetings before the house of Santerre the brewer, and from the cold grey stones of St Antoine came the smouldering odour of revolt. Deputations were sent to the Convention, to return with court promises[20] and empty bellies. The discontent erupted on the 20th May with the insurrection of Prairial when the fauxborgs stormed the Convention to cries of "bread and the Constitution of 93"; where Ferand was shot and had his head cut from his body, and desperate hand-to-hand fighting continued in the gardens until dusk. The following day the people formed their own government at the Town Hall, and it might have been all up with the scum of the Convention had they not promised the mob most of their demands, speaking them fair while sending secret messages to the generals to come to their aid. The next day, surrounded by armed troops, they refused to even see the people's spokesmen and shortly thereafter sent in the troops to restore 'order'. The sections were disarmed and a military commission imprisoned many and shot a few more.

A trifling victory, you might suppose, against ill-armed,

---

[20]   *Court promises – fair words without action*

starving civilians already half-dead with fatigue. But you'd be wrong. It was a turning point in French history – eventually. Although most Parisians missed its true importance even then, this bloody repression was seen as the end of one of the mainstays of the revolution: that the army would never act against a mass protest. From the first stirrings of revolt in '89 all sides, Royalist and Jacobin alike, took it for granted that the King's troops would never fire on the people. It was this alone that had made the revolution possible. Had the Baker believed for one second that the army would obey his commands he would not have thought twice about sending in *les soldats* to teach his uppity lower orders a lesson. A quick bloodbath, and it would have been the noble in his chateau and Peter Peasant back to his pigsty.

But times had changed. The generals, Dubois, Kilmaine and the rest, had all been kissed by that strumpet Corruption, and they'd be damned if a few ragged-arsed beggars were going to kill the golden goose who was a-busy laying them all fine eggs of specie. The army, you see, had abandoned the people, and was now hand in glove with windy charlatans and gross-gutted speculators. A singularly dangerous development, had the politicians but stopped to think - for the whip hand now lay with the soldiers. It was their armed might, their power, that had saved the privileged few from the wrath of the people; and once this precedent for repression by force of arms had been set, what was there to prevent any bold general from making a grab for supreme power? It was lesson they were to learn later in tears and sorrow. The way was now open for military dictatorship.

I tell you all this only because it is necessary in order to understand the momentous events that followed. From this mass revolt arose the Constitution of 1795, and a new form of government - the Directory - devised by those in power with the sole purpose of allowing them to retain their high positions. They knew the masses would seize the opportunity of an election to turn them out, so Tallien,

Fouché and the rest of that foresworn pack of rogues simply abolished universal suffrage and gave the vote only to those with property. The new Government comprised a double Chamber of 250 Ancients (who had to be at least forty years of age) and a younger house, the Five Hundred, whose minimum age was thirty. This conclave of dullards was headed by five Directors, chosen from the Ancients, who formed an executive. Well and good. But so hated were the erstwhile heroes of Thermidor that even these betrayals of revolutionary principle were no guarantee they would keep their place of safety in the government. Nothing daunted, Talien and the rest proved themselves equal to the challenge. If the population would not elect them, well then, they would elect themselves.

And this is just what they did, in a decree which allowed for two-thirds of the old Convention to be elected *automatically,* to one or other of the new Chambers. The result was less violent than many expected; there were a few marches, a smattering of riots, but a new spirit of lethargy seemed to have descended upon France. It was as if the people had given up; that they had lost belief in the principles that had sustained them since '89, and had buttressed their victorious fight against all the nations of Europe; that they despaired of ever being rid of the devious crew of sophists who clung so tenaciously to power. When the decree was put to a plebiscite (of property owners only of course) few bothered to vote, and the count, to no one's surprise, went in favour of the incumbents.

Which set the fox among the chickens in no small way. The brazen effrontery of it all fanned the embers of revolt and set patriotic hearts once more aflame. Royalist agitators immediately saw an opportunity of stirring things up and on October 5th, just before the new 'Directory' was to be inaugurated, yet another rising took place. It was led by the hotheads of the St Pelletier Section, but soon everyone had joined in, shopkeepers, workmen, waiters, clerks, and within hours there were upwards of 20,000 of them, including a stiffening of National Guard battalions who had gone over to the Sections, marching to the beat of the drum towards the Convention to finish the 'rotten bellies' once and for all.

I was drunk at the time. Deadly, deeply drunk in a cellar in the bowels of the Tuilleries whence I retired with several bottles of good wine whenever the black devils of depression looked set fair to overwhelm my mind. Which, to speak truth, was most nights. First thing I knew was when a hand shook my shoulder roughly and I raised my bleary eyes to see some thin-shanked ginger pate, a clerk doubtless, regarding me disdainfully down his long nose and squeaking out that Monsieur Fouché (*Monsieur,* not *Citoyen,* you'll note, so soon were the revolutionary niceties abandoned), Monsieur Fouché desired the pleasure of my company toute de suite. It was, says this officious little durgen, pulling vainly at my collar, a matter of the most extreme urgency. Monsieur Fouché must not be kept waiting.

So I rose, straightened my crumpled clothing, and forced my drink-sodden limbs to follow his mincing steps up a series of stairways until we ascended into the dim light of an early dawn, on a ground floor corridor, full of flunkeys scurrying hither and yon, their hands crammed with cahiers and documents, and a look of terror on each face. That sobered me somewhat – mischief was plainly afoot, though in my drink-befuddled state I could not imagine what. We climbed another set of stairs, wide and imposing, which brought us onto a landing from which three spacious passageways led off, each decked out with elaborate wall hangings and ornate candelabra. You'd have thought Louis and his overdressed Court had never left Paris.

I was led to a wide oaken door, past half-a-dozen bureaucrats with worried looks; a discrete knock, a muffled reply, and I was ushered into the Adytum to find my master sitting head down behind a wide walnut desk, papers, quills and inkpots scattered across its width, and at least three empty wine bottles lying on the carpet beneath. He looked up, grimaced a smile, and waved me to a chair while he completed his reading.

But that one look had set me back, I may tell you – whatever had happened, it had to be momentous - the man had aged overnight. I'd seen Fouché at two the previous afternoon, and he had appeared his usual smooth-faced imperturbable self. But a single night had done the work of years. There were worry lines etched deep into his usually sleek forehead, the skin was stretched over the unshaven cheeks, and there were dark sunken rings beneath his pale eyes. His hair was dishevelled, cravat awry, and his coat and pantaloons looked as if they had spent the night in the cellar with me. But I doubt he had slept since I saw him last.

He looked up suddenly and caught me staring at him. "By God Francois" says he throwing down his pen and rubbing a palm over his face "I warrant you look even worse than I". Which may have been true, through I doubted it. Any worse and I'd be jackined*[21], or dead. "We have a pretty pickle here" he continued, "it seemed of small account yesterday, but it has grown into something that may well bring us all down. Or, as that pompous fool Barras would have it 'destroy the sacred purity of the Revolution'". He laughed shortly at his own sally then rose and began pacing the carpet in front of me. "Attend me well, my friend" he rumbled portentously, "I do not wish to have to repeat myself, time is too short". He took a long deep breath, "Well now, matters stand ... Ah Michel" this to the carrot-top who had brought me here and still stood by the door "you may leave us for the moment. I will call when I need you."

He waited until the door had clicked shut before resuming his pacing. "As I say, matters stand in this wise. Royalist agitators have stirred up the people, and along with the usual riff-raff and ne'er-do-wells, are declaring against the new decrees." He paused, pulling at his long nose. "Without realising that they are acting against their own

---

21   *On the point of death

196

best interests, the citizens of Paris are in revolt and wish to prevent the inauguration of the Directory. They have some silly idea that the revolution has been betrayed, that their rights have been compromised - the Royalists and Jacobins have made common cause and persuaded the citizens that a resort to arms is their only recourse."

He paused, and stared at me. I stared back, nodding sagely. It was all complete twaddle of course, but hell would sprout icicles ere I ever told him that. The truth was the people's rights *had* been purloined, the elections rigged, and the democratic ideals of '93 sold far down the Seine. But the masses would have endured all this, and more belike, but for the one factor Fouché studiously ignored. While he and his friends nightly guzzled the best wines and liquors, and forked foie gras and Blanquette de veau into their rotten bellies, the people were starving. Literally starving. They wanted their rights and freedoms, past question - but far, far more they wanted bread.

However, the main thing was that, while I'd been sleeping off the effects of my solitary bacchanalia, at least part of Paris had risen in rebellion. And no small part, to judge by the worried look on Fouché's pallid face. "Details are sketchy" he was saying "we know that the rebels are led by a former soldier of the Republic, but his identity remains obscure. While you were.." he sniffed ".. otherwise engaged, this rebel has moved his men. They are now on both sides of the Seine, to the South in the Faubourg St Germain, and on the north side of the river in the St Pelletier Section. Both groups are readying themselves for an attack upon the Tuilleries. We do not know when the crisis will come, or from what direction. Intelligence is in short supply, I do not even know who commands the defence of the Tuilleries, or even if there is a defence, Barras has not taken me into his confidence. But one thing I do know – unless we can insert someone into the ranks of the rebels, someone skilled in disguise who can impersonate one of the rabble and return with solid reliable intelligence, then we are lost."

My chitterlings had already plunged at these words and I was suddenly as sober as a parson at Pentecost. For I knew what was approaching, and it could bode but ill for poor Sidney. "We must know who these rebels are, and what they plan". He looked at me askance and I thought 'Oh Christ, here it comes!' And it did. "Naturally, Francois, I thought of you..."

There was no help for it. Ten minutes later, armed with the few scraps of rumour my master had already acquired, I stepped out into an early dawn, the sky clear, promising a fair day, and discovered that Fouché's tattle was already well out of date. There was a buzzing in the air, like a swarm of angry hornets, a sound that resolved itself gradually into the clamouring voices of Captain Tom*[22], vaguely discernible through the mist that still hung over the Seine. What I could see of the southern end of Pont Royal was alive with a dark mass of people, banners aloft, pushing their way eagerly over the causeway, the morning light picking out pike tops and the copper-red of muskets. The rattle of drums carried faintly over the foggy water, mingling with the high-pitched trill of a fife and massed angry voices belting out the *Ça ira.* It was an impressive sight – this was no royalist forlorn hope, but a fully-fledged revolt that bid fair to topple Fouché and all his friends.

The rebels looked as if they were readying themselves to mount an immediate, concerted attack on the Tuilleries. If there were as many to the north as the south, then the future of the government looked bleak indeed. Hopefully they would hold off until I had gathered some useful information and reported back to uncle Fouché.

But hold - if I was with them when the assault began, then so much the better – I could *Nom du Chien!* and *Vive le Republique!* with the best of them, from a safe distance naturally, and wait to see who held the field at the end of the day. If the rebels, then I would already be in newly fashionable sansculotte attire; should the government

---

[22]   *The Mob*

win the day a swift disrobing would leave me once again a firm supporter of the new Directory. I would make my apologies to Fouché... not sufficient time to amass useful information, the rebels moved too swiftly, impossible for me to do anything, etc etc., and await the opportunity to seek solace in my cups. I might be tired of life, but I wasn't going to willingly put my head in a noose if I could help it. Either way, I couldn't loiter; I must be about my business.

Hurrying forward, I made my way along the south facade of the Tuilleries, aiming for a narrow alley which debouched onto the Rue St Honoré. In one end as Carton, out t'other a sansculotte, then up the Rue de Richelieu in the Section St Pelletier. That was the plan. But as so often in my long eventful existence, I ran into slap-bang into History.

Head down, collar up, I scurried round the west end of the Tuilleries, tripped over a powder keg and careered into some little fool of a man braying out commands, and down we both went, arse over tit. Which was just as well. For at that very moment some of the rebel forces let fly with a ragged volley, and the wall above us exploded in a haze of dust as a dozen musket balls crash into the spot where, moments before, the little fellow had been standing.

I scrabbled to my knees, but the little chap was already on his feet. I had the impression of officer's gold epaulettes, long lank hair, a narrow face and brilliant eyes that seemed to dance with an intense inner flame. "My thanks, citoyen" says he clapping a hand on my shoulder "rest here I pray you, while I deal with this rabble. Then we may talk"

I was nothing loathe. I'd fetched up behind a nice stout balustrade, safe from musketry, and had no desire to attempt a crossing to the foe at this point. I scrambled along, deeper into the masonry, settled myself against the comforting stones, looked round and saw that the little fellow was already some thirty yards distant, giving his orders laconically, but with a quick, quiet confidence that stiffened the backbone of every *soldat* who heard him speak. And they all did, for he was everywhere at once, checking

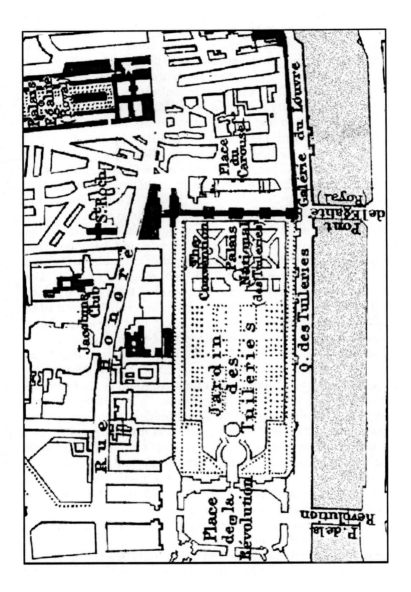

shot, sightings, powder, the supply of food and water, and whether Jacques had sent his mother her birthday bouquet this morning, doubtless.   He knew his work, this little furnace of a man, that much was obvious from the way he was disposing his cannon.   Where the devil he had got them I'd no idea – I didn't learn until later of Joachim Murat's desperate dash to Les Sablons[34] - but I could see plainly that this ordinance made all the difference to the defence of the government.

You'll understand the position better if you take time to cast your eyes over the rough map I've penned for this memoir. The Tuilleries is a thin, L-shaped building, with its bottom arm (along the Galerie de Louvre) protected by the Seine and approachable only via the Pont Royal.   However, the remainder of the building is very vulnerable to attack, from the north across the Rue St Honoré, eastwards via the Rue St Nicaise into the Place de Caroussel, and through the Gardens of the Tuilleries to the west.   My new friend realised all this, thank God, and had stationed his pieces to cover all approaches.   Except in the west.   Filled with apprehension, I strained my eyes through the mass of trees and bushes and saw with some relief that beyond the gardens the Place de la Révolution was filled with horse and rider, men loyal to the Convention, lance and sabre at the ready..

And they had need, I may tell you.   From the south came the rumble of cannon as the rebels made their assault across the Pont Royal.   At the same time, the crowds to the north were massing about the steps of the St Roche Church, brandishing their weapons, screaming imprecations and working themselves into a fine frenzy for a charge.   The mob would be upon us soon, no error, and my heart was already beating the retreat.   There was a movement beside me, I looked up, and there was the little fellow again, one arm aloft and smiling grimly as he watched the mob move of one accord down the steps of the church and onto the street. "Steady now" he calls out and he might have been watching a flock of sheep approach for all the concern in his voice. The crowd was rolling forward now, and a deep roar issued from its collective throat. I could feel my bowels dissolve, they'd be on us in moments, rolling over our positions, we'd never survive-

"Now!" the little chap's hand went down and all along the line I saw the slow match stroke the touch hole. The roar was appalling, and as the echoes died away the screams began. He'd loaded grape, you see, and the small shot wreaked a bloody destruction on the massed front ranks of the mob, and left the rest with little stomach for the fight. Off to my left a bugle sang out, and Murat and his bonny lads came cantering out of the gardens, dressing well, boot against boot, sabres on shoulder, heading north passed the Garge Meuble and disappearing from our view. But the rhythm their hoofbeats could still be heard and presently it changed from canter to full gallop and we saw the remnants of the mob at the St Roche turning to flee as Murat's riders bore down on them full tilt along the Rue St Honoré. One group of stout-hearts stood their ground and swiftly fell beneath the hooves and sabres. The rest bolted for the colonnaded sanctuary of the church or the safety of the narrow alleys.

And suddenly the streets were silent. It was over. The Insurrection of Vendremiaire had failed. And the hero of the hour was undoubtedly the wiry ball of fire and energy who now came towards me, a tight-lipped smile of satisfaction garnishing his sallow features. "Well monsieur" says he conversationally, and I noticed for the first time the marked Corsican accent of his French "amazing what a whiff of grapeshot can accomplish, *hein*? And I must thank you sir. I owe you my life."

I made the required deprecatory noises and would have left it there and hurried back to Fouché with my eyewitness account of the victory – for it would do no hurt to be first with the good news. But the little fellow seemed to feel that he was under some obligation for my upending him in the course of his duties, and with his startling eyes and imposing presence I must say he was a difficult cove to refuse. "You will come to dinner with me tomorrow night sir" says he, in a voice that brooked no argument "no.... please, I insist. Rather, I implore you. Your courgae today demands my utmost respect. It would be an honour and a privilege. Let me show my appreciation for the strange way Fate has thrown us together. I am unmarried as yet but" and to my utter surprise he coloured a little "but I soon hope to remedy that omission for I have met the most adorable of creatures..." he seemed momentarily lost for words as some vision of feminine beauty doubtless passed before his inner eye "yes, yes, the most adorable... as you shall see yourself if you will be good enough to accept my invitation. You smile? You will attend? Bien. Ah, good sir " says he shaking my hand, "I am more gratified by your agreement than with this victory for our glorious ... Revolution" and I could not help noting the contemptuous emphasis on the final word. I said nothing, but made a mental note nonetheless – such seemingly trivial details were the corn I ground daily for Fouché's reports. We embraced and arranged to meet at eight the following evening, at a house on the Rue de Chantereine. "It is settled then? Good, good. Until then, *bonne chance*" and he swung rapidly away, only to turn back almost instantly. "But Sir, I do not know your name" I satisfied him on this head, or rather, I gave my French name-of-the-moment, and he nodded, well satisfied. "An honour to make your acquaintance, monsieur" he says, very soldier-like. "I am Brigadier-General Buonoparte, but", and the white teeth flashed again "my friends, amongst whom I hope I may number your good self, they call me Napoleon."

Chapter Seventeen

I dutifully arrived for dinner at eight the following evening
at what turned out to be a not very prepossessing house
at number 6, Rue Chantereine. But there were servants
at least, and I was ushered into the reception room where
several guests had foregathered, speculators in frock coats
and tie-wigs, alluring half-naked *merveilleuses* in their
cashmere shawls, skin-coloured tights and transparent
figure-hugging dresses and... and without warning, the
people seemed to fade into the background, the very walls
of the room slipping away, and I was back in a cell of the
Conciergerie, and a husky Creole voice was whispering
"Dear Monsieur... kind Monsieur...you will oblige me...? "
Standing before me, exquisitely dressed in a beautifully
embroidered chemise a la Grecque, a golden girdle just
beneath her breasts, a newly fashionable hand-bag in one
hand, roman sandals on her shapely feet and with my
new military friend hanging devotedly on her arm - was
the Comtesse de Beauharnais! She who I had believed
dead these long months past, now most obviously alive
and looking very fetching indeed. Our gaze joined, her
eyes widened and I was gratified to see that she was, if
anything, even more shocked and embarrassed by our
unexpected meeting, no doubt believing that I had visited

the revolutionary barber shortly after she had departed our love-nest at the Conciergerie. "Ah you have arrived" cried Napoleon, striding forward with a reluctant Comtesse in his train and slapping me on the back in hearty soldier-like fashion "I was afraid you would change your mind and stay away" Which, at that moment, was exactly what Comtesse de Beauharnais was wishing I had done, I've no doubt; it was, I swear, the only time I saw Josephine de Beauharnais, the Empress Josephine as she finally became, blushing and discomfited. We were introduced, I kissed her hand chastely, then Napoleon was pulling her away towards the door as another newcomer entered the hallway.

My mind in a whirl, I mingled with the other guests, the usual motley crew of politicians, speculators, wine-bibbers and whores, and tried to draw from them what information I could concerning the recently resurrected lady on Bonaparte's arm. I gathered that her removal from the Conciergerie had been even more fortunate than my own. All charges against her had been dropped (a wonder in itself), her reputation had been restored, and she had been freed early that same afternoon. It was by any light a miraculous escape and I confess to conjecturing - unworthy thought – what particular reward the lady may have offered during that long morning's interview for so fulsome an acquittal. Yet all power to her - she had survived the worst excesses of the Revolution, and thrived wondrously following Robespierre's demise. Now, as I already suspected, I learned that the Comtesse was my new military friend's " most adorable of creatures", having been recently handed on as a thank-you for Vendemiaire's 'whiff of grapeshot' by Director Barrass, whose lover she originally was. Despite the age difference – Josephine must have been at least ten years older than her present paramour – Buonaparte was apparently besotted, and even then there was talk of a marriage in the offing.

Over dinner I was able to discover the depth of Comtesse Beauharnais' feeling for her military hero. We had hardly sat down when I felt a stockinged foot sliding up my calf, and higher still, if truth be told. After our meal there were charades and other pastimes and Josephine contrived to engage me in innocent conversation, at which she took the opportunity to give her own account of her escape from the guillotine - and to make it obvious that she would not be averse, indeed she was passing eager, to renew the close friendship we had established in the condemned cell. She had, apparently, the fondest memories my obliging behaviour and, if nothing else, she was a lady who took her obligations extremely seriously.

Which was an intoxicating piece of good news to one of my amorous complexion, and I fell in with the game willingly enough.[35] A good bout of clicket is as fine a physic as any man can expect in this life, and although the relief may be temporary, the remedy - should the lady be willing – can be resorted to once or twice a day, 'as necessary' as my apothecary is so fond of saying.

So I took to visiting the Rue Chantereine often, in a variety of personas: vintner, footman, beggarman, tinker and once, I recall, as the road's nightsoil collector; I would knock discreetly or loudly, as befitted my character, at the tradesman's entrance, a giggling maid would usher me through to Josephine's boudoir where there would be a glorious disrobing, and we would give ourselves over to guilty pleasures. Often, she'd require me to remain clothed and in character during the bout, and then she'd be especially boisterous. She particularly enjoyed the tinkerman, I remember. I've no doubt that, for her, the disguises added a certain piquancy to our coupling, for she was a wanton baggage when all was said, and would have given Messalina a run for her money in any cavaulting school*[23]. But her predilections made my own part all the harder - it's wondrous difficult to perform the capital act quietly when festooned with pots and pans. Impossible in fact. Doubtless the neighbours were greatly impressed

---

[23] *Brothel

each Wednesday by the ardency with which Josephine's old tinkerman banged away at the kitchenware.

And so I began a second double life, of matinee performances with Josephine and regular evening soirées with her intended, for the couple were becoming famous as impeccable hosts. Napoleon's adoration was obvious – when she was in the room it was hard to get a word out of him, he seemed mesmerised by her every movement and when she lay upon the chaise longue he would spend minutes drinking in her figure or just staring at her face. For Josephine, it was much less of a grand passion, indeed there was no passion at all. I remember after one particularly joyous engagement – I'd been Francois the Footman that day, I recall – when she lay back on her cushions and began a long, detailed comparison of her lovers' abilities – for you must know that, despite my undoubted prowess at slapping the mattrass, even Sidney's many faces were not enough to satisfy her lust and I was just one of many with whom she danced the feather-bed jig. She was quite ruthlessly honest about her lovers, and had us all neatly graded, which was refreshing in a way, though it was obvious that she regarded all men as mere instruments of her pleasure, as varied dishes in a self-indulgent feast of fornication. I doubt she had cared for anyone in her life, and love-struck Boney least of all. He did not even figure on her festive board, and I could not help but comment on the omission. Her reply surprised me. "My leetle soldier boy? You have seen the way he fawns on me? No? Pah, it is sickening. He's the man who wants to father Alexandre's (her unlamented husband) children, and for various reasons I am inclined to accept the offer. You will ask me do I love him. No I don't. Do I dislike him? Again, no. I'm indifferent. Lukewarm."[36] Thankfully, I was rated somewhat better in the love-stakes. Joint second, in fact. Which is something I suppose, when you consider her vast experience.

Her feelings for Napoleon, or lack of them, were all one to me, though I always took care to remain incognito during our amorous assignations. I can't really say why. After Robespierre's short-lived Age of Virtue, the pendulum of public morality had made a rapid return swing, and *quae fuerant vitiae, mores sunt***24*. Infidelity was the norm in those days, and the whole of France descended into a time of licence and debauch. No one would have turned a hair if Josephine and I had paraded stark naked along the Champs Elysee and fornicated publicly amongst the verdure of the Jardin de Tuilleries. Many did just that. But Napoleon held to a different code of honour, and I had the odd notion that this intense, sallow-faced young soldier was not one to be crossed, that his 'star' – as he himself called it – was in the ascendancy and I would do rather better as his friend than a focus of his enmity.

Nevertheless, Josephine's attentions and the endless round of parties and soirees did help me through the worst of my melancholic bouts, and spread a counterfeit balm on my hopeless, unreasoning desire to see Lucie again, to speak with her, just once more, to understand her reasons, to understand the *why* of it... But while I could now laugh, joke, and flirt *en cavalier* in fine style, produce the odd *bon mot* and discuss everything from courtesans to Cato with that jolly creedless crew of political rogues and painted jezebels, another part of me, at my heart's core if you wish, remained utterly untouched. A cold black stone at the centre - impervious alike to love or hate. Dead.

---

24 **What were once vices are now in fashion*

Chapter Eighteen

As the weeks pressed on I found I could tolerate this cynical mix of parvenu and nobility, with its stifling atmosphere and false gaiety, less and less. Even Josephine's inventive, enthusiastic and admittedly ecstatic romps began to pall, and I despaired more and more of my shallow, pointless existence in France, of the endless sense of loss and remorse that assailed me. Every street, every boulevard brought memories of Lucie, her betrayal and my violent response, of that hellish tragedy which I knew an infinity of guilt and remorse could never wash away.

And behind all this, though I tried my cynical best to deny it, there was yet another incubus to gnaw nightly at my soul. I was, after all, an Englishman in the pay (albeit involuntarily) of a foreign power, and try as I might I could not help regarding myself a traitor to my country. France and Britain remained at war, and although at present Fouché had me working on matters of internal security, it could only be a matter of time before my talents would be required to help the Revolution against the vile machinations of perfidious Albion. What would I do then? There were but two choices open to me: refuse Fouché's commands and find myself once more in the tumbril, or submit and do my part in bringing England to its knees.

No, I would do neither. Before that choice was laid before me I would resurrect my original plan of escape and make for England, even at hazard of my life. Once in Rumeville I knew I should be well received. My time with the French had given me a store of detailed information that would be invaluable to the Crown and should set me up for life. Better by far to live in sorrow at home than here, with its daily reminders of my woe, and where at any moment I could be asked to work against the country of my birth.

But it would not be easy. It was past question I must be careful - Fouché had spent the long months since Robespierre's demise diligently building up his already formidable web of informants. That downy bird trusted none; he had files on every member of the Directory, the Army, the bureaucracy - and on the one-legged cleaner of the *pissoir* by the Rue Dauphine too, I'd wager. Nothing happened in France, in Paris especially, but Fouché had word of it within hours, and should I attempt to cut my cable and make for England he would doubtless sniff out my intentions long before I was ready to act.

Then again, that was true only if I attempted to involve someone else in my schemes. There was only one way to have half a chance of keeping this enterprise beneath the rose, and that was by acting strictly alone. So, I laid my plans in the deepest secrecy, slowly amassing cash and equipment. The old revolutionary passports I had purchased for Lucie and myself were useless now, but fortune began to wear a kinder aspect just then, for my work took me to the fauxbourg St Antoine, where I struck a master counterfeiter, a little withered old dommerer, but as skilled an artist as ever held pen, who produced certificates and documents in a host of languages and styles for Fouché's many spies. I made it my business to be pleasant to the old fool, and took to drinking with him at a tawdry tavern of his acquaintance, surrounded by draymen, carters, chairmen and the odd footman out of place, swilling down bad wine and eating cowheel and execrable raw-pork sausages called, very fittingly I thought, *Morteau.*

But as I never tire of telling the young men of my acquaintance (not that they listen) it pays to take pains; the old man lived for his art and would talk of little else, and so, after four weeks of brain-numbing conversation, I had extracted sufficient knowledge to try my hand at his art. And thanks to countless solitary hours experimentation in my room with parchment and papers, nibs and inks, I was soon able to produce my own passable imitation of an official passport – a little rough and ready to the practiced eye, no doubt, but with a genuine enough look to get me to the coast, from whence I could bribe a ship's captain to stow me on board for a short trip across the Channel. I was ready.

Though he had served his purpose, I continued to visit my mentor, and to drink with him at the Augean hostelry he insisted on frequenting. Any change in routine would have alerted Fouché's informers (and doubtless others too), and I was too close to my prize to have my plans miscarry. The very night I was to slip my French collar I made a great show of bonhomie, and all the company declared I was a first class chap and a thoroughly good egg, though none knew that I was liquoring my boots and, if luck held, would nevermore clap eyes on them again. The result of all this revelry was that it was past eleven of the clock before I managed to bid my adieus to the garrulous old sot and his irksome cronies. I trudged back to my lodgings deep in thought, petrified and exhilarated in equal measure by the ordeal ahead and going over for the hundredth time how I would circumvent the many traps between Paris and the coast, when out from an open doorway steps a bonnet and shawl. It was but a small bump, yet it sent her basket of apples flying and I was about to curse her for a clumsy bitch, when the oath froze on my lips as I took in what a luscious peach she was, and I hurried forward with many a courteous apology to help her gather up the fruit.

"My stars, monsieur" says she, bending once more to collect

a last apple, her loose calico blouse opening revealingly while I looked on, bedazzled by the sight of her. She was a forward wench right enough, a bouncing damsel with a pair of cupid's kettle drums so bountiful they'd have had even Simeon the Stylite abandoning his pillar, shimmying down and laying hold with both hands. "What a shock ye gave me, rushing into me like that so unexpected an' all" She stood and patted a trembling hand against her heart, or as close as such a bushel-bubbied doxie could come to that organ –a good ten inches I thought, in my humble and admiring estimation. "Oh sir, I'm all of a flutter I am, come over quite faint I 'ave" and she made free to lean on my arm, and place her chestnut locks against my shoulder, which I allowed with mounting agitation. She lingered there a breath or two, then looked up, and I was staring into the biggest long-lashed eyes of emerald green that I had ever beheld. "'Ere though" she whispered "I don't s'pose you'd like to help a defenceless maiden back to her room, would you? Carry me basket for me? I don't fink I've strength enough to hold me stuff" she cocked her lovely head towards the doorway. "It's jus' up those stairs. What d'ye say?"

I was nothing loathe, for by this time I was in a fine old fever, sufficient to convince myself that an hour or so's dalliance would do my plans no scathe. So I rose manfully to her request, settling the basket on my arm and allowing myself to be persuaded to her apartments. Moments later and I was climbing narrow stairs behind delightfully swaying hips, well pleased with my good fortune and imagining all sorts of carnal delights with this light-heeled doxy. We crossed a darkened hall, the boards creaking underfoot, and entered her apartment. The room was small, lit by a single candle and tastefully but cheaply furnished with a table, chair and writing bureau in one corner and in t'other a large four-poster, the sheets turned down invitingly. Better and better thinks I. She had made her way to the table, her back to me and as I advanced she swung round, a glass of wine in each hand. It was then I half-noticed her fingers, long and delicate with perfectly formed nails and certainly not those of an apple-seller. But as you'll allow, it was not her fingers that concerned me at that time and the stray thought was swiftly lost: I wanted only to begin the good old work of making feet for children's stockings, and sooner rather than later. She held out a glass to me but I was in full lustful flood by now, and set it aside with an oath as I swiftly made to come to grips, a hand on her rump and another upon one of her plump pumpkins.

"'Ere now, 'ere" says she in mock alarm, resisting gently, pushing me away, her voice teasing. "Gently now, monsieur, you're such a big strong man, you wouldn't want to hurt a poor girl, now would you?" I allowed myself to be disengaged - that one squeeze had been enough to divine her intentions, for she was as hard aloft as I was below. We would come to it in time, I knew, but while I have never been averse to playing out a long game, in the current circumstances time was of the essence. Besides which, this chance encounter with so frolicsome a wanton had set my blood a-boil, and I was at that moment as eager a mutton-monger as ever slapped mattress. As if divining my thoughts, she brushed up against me, pressing those delightful bouncers into my chest and teasing her lips across my lobe. "Let's not to rush things dearie" she whispered "its always better, don't you think, if you make it last?" Her voice was mesmerising and the thought that an extra half-hour would make no difference insinuated itself contentedly into my lust-befuddled brain. I nodded dumbly, panting like a wounded horse as she leaned languidly to one side and drew my wine from the table. "Here now. Drink a glass with me before we fall to, as a token..." I seized the wine and quaffed it down in a trice, watched impatiently as she finished her own, then reached out greedily towards her swaying luscious form.

She moved swiftly aside and I stumbled against the table upsetting the wine bottle which fell oh-so-slowly to the ground. I tried to turn but something was wrong. The lady seemed to be moving in and out of focus in the most alarmingly manner, as was the furniture, and everything else in the room. I tried to step forward, hands outstretched, but the wavering, smiling face before me receded with every pace. The room was spinning. I stumbled on, the scarlet haired beauty stepped neatly abeam, there was a roaring in my ears and my last thought as the wooden floorboards rushed upward to extinguish all light and noise was that her fingers had been too clean.

Chapter Nineteen

Fouché's voice was in my ear and for an instant I wondered how in hell I had fetched up in his office, but the question seemed to slip away as he hove into view and it was not Fouché at all, but a languid St Just holding a basket of apples, who smiled sardonically and beckoned me to follow, taking me off towards a large wooden door. It opened and there was Collot d'Herbois slapping the mattress with Mistress Defarge, who clutched the bedhead, gasping with delight at his attentions until on a sudden the brazen voice of Danton filled the room asking "Why? Why?" and I swung round to see Danton's huge severed head on the *escritoire*. "Why?" he repeated "why did you kill her?" I tried to speak, wanting desperately to explain, but the damned choke-pear was in my mouth again and I turned away in pain and confusion, pushing past a wounded Robespierre, broken jaw agape, whispering "handkerchiefs must be banned for the sake of Virtue!" and now it was no longer Suzanne Defarge beneath the vile Collot but my own Lucie and the barker was in my hand once more and I was blazing away at her lovely face and Samson was tapping the guillotine's blade against my temple as the seamstress' head lay in the basket calling "Traitor! Traitor!"-

And I awoke with a start, a pistol tapping at the side of

my head and the words "Traitor! Up you bastard, and sharp about it!" ringing in my ears. But I knew this too was all a fantasy, one of those dreams within a dream, where you think you wake and dress and have breakfast only to suddenly discover you're still snug beneath the covers. I was absolutely certain of it because the voice I had heard calling me traitor had metamorphosed from the seamstress's mellifluous tones to the equally improbable pompous braying of my old lawyer friend Stryver. And *he* was 300 leagues distant, in London, where I would soon be myself, once I woke and put my escape into action. Yes, in London, fêted, lionised and-

A sharp tap to the temple brought me swiftly to my senses. "Up you bastard. Up I say!"

I rose in the most terrible confusion, swinging my legs over the bed and staring blankly at the man in front of me. His face looked familiar, but if this was Stryver, then by God he had grown from a horseload to a cartload. The man was of enormous bulk, almost as wide as he was tall. His costume too was greatly changed, for when I had last seen Stryver he was resplendent in sober lawyer's weeds of impeccable cut whereas now his dress consisted of an untidy brown stuff coat, buttoned behind and at the wrists, with an old fashioned cap of the same material upon his head. But when I looked more closely there could be no doubt. The familar florid, prematurely aged visage stared back at me with the same stern bullying mien (I have to say that, unlike myself, young Charles the Scribbler managed to portray friend Stryver's obnoxious ways to perfection. Pity he went badly astray with so much else).

But what disconcerted me most was the lack of any friendly twinkle in Stryver's small piggy eyes, which in times past would always soften his belligerent appearance. This was Stryver, my old friend and drinking companion, devil of a doubt - but a Stryver who returned my gaze with a grim implacable hatred.

My first inclination was to bolt for the street – Stryver's

bulk would make him slow and I doubted the fat bastard could even get through the door without a lever of some kind. But a quick look around the room soon changed my mind. There were more candles now, and in their bright glow I could see two large bully boys standing either side of the door, each with an oaken plant under his arm, while my erstwhile companion, the beauteous apple seller, sat the room's single chair, swinging her legs languidly and drinking wine. She caught my gaze and toasted me with raised glass, smiling ironically and, I thought, somewhat sadly too. Duped again - I'd been sold a pup, no mistake. I looked away and back to Stryver, standing there grim as Death itself. Whatever was afoot this was no joyous reunion of old friends.

"You're a hard man to catch up with Sidney" says Stryver conversationally, sitting down so heavily at the end of the four-poster that I swear the bedhead rose a good half-foot in the air. "But now we have you, you bloody traitor, they'll be no escape."

"What in God's name are you talking about" I gave back hotly "I'm no traitor. I've been forced to work for the Frenchies, yes, but upon my honour I've not done one jot or tittle to risk the life of even a single Englishman. Anyway, what's all this to you? You're only a bloody lawyer with no interest in anything but the size of your fee."

Exuding importance, I watched my former friend inflate with his own self-conceit until I feared he must burst. "Only a lawyer? *Only* a lawyer? Ah, but a lawyer in whom the Crown has chosen to deposit the highest trust and the most difficult tasks. I am under the orders of the Alien Office-" he preened, but seeing my blank look shook that great fat head 'til his jowels quivered "-ah, but of course, you would not know. However, it will do no harm to tell, not where you are bound. The Alien Office" says he, warming to his subject "is a most secret arm of government, the centre of Great Britain's intelligence service, and directs an international band of agents around the globe. We're spies." he added helpfully, lest I had misunderstood[37].

My first thought was that Britain's spymasters must be in sad plight. If they were reduced to recruiting the likes of Stryver for 'intelligence' then God help the country. But such pleasantries would not aid my own case and I decided instead to put the best gloss I could on my situation. "Agents of the Crown" I crowed in sham delight, "upon my credit Stryver, you have risen immeasurably in my estimation. I would never have thought it. And praise be to God you've rescued me now. I was just about to make my own way to England – I have forged passports and all in readiness – to tell what I know of French plans to the Crown authorities. Now, if you can just get me away-"

"Oh we'll take you away right enough. We'll take you all the way, via England post haste for Hell! Damn your pitiful soul, Sidney, don't try your tricks with me. We've been watching you see? We know you work for that scoundrel Fouché; 'Just about to make my own way to England' indeed! Blood and sand! you're as arrant a turncoat as ever was shot before a regiment or forced to cry cockles at Tyburn." I made to object but he quashed my protests with that overbearing voice of his, his tone as cold as when I had heard him at the Old Bailey – what, just a twelve-month past - demanding the death of a felon. I could almost see the gown, and the wig upon his fat balding head. "No Englishman harmed, you say Sydney? Upon your honour, eh? I think not sirrah!.."

He rose and loomed threateningly over me looking, as ever, too large for any room he occupied. "What of young Edward - you remember him surely? You named him to the Frenchies as soon as he tried to make contact -" I started at that, as an image suddenly sprang into my memory, as clear as day: the young cribbage-faced fool who had slipped me a note on the Rue St Antoine, in full view of Defarge and his cronies- " I see you remember, Sydney. They tortured him, you know. Thumbscrews, wedges beneath the fingernails, and the rack. He broke in the end, poor young Ted, - on the rack, who withstands the rack eh? - after a day and a half of torment. Long enough for us to get most of our people away and to change our codes. But we lost two others. Three men, Sydney, three brave Englishmen dead because of your treachery. And how many more we know nothing about? Five? Ten? A hundred? No, Sydney old friend" and he stepped back, grinning maliciously "you're bound for Old England right enough, as soon as we can slip you safely past the Frenchies and over to Dover. But you'll see no joyous homecoming. It's Tyburn and the Paddington frisk for you. You'll ride the three-legged mare and I'll stand by and laugh as the life chokes out of you ".

"But no! You don't understand! I was forced to this. It was help them or the axe-"

"A gentleman would have taken the latter option."

"Not any bloody gentleman I know. It's one thing to fight and die in hot blood, Stryver, but I tell you it's another to go like a sheep to slaughter, trussed tight with the hair shorn to its roots on your neck so the glaive will slice clean. Dear God I've been on the scaffold, I know!

"Yes, we heard of your gallant attempt to save Darnay" he sneered "Pity it didn't work, or perhaps it was divine justice." He was resting his back against the fireplace now, watching me carefully, as were his henchman and my erstwhile dulcinea. "I never did believe that tosh you served up at his trial, even though it did my reputation a power of good to see the Frenchman acquitted[38]. Guilty as sin, in my opinion. He got what he deserved, most like" and he heaved himself away from the mantle and paced slowly towards me, speaking slowly, a judge gravely summing up the case. "But even if we grant extenuating circumstances in your particular case, the evidence against you remains damning. Young Edward for instance-"

"But Sweet Jesus" I burst out "it was his own damned fault"

"Howso?"

"I was being watched. Constantly, couldn't move without one or two of them on my tail. Robespierre didn't trust me, y'see" I was on the edge of the bed, leaning forwards, ready at any moment to fall on my knees, grovel and beg, kiss his hands, his fat arse, anything to end this horror. "He feared, Robespierre I mean – and rightly I tell you – he feared that my true allegiance remained with England!" Stryver had stopped pacing. He seemed interested, his head cocked to one side and I took a swift breath and gabbled on for my very life "The young idio- what was his name? Edward? Yes, Edward, he comes up to me in broad daylight, bold as a Miller's shirt, and hands over a note before striding away as if he were taking the air on the Strand. God Almighty Stryver, what was I to do?" there was no response so I plunged on. "The poor bastard was dead already, whether I'd cried hearty on him or no. He'd been *seen*. What was the point of keeping my trap shut? It could only mean both of us would be taken. I had to peach!"

He stood there in the candlelight, looking into the fire, hand to his greasy chin, considering, and my mind danced a quadrille between hope and despair. Surely he could see the logic of my position, he was a lawyer, after all. Yes, he must, he had to- And then he was turning that great fat face in my direction, staring towards me like a stoat with a trapped cony.

"No, Sidney, it won't do" he says at length. "It is a splendid defence, I grant you. But you forget that you were long my jackal – and an excellent jackal at that – and I have seen how you work, your skill in coming to the nub of any dilemma, and devising a path to circumvent each problem. And now you're trying that same sure touch on me, you godforsaken traitor, to save your own worthless carcase." He bent suddenly so that his mouth was against my ear.

"Have you ever smelt your baubles a-roasting? For that's what's waiting for you, Sidney, a traitor's end - hung 'til you're half-strangled, then brought down and your trinkets, and your *arbor vitae,* cut off and thrown on the fire to cook before your eyes; then the hook, that horrible sharpened hook, in at the base of your chest and ripped straight down, spilling your entrails. They'll drag them out while you're yet living, and on the fire they go too, spitting and sizzling as they roast. Only then do you have some degree of mercy, for your head's next. Down the axe will come, and that's the end of your troubles - though not your humiliation. For they'll split your body in four and send a part to be displayed at each of the four quarters of the Nation..... Aye, a horrible fate, you'll agree. And inescapable, short of ...."

My head came up so suddenly I caught him a glancing blow on the mouth "What Short of what for God's sake?"

He rubbed his injured lips with his hand. "Interested are you? Drawing and quartering not your style? Thought not. Well now Sidney old friend, we don't trust you or believe you. And I'd not weep to see you dangle in the Sheriff's picture frame, that's plain enough. For my part I'd just as soon see you ride backwards up Holborn Hill and choke your life away before the Newgate mob. But that would be a waste, possibly, for you may well be of more use to us alive. *If* you decide to help."

I could have kissed his feet, or any other part of his anatomy. "Anything, I said abjectly "anything at all", hastily adding "For England" and hoping it did not look too much like an afterthought.

"Splendid! I thought we might find a patriotic bone if we sought hard enough" says the gross sarcastic bastard pleasantly. "Now, you may not have considered it, but you hold a unique position in French intelligence; one that would take us years to achieve by infiltration. Fouché's right hand man, the *Chameleon* no less"

That was a shock, I warrant, these lads knew more than I'd supposed. "That was why I was about to flee to England with my information-" I began, but he held up a withstraining hand. "Well, we're agreed on one thing at least Sidney – that your position with Fouché gives you access to much that the Frenchies would prefer to remain *sub rosa*: you'll be privy to maps, documents, resumés of meeting, plans, schemes, and much other secret tittle tattle

I've no doubt. All of which the British Crown would wish to know about. They might look more leniently on any former miscreant supplying such information, on a regular basis of course" He paused and smiled at me, looking for all the world like a hippo with constipation "You see the way the world wags, old friend?" I nodded sickly and let my head fall into my hands. "'Course you do; you may be traitorous dog, but you've lost none of your wit, I'll warrant. Nor your instinct for self preservation..."

He sat beside me on the bed, bowing the mattress so that I had to lean away from his massive bulk to prevent myself falling into his ample lap. "Yes Sidney, the only way for you to save your miserable carcase, the only way to prove your loyalty and make us certain of your constancy, is for you to stay in France and to spy against Fouché and the Directory - for England". He dropped a plump hand on my knee and squeezed, "Nothing else will do old friend. And if you are as true a patriot as you claim, ye'll jump at the chance of doing your duty for God, King George and Merry England, eh Sirrah?"

And what was there to do but acquiesce? If you, dear reader, can see a way out of the irredeemable hole I was in, then I wish that you had been there by my side to offer aid and comfort (or better yet, there alone and in my place). Where were you, I wonder, as I fumed and fretted impotently over my fate? Finishing a good meal, rogering your light-o'-love, or sleeping soundly in an English bed mayhap. Or perhaps, not yet even born?

Strange how disaster can strike one person and leave another completely untouched. Even as I sat that bed in utter misery I could hear, not ten feet distant through the thin partition wall, the joyous sounds of a happy couple dancing the featherbed jig, while below on the street, one chap was whistling cheerfully as he went his merry way to home, tavern, mistress or heaven knows where.

But Stryver was talking again. "Now Sidney old lad, I have to tell you this, so that everything is clear between us, nothing hidden, and all above board. Just in case – perish the thought – you were minded to accede to our demands and then, once out of our power, to turn renegade with the French ... yes, yes, I know you were forced to it, but I tell you this lest you are tempted to turn your coat again. If we suspect you've changed your allegiance, if I get even a sniff, then we will simply let the Froggies know you are one of Pitt's spies. Compelling, incontrovertible evidence of your guilt will appear and you'll be arrested and following the footsteps of young Ted faster than shit off a shovel. You understand? Yes, I see by your eyes that you do. Well then" says this overbearing whale, slapping his flippers together "we understand each other. I'll leave you in the capable hands of Yvette here. She's a past master of this game – been here three years, haven't you Yvette, and devil a problem all that time. She will be your contact and I've no doubt" here he gave *la belle Yvette* a peery glance "that she will find an appropriate cover for your clandestine meetings." He stood abruptly. "I won't shake hands Sidney, but perhaps in a year or so – if you're not already with the majority – we can take up where we left off in London." And with a nod to Yvette he and his bully boys made their departure. I noted with perverse satisfaction that my overweight tormentor had particular difficulty negotiating the door. Fat bastard.

And I was left alone with Yvette to be initiated into the passwords and codes that were *de rigeur* for this perilous business. It was not her real name, of course, but the *nom de guerre* of an English lady of good family whose French cousins had perished in the Terror and who was determined to do her bit to bring down the dastardly revolutionaries, against whom she fulminated with right good will. But with me she was all sweetness and apology, decrying the need to trepan me into Stryver's ambush and hoping that we might still remain on amicable terms. "Especially as we must see each other quite often in the course of our work" she says, all doe-eyed and beseeching, and before those green sparklers and that delicately quivering bosom how could I refuse my assent? We were, she said, colouring delightfully, to cover our weekly meetings by the pretence of an *affaire*. Would such a suberfuge be acceptable? I nodded, feigning indifference, for though my present ordeal had left me with little present inclination for the two-backed beast, I saw that there could well come a time when Yvette and I might make quite as much noise as the spirited couple next door, who had now commenced on a return bout with no diminution in enthusiasm.

"One thing remains." says my luscious tutor, all sombre business once more "Take this" and she placed into my hand a small wooden token about the size of a sovereign, painted with a curious device: three little red flowers, roses or somesuch, surrounded by tiny green leaves[39]. "Keep this safe, at all costs," Yvette stated solemnly, pressing the token into my palm, closing my fingers over it and taking perhaps a little longer than necessary to take her hand from mine. "It will identify you to any of our fraternity. We each have one and, despite Mr Stryver's optimistic sketch of my time here, this little pledge has saved my own life on at least two occasions. Now come" and she raised me gently by the elbow, and led me down the stairs to the door. "I would that we had more leisure to converse" she whispered at the threshold "but, taken with Stryver and his friends' extended visit, you may already have spent too long in this place". As I stepped out into the cold night air, she called me back. "If we are to succeed in our charade as lovers" says she with eyes downcast, and a voice a touch more husky than of late, "then we should perhaps more fully act out our parts" and with that she pulled my head down and gave me a kiss that was anything but ladylike, though none the worse for that. "We should meet not once, but twice a week" says she somewhat breathlessly as we broke away "lest these vile republicans see through our schemes." I nodded my eager approval. Twice a day would have suited me.

She stepped back into the shadow of the hall so that only her auburn-framed face was visible, an angel swathed in moonlight. "Always remember, we may be watched or listened to at any time. The walls are thin, as you no doubt appreciated tonight." A shy smile crept over her perfect face. "We shall be just as easily overheard." I made to speak, to reassure her of my full commitment to our task, but she silenced me with a finger against my mouth. "I think it best" she continued, gently stroking my nether lip "and solely for the sake of our mission, that everything be done to keep up the pretence of our *affaire*. Yes," and there was much promise in those large green eyes. "England expects no less. You and I must do *everything*." And she sank back into the shadows, the door closing quietly in my face.

Which just goes to show - as our local blackfly is forever declaiming from his pulpit - that no matter how dark the day may seem, there is always some good in every situation, if only you strive hard enough to find it.

Even so, the promise of Yvette's undoubted charms was but a dog's portion set against the sudden reversal of my fortunes, and the dashing of all my hopes for freedom. France or Britain, I was damned coming or going. And nothing for it but to endure, to trust to a Destiny that, thus far, had been anything but benign. I turned and began to tread a disconsolate path back to my lodgings, heart in my boots and my plans in tatters. Fate had vomited into my britches yet again. A bare two hours had passed since my collision with the counterfeit apple seller, and I was back on the Paris streets a British spy, my life once again hanging by a thread.

NOTES

1   Carton was not suffering from stress-related delusions when he penned these lines. Robespierre considered himself an accomplished poet and we have many examples of his work, including the marvellously improbable The Art of Spitting and Blowing One's Nose, from which Carton gives an admirably accurate quote.

2   Here Carton is referring to Danton's Rabellaisian riposte to another of Robespierre's eulogies on Virtue. "There is no virtue more solid" Danton retorted "than that which I practice nightly with my wife." Nor was Robespierre the only victim of his sharp tongue: on hearing that his opponent Vadier had called him turbot farci, no better a huge fish to be gutted, Danton responded with typical earthy wit: 'I'll eat his brains and use his skull to shit in.'

3   "The Baker and his Wife" was a popular phrase at the time for King Louis XVI and his Queen Marie Antoinette. Carton's recall is perfect - the French Queen was beheaded on Wednesday 16th October 1793, at 10.00 am.

4   Carton is repeating a well-known fallacy. The truth is that Doctor Guillotine merely endorsed a British-invented machine, on the grounds that its action was swift and humane. During the revolution, his name somehow became erroneously attached to the device as its inventor.

5   Count Alexander Beauharnais was certainly under suspicion during December 1793, and we know his sister-in-law Francoise to have been imprisoned at Sainte-Pelagie Prison around this time. But we have no record of the arrest of the Countess in Paris. While Carton's testimony remains uncorroborated, given the tumultuous times it is by no means unlikely that the Countess was seized as he describes and that, despite its startling conclusion, his account of their meeting is, in the main, accurate.

6   Danton was away from Paris, with the army in Belgium, when his wife died giving birth to their fourth child. On his return, consumed with guilt, he ordered her coffin disinterred, tore open its lid and, before the horrified gaze of workmen and friends, drew the body from its resting place, embracing the corpse, murmuring endearments and smothering its dead lips with kisses.

7 A Homosexual. Carton's writings are peppered with Latin aphorisms and criminal cant, the latter no doubt picked up from his constant association with the dregs of society, an unavoidable adjunct to his profession as a London lawyer.

8 Thomas Hughes' novel Tom Brown's Schooldays was published in 1857, and Carton must have seen the book very late in his career. As a parent, albeit an unknown parent, it is only natural that Carton should see the rather uncomplimentary account the author gives of 'his' boy as biased.

9. Revolutionary banknotes whose value declined almost from the moment of printing.

10 This is Carton's second reference to an earlier period of his life spent in North America. How he made his way thither, and the nature of the terrible disasters he endured, will no doubt come to light when the remainder of his voluminous papers are edited.

11 Carton's memory fails him here: Hebert and his allies were executed two days later, on March 14th 1794. His account of the actual proceedings is, however, commendably accurate.

12 A rather grand carriage pulled by four horses.

13 Carton's account confirms a persistent rumour that the Incorruptible's family had strong Irish links. Indeed, it is likely that Robespierre initiated the plan that culminated in the disastrous 1796 invasion of Ireland by 14,000 French troops under the command of General Lazare Hoche. Incomprehensibly, the invasion force set out on December 15th, at the height of the worst sailing season, and was scattered by winter storms. See Hayes' Ireland and Irishmen in the French Revolution. London, 1932.

14 Carton's account of the meeting accords with other witnesses, even to the dialogue between the two men, though no one else heard (or thought it wise to record) Danton's parting bon mot. It seems, however, to have been a favourite phrase of Danton's and is reported elsewhere on at least one other occasion.

15 The blue plum (or plumb) was a lead musket ball. To surfeit with a blue

plum was therefore, in modern parlance to "fill them with lead".

16 Here Carton gives us a little more detail of the disaster that overtook him in the Americas - he appears to have been involved in a massacre of some kind and to have lost someone very dear to him. The specific nature and location of this disaster remain, at the present time, unclear.

17 As common as the barber's chair - in which all men may sit to be trimmed.

18 Following a number of setbacks to the revolution, rumours flourished of plots hatched in the overcrowded Paris prisons. From the 2nd September 1792, mobs invaded the prisons and over a period of five days massacred more than 800 inmates. Danton, then Minister of Justice, refused to intervene, saying "I do not care about the prisoners. They will have to take care of themselves."

19 The Compagnie des Indes was founded by Louis XIV, and was ordered wound up in 1793 as a vestige of the *ancien regime*. It possessed huge assets which various 'entrepreneurs' attempted to acquire illegally.

20 Perhaps the most famous example is Abbé Edgeworth, an Irish priest settled in France, and who, at peril of his life, attended the unfortunate Louis XVI at his execution and left a moving account of the King's last moments.

21 While many revolutionaries were atheist or agnostic in their views, Robespierre retained a religios outlook and wished for a de-Christianised worship of the Godhead, a concept he later proclaimed in early 1794 as The Cult of the Supreme Being. His high-handed actions during the first Festival of this new state religion (in which many thought he took upon himself the attributes of a King) may well have been a contributing factor in his eventual downfall.

22 Robespierre must have been pleased with this extempore oration; he re-used many of these phrases in his famous speech of 8th Thermidor to the National Convention.

23 The 'Glorious First' or Battle of Ushant was fought in mid Atlantic by the British Channel Fleet under Lord Howe and the French Atlantic Fleet commanded by Vice-Admiral Louis Thomas Villaret de Joyeuse. The British were intent on taking an important grain convoy, bound

for France from the United States. Despite the British victory in this engagement, they were unable to prevent the grain reaching France.

24 Better known today as *War and Peace*. The title of Tolstoy's masterpiece suffered a mauling after 1917 at the hands of the Bolsheviks, who abolished a number of features of the Russian cyrillic alphabet, resulting in one of literature's most famous mistranslations. Chekov suffered a similar fate - The *Cherry Orchard* began life as Dark Orchard. Strangely, Carton appears to have had an unknown edition of the book in his possession some time earlier than its known publication date of 1869 (Tolstoy completed the first draft of his masterpeice in 1863).

25 "The Father of Spanish Fencing" Don Jeronimo wrote his classic *Of the Philosophy of the arms, of its art and the Christian offense and defense*" in 1582, establishing a school of swordplay that exists to this day.

26 'crimped fish' were cut up alive, a practise said to produce firmer flesh for eating.

27 Carton's memory has failed him at this point, but we know from other contemporary sources that the speaker was Jacques Nicolas Billaud-Varennes.

28 Imprisoned by Robespierre, and under threat of execution, Tallien's mistress Therezia sent a letter to her lover on 26th July, berating him for his failure to obtain her release: "I shall die in despair" she wrote "at having belonged to a coward like you!" With the note was a dagger, on whose blade Tallien then swore to either free his love or die in the attempt

29 Carton is probably referring to the Company of Surgeons, later the Royal College of Surgeons, who had their headquarters at Lincoln's Inn Fields until the end of the eighteenth century.

30 Carton must be alluding here to Merda, who claimed after the assault that he had fired the shot that wounded Robespierre. Few of his contemporaries believed him – with good reason, as we now find that it was Carton himself who struck Robespierre down.

31 the identity of the charitable person who did this act of kindness has long been a mystery.

32 It had been moved because of complaints about the smell that arose from the dried blood all around the fatal machine – it is said that cattle refused to cross the square. Robespierre's apartment was close to the Place de la Revolution and it is likely he was one of the prime movers in the relocation of the Guillotine.

33 The ancients called the living 'three-times blessed'. Those 'four times blessed' were the dead.

34 The revolutionaries sent men post haste to the camp of Sablons to secure above forty cannon, whose possession would mean disaster for the government forces. Bonaparte ordered Murat with 300 cavalry on the same errand. Murat scattered the rebels, seized the guns, and brought them back to the Tuilleries.

35 Josephine is known to have taken many lovers, before and during her marriage to Napoleon; Carton, it seems, was one of their illustrious number.

36 Carton shows himself a reliable witness here. Josephine makes an almost identical comment in a letter to one of her close friends, some time before her marriage to Napoleon. See Knapton, Ernest John, *Empress Josephine*. Harvard University Press. 1964.

37 The Alien Office was indeed the forerunner of MI6 and the modern-day British Intelligence Service. Still somewhat shrouded in mystery, it began as a simple surveillance unit in England for French refugees and émigrés, intercepting letters and observing movements. In 1795 the organisation extended its operations to Europe, and especially to France, where its agents attempted to provoke uprisings, infiltrate the Paris police, bribe politicians and, on at least one occasion (and probably more), to assassinate troublesome opponents.

38 See Dickens' *A Tale of Two Cities*, Book the Second, Chapter III, for details of Carton and Stryver's 'doppelganger defence' of Lucie's husband, Charles Darnay.

39 This small token, bearing a red rose, was indeed standard issue for British agents at the time, and seems to have been the inspiration behind Baroness Orcy's novel The Scarlet Pimpernel.

Books by Keith Laidler

The Talking Ape (Collins)
Squirrels in Britain (David & Charles)
The River Wolf (Allen & Unwin)
China's Threatened Species (Blackwell)
Pandas (Collins/BBC)
The Head of God (Orion)
Divine Deception (Hodder Headline)
The Last Empress (Wiley)
Female Caligula (Wiley)
Surveillance Unlimited (Icon)
Animals (Quercus)

Keith Laidler is an anthropologists, film-maker and author of twelve books including the best-selling Female Caligula and Divine Deception, also available from Aziloth Books. Originally concentrating on Natural History, Dr Laidler has travelled in many of the world's wild places, from the rain forests of South America to the deserts of Arabia and the mountains of Tibet. He worked with Sir David Attenborough on The Living Planet, and his production company, Wolfshead, has made a number of highly acclaimed documentaries for the BBC, National Geographic and other quality broadcasters. Dr Laidler has a first class B.Sc. (Special Honours) in Zoology and holds a Ph.D. in Anthropology from Durham University. He is a Winston Churchill Fellow, a past member of the Scientific Exploration Society and a Fellow of the Royal Geographical Society.

Aziloth Books has already established itself as a publisher boasting a diverse, modern list of powerful, high-quality titles. We will continue to bring novels of flair and originality to the reading public, together with factual publications on important issues that have not found a home in the rather staid and politically-correct atmosphere of many publishing houses. View our list at

www.azilothbooks.com

We are a small, approachable company and would love to hear any of your comments and suggestions on our plans, or indeed on absolutely anything. Aziloth is also interested in hearing from aspiring authors whom we might publish. Contact at info@azilothbooks.com.

Lightning Source UK Ltd.
Milton Keynes UK
172667UK00007B/26/P